THE
AUTOMOTIVE
HISTORY
OF
LUCKY
KELLERMAN

THE
AUTOMOTIVE
HISTORY
OF
LUCKY
KELLERMAN

STEVE HELLER

CHELSEA GREEN PUBLISHING COMPANY
Chelsea, Vermont

The Automotive History of Lucky Kellerman
was designed by Hans Teensma of Impress.

The people and events in this novel
are fictional. True mechanics, historians,
and Okies will recognize certain liberties
the author has taken in presenting
the world of this story.

S.H.

Library of Congress Cataloging-in-Publication Data

Heller, Steve, 1949-
The automotive history of Lucky Kellerman.
I. Title.
PS3558.E47624A93   1987   813'.34   87-14816
ISBN 0-930031-09-1

*For my father, Stephen Francis Heller, Sr.,
and my mother, Elizabeth Hale Heller, and
for Mary, David, Michael, and Daniel.*

My gratitude to the
National Endowment for the Arts
and to Yaddo.

Nobody with a good car needs to be justified.

HAZEL MOTES

1

ON HIS SIXTY-FIFTH birthday Frank Kellerman locked himself inside an old stone schoolhouse filled with honey bees.

"Just you and me now, honeys," he said to the bees buzzing around the solid oak door. He bolted the heavy lock and smiled. Although he had seen no one else this morning, Kellerman knew the sharp click of the bolt locked do-gooders, intruders, and betrayers outside. Inside was his project.

Against the door he propped the double-edged ax he had used the day before to chop his new color console television to pieces. He had left the debris — slivers of mahogany, steel, and glass — scattered over the living room floor. Until yesterday the TV had been merely a nuisance, another distraction from his work. Yesterday he had seen something on the shimmering blue screen that shamed him.

"Privacy, that's what we need, honeys," he said to a couple of bees buzzing around his head. He checked the windows, making sure the thick cedar boards covering them were securely nailed. He had left a peephole in the south window above his worktable. He had only to glance through the peephole to see, across the yard, the old two-story woodframe house he'd lived in for the last thirty years. But Kellerman wasn't interested in looking at that anymore.

Instead, amid the constant, throbbing hum — the trapped echo of a hundred thousand tiny beating wings — he turned and surveyed the once-spacious classroom that now served, barely, as his workshop. For a moment, in the pale yellow light of the single naked bulb that hung on a wire from the ceiling, what Kellerman saw resembled a miniature city being rebuilt at a fanatical pace after a holocaust. Tilting columns of overstuffed cardboard boxes rose like battered skyscrapers above the general debris. And swarming over and around the columns, like thousands of gold-uniformed construction workers, a swirling cloud of honey bees — flying, crawling over each box, rebuilding the city. The movement made Kellerman dizzy until he adjusted his bifocals. Then his eyes focused on his project.

Perched on four heavy jack stands amid the columns of boxes and piles of junk was the shining silver steel frame of an ancient automobile.

"Good bones, honeys," Kellerman remarked to the small squadron of bees hovering above the naked steel rails he had finished restoring only yesterday. "This baby's going to have good bones." Around the room, fenders, bumpers, and other large parts were stacked and propped against the columns of boxes. Each box bore a crude label: RUB BUSHINGS. REAR 1/4 PANEL. And so on. Next to the east wall by the sink and toilet, a lumpy gray canvas covered the two most important parts.

"Her heart and soul," Kellerman proclaimed, stepping over to the canvas where half a dozen bees crawled over its dusty surface. Kellerman grinned as he imagined himself rolling back the canvas to reveal his prize: a perfectly restored vintage

V-8 engine and drive train he'd recently picked up (*stolen* would be a more accurate word) from a 1932 Model 18 Ford (the very first Ford V-8!) Deluxe Roadster in Carl Vukovich's salvage yard down in Yukon.

"Vukovich probably thinks it was punks or hot-rodders," Kellerman said proudly, recalling the sneezing howling fury of Vukovich's two purebred Doberman pinscher guard dogs when the pepper bombs exploded on their slavering snouts. Kellerman lifted one eyebrow and curled his lip in an impish grin. "Maybe this squares us, honeys."

Even as he said the words, he realized they weren't true. Carl Vukovich had stolen a lot more than a junkyard engine from Kellerman. He'd stolen a life's dream. There was no getting even for that.

Kellerman bit his lower lip, then stiffened. All that was past. Outside. It didn't matter now.

He patted the canvas, then pulled a rag out of his pocket and wiped his glasses. The room, his project, everything was in good focus today. Kellerman rebalanced his bifocals atop the swollen parrot beak that was his nose. Over the years he'd learned to take a kind of cynical pleasure in the nicknames his nose inspired: Rocky, Jewboy (though he was baptised a Catholic), Beaversniffer, Cyrano (he had to ask about that one), El Schlabong. The black custodians at the Oklahoma State Capitol where he'd worked for seventeen years called him Honker. That's what his neighbor Charley Bluefire had called him only yesterday when he had tried to pay the god-damn blanket-assed half-breed with a check.

One A-frame hoist, one crowbar, twenty pounds of white sugar. That's one sixty-five, cash, Honker. Charley had piled the last sack of C&H on the schoolhouse porch, then raised up, spit, and eyed Kellerman, who was blocking his view of the in-side. *Tell me something, Honker. What's an old sugar junkie like*

*you doing with all that sweet stuff? What you building in there
with all them bees — a gingerbread house?*

Never mind that, Kellerman had said. If anyone could
guess what he was building in here, it was Charley.
Hadn't he helped Kellerman find parts for the Model
18? But if Charley knew about the automobile, he also
knew to keep it to himself. Kellerman had been more con-
cerned about what Charley might have seen on TV that
morning. Had the only neighbor he still talked to seen
his shame?

What do you mean cash? Kellerman had snapped. *You and
me worked side by side for seventeen goddamn years. And even
before that, I used to fix your boy's GTO whether he had the money
or not. And now you tell me my paper's no good? Besides, you
forgot the damn ice.*

Charley Bluefire, who was half Pawnee and half something
else, hadn't blushed at Kellerman's accusations. Instead, he
leaned back on the tailgate of his pickup, his Adam's apple
sticking way out as he looked Kellerman up and down. Kellerman swallowed and tried to guess from the cool look in
Charley's eyes whether he knew.

Cash on the barrelhead, Honker, Charley finally insisted
and lifted his eyes to watch the bees buzz around the
boarded-up windows and tiny cracks between stones. *My
old lady's already giving me hell about buying this sweet stuff
for you.*

Tell her my biggest problem is butt-in-skis.

Charley nodded and leaned sideways far enough to see
through the doorway to the green army cot Kellerman had
carried over from the house. *I don't doubt it, Honker,* Charley
said, then pointed to the cot. *You sleeping in there with them
bees now?*

Kellerman said nothing.

Charley stared at Kellerman for a long moment, then shook his head. *So how come? Wouldn't have anything to do with the Crow Woman, would it?*

As Charley spoke, Kellerman first felt the taut muscles around his stomach relax — *He doesn't know, at least not yet* — then in the next instant his belly contracted again, this time with the quick dread he always felt at the mention of the Crow Woman. He laughed, a bit too loudly.

Mabel Zucha? What do I care about that flap-assed old crow?

Charley ducked as a bee flew close to his head. *Orville says she's been getting loose again. Says he caught her out here the other day, peeking into this old schoolhouse again.*

Kellerman started to make a fist, then stopped himself. *So?*

Charley kept his eyes on the bees as they buzzed in and out of the doorway in two separate streams. *So nothing, I guess. She gives me the creeps is all. All that cawing and flapping and carrying on. Black eyes staring at you like you was a corpse. Why you think she hangs around this old schoolhouse anyway? You think it's because she got married in there way back when? My mother was at that wedding, you know.*

I don't care if she was married in the Pope's shithouse! Kellerman shouted. *I ain't responsible for no eighty-one-year-old crazy woman thinks she's a damn* bird. *You tell Orville she better not come crowin' around here. You tell him he better put her away down in Sunnyview before I catch her and lock her up in a cage where she belongs.*

Charley Bluefire raised his tailgate and latched it. *OK, OK. I'll bring your ice by tomorrow evening. Just don't do anything dumb with that sugar, OK?*

Kellerman laughed again now at his neighbor's concern. "Stupid Indian thinks all this stuff's for *me*, honeys."

He swallowed, feeling the familiar craving, the dry crackle under his tongue, as he watched several bees crawl over the

the sacks of sugar stacked on top of his big automatic air compressor.

"Hungry, honeys?"

Under the sink he found a large iron skillet. He filled it with water, then heated it over a can of Sterno. When the water came to a boil, he snuffed out the flames and poured sugar into the skillet, watching the granules dissolve in the bubbling water. He let the mixture cool.

If Babe were still alive she'd raise holy hell about feeding the bees, he thought. He paused, half expecting to hear her starting in on him:

Now Frank . . .

He had lived alone for nearly a year now, but it was hard to break the habits of most of his adult life. Only a few nights ago, shortly after midnight, he heard his name — *Frank* — crack in the darkness like an invisible snap of her fingers. Then something else, one of the little sayings she had that infuriated him: *Live and let be. Car crazy. I'll swan.* Half asleep, he rose from the bed in anger. "The hell you say," he growled, and pursued the echo of her voice down the unlit hallway. He stumbled through the darkness cursing her until he flipped on the light in the kitchen, stood squinting in the bright empty silence, and remembered.

"Damn woman never paid me such attention when she was alive," Kellerman complained to the bees. He shook his head and took the pan of sugar water over to the barstool beneath the large crack in the south wall.

There were cracks everywhere in the uninsulated plasterboard that hid the exterior stones, but the largest crack was in the south wall just a few feet from the window above his worktable. The crack was the main inside entrance to the "hive," if you wanted to call it that. All four walls were inhabited by honey bees — so many bees that the sound of their buzzing made the walls hum like a chorus of a million tiny voices. Not that it bothered Kellerman. The old schoolhouse had long been his workshop, a bonus coming with the house and five acres he'd bought after moving to Oklahoma thirty years ago. The bees had been here for only fifteen of those years, but he was long accustomed to them. The first two years he fought them with everything he could think of: bug spray, poison, cement. *A clear and deliberate invasion of privacy,* he had complained to Babe, and vowed to drive them out at any cost. He did his best, stuffing fly paper and no-pest strips into the cracks, and caulking up their entryways. In a rage, he put on a heavy rubber raincoat, gloves, and a mosquito net, then attacked them head-on with a chemical fire extinguisher — only to retreat after being stung half-a-dozen times on the arms and neck. As a last resort he hired a professional beekeeper to steal the queen and cause them to swarm.

Biggest natural hive I ever saw, the astonished beekeeper said. *Every time I get close, they move the queen to a different location. I think you're going to have to tear down at least one wall.*

At that point Kellerman gave up. *Share and share alike,* he said. He tore down the battlements and offered sugar. *A man can learn to live with just about anything,* he said to Babe as the hive spread into the east wall.

By the fourth year the walls of the schoolhouse were filling up with honey, steeping his workshop in a musky sweet smell he came to love. Curly had left home for good by then, having never entered the schoolhouse since the bees' arrival. *It's your hive, Dad, not mine.* Babe stayed away too, frightened of the bees and refusing to believe he had not been stung since the day the beekeeper left. Kellerman shrugged it off. *Nature's way, I guess.* Over time the bees became Kellerman's confederates, his honeys. *You rattle like a goddamn snake,* he would snap at Babe whenever he was losing an argument, then storm over to the schoolhouse to surround himself with a more harmonious buzz.

He had escaped her then as he planned to escape her now. The schoolhouse had become his sanctuary. Inside its humming walls he was free to think and work. His honeys went about their own business, sucking up the sweet water from his feeding stations with incessant, reassuring energy, oblivious to him and his moods. He had to take care not to squash errant worker bees by accident, dutifully checking his chair and sliding his hands gently down his backside before sitting. These precautions became second nature.

The only bad thing about the schoolhouse workshop was that he couldn't use it to work on cars — his first and only passion, Babe used to say. Until now, that is. Once or twice he'd considered knocking out the west wall to make the schoolhouse into a garage, but that would have meant evicting his honeys.

A couple of bees landed on the skillet. Kellerman looked at them for a moment, then sucked in a quick, deep breath, like an impatient, younger man. "You don't remember it, honeys, but I was once the best goddamn automotive mechanic the town of Yukon ever had. The best in this part of the state."

It was true. In the fifties, Frank Kellerman's auto repair business thrived in a white cinder-block building just east of the giant twin high-rises of the Yukon's Best Flour Mill and the MFC Farmers Co-op grain elevators. For a decade people drove in from El Reno, Piedmont, Bethany, even Oklahoma City, to bring their rough-running cars to Kellerman, the best engine man in central Oklahoma. He could make even the sickliest motor sing.

But those days were long gone. Carl Vukovich and the Yukon National Bank had seen to that. The last two decades had been a humiliation. Kellerman had spent all but the last three years of that time working with bums, retards, and relatives of state senators on the maintenance crew at the Oklahoma State Capitol.

Bees lined the entire rim of the skillet now, dipping low to reach the sugar water. Kellerman looked at them and forced a grin. "A birthday present from me to you, honeys. Sweets for the sweet-makers."

The bottom of his tongue tingled as he watched them dip into the pan. Getting a little warm in here, he thought, and wiped a ribbon of sweat off his forehead. He noticed himself stooping again. Goddamn hip. He drew himself up to his full five feet, three inches — used to be five-five, he thought sadly. He rolled back the sleeves of his checkered workshirt and stared at the withered, liver-spotted flesh of his forearms. He'd always been proud of those arms — lean and rock-hard from six decades of gripping and lifting. And his shoulders: not broad, but strong, from carrying gunny sacks of coal up Mulligan's Bluff from the old Burlington Railroad yards in Kansas City.

"Deflated, that's what I am now."

The sudden weight loss three years ago had terrified him, though he hadn't let on. From 155 to 120 in only a month. He was still working on the capitol maintenance crew then. Charley Bluefire had gotten him the job back in 1961, after the bank had taken his garage. Charley was the first to notice the weight loss, late one afternoon when Kellerman was replacing the hall light in Senator Gandy's office. Kellerman remembered it well.

Honker, you fixing to drop your pants for my benefit or Pearl's?

Behind the glass, Senator Gandy's blue-haired secretary worked her mouth up and down like a large-mouth bass as she typed personal letters from the senator to the registered

voters in his district. Kellerman said nothing and continued
to balance himself on the ladder as he screwed in a bulb with
one hand and tried to tighten his belt with the other. He
thought the weight loss might have something to do with
the craving he'd lately developed for candy. Babe had been
complaining that he ate almost nothing but Baby Ruth bars
anymore. He'd promised her he'd have a ribeye steak tonight.
To get my strength back, he'd said. But just then, balanc-
ing himself on the tall ladder, he felt fine. Peaceful, in fact.
More peaceful than he'd felt in years. And so *light*. Looking
down the long arching hallway toward the central rotunda,
he felt like he could almost float. Rise off the ladder, then
drift free and easy right over Charley Bluefire's head, down
the hall over the third floor balcony into the tall cylinder
of the rotunda, where he could soar, up, up — four, five
stories above the big marble floor map of Oklahoma, past
the giant fourth floor oil paintings of Will Rogers, Sequoyah,
Jim Thorpe, and Robert S. Kerr, 105 feet up to the very
top of the rotunda, where the base of the capitol dome should
have been, if the Oklahoma capitol had had a dome, to the
spot where the five-point star of the Great Seal of the State
of Oklahoma was encased in leaded glass.

It took three of them to get him down off the ladder.
Easy, Frank, we'll take care of you, he remembered Merle
Coats, the boss of the building maintenance crew, whisper
in his ear as they led him to the elevator.

"Take care of me for sure," Kellerman fumed at the bees.
The Board of Affairs eased him out of his job shortly after
the V.A. told Coats it was diabetes. Coats the Betrayer: *You
just can't cut it anymore, Frank, what with your bum hip and the
diabetes and all.* "Early retirement" was what they called the
monthly check he had received for the last three years. The
bleeding hearts in the Affirmative Action Office claimed they

could do nothing for him because of his absenteeism since the onset of the disease. So he'd missed a few days lately. Maybe more than a few. So what? He'd put in seventeen years with the state. *Deliver me from do-gooders and false friends,* Kellerman said on his last day. He refused to shake Coats' hand.

"Three years ago today," Kellerman noted aloud, for the record. A shitty gray day in June, he remembered. After he pulled the Corvair — he hated that car, always had — into the garage attached to the woodframe house, he paced straight across the yard, past the tin-roofed carport he'd built to house his automobiles, to the sanctuary of the schoolhouse and his honeys. Tacked on the schoolhouse door was a postcard from Curly. On the front of the card was a picture of an enormous pink rose in full blossom. Superimposed over the rose was a picture of Curly standing erect on the bottom-most petal — slim, tan, oh-so-smooth — and wearing the brightest, gaudiest, most ridiculous-looking suit Kellerman had ever seen. Red, white, green, yellow, pink, and blue stripes ran from shoulder to cuff. His "rainbow suit," Curly called it, the suit he wore to host "The Dream Game."

"The Dream Game" had been on TV only a couple of years then, but already it had made Curly Kellerman famous. The purpose of the game was to win a dream vacation. Each contestant designed his own trip to anywhere in the world, then tried to win enough money to pay for it. It was all or nothing; the dream either came true or it didn't. Only one contestant at a time played the game, answering a series of questions that became increasingly difficult as his winnings approached the required total. Curly asked the questions in an important but encouraging tone, his oh-so-smooth face and his rainbow suit beaming at the contestant. About one out of three contestants won his dream trip. The rest went home with a round of applause, a $100 gift certificate, and a kiss from one of the tall, beautiful young women in evening gowns or bathing suits who helped Curly host the show. Throughout the game the beautiful young women would pose on sets (a palm tree, a pile of sand, a chaise lounge) representing the place the contestant would visit if his or her dream came true.

Five years ago a letter arrived, addressed to Babe, containing a picture of Curly and one of the women on the show. The woman wore a traditional Hawaiian wedding dress of green kapa cloth with three enormous leis of plumeria and pikake blossoms (Babe recognized the flowers) heaped on her chest. Curly wore a white suit and four leis, a dozen different colors of carnations.

The letter was brief:

> *Dear folks —*
>   *A sudden dream romance. We couldn't wait even a day. Her name is Marlene. We're honeymooning in Tahiti. See you soon.*
>
>   *Love,*
>   *Curly*

They never got to meet Marlene, though Kellerman occasionally saw her on TV doing feminine deodorant commercials. The marriage lasted five weeks. One of the janitors at the capitol showed Kellerman the article in the *National Enquirer.* Babe continued to watch "The Dream Game" every morning at ten o'clock on Channel 9, though they must have taken Marlene off the show soon after Curly's letter. *It's such a wonderful show,* Babe maintained, even after the rumors of cheating and payoffs developed into a national scandal and the show's producers took "The Dream Game" off the air. *It's made so many people happy,* she said.

Kellerman couldn't bear to watch it himself. Curly's rainbow suit reminded him of the most desperate days of his own
youth — when the hollow sucking feeling in his gut got
so bad he humiliated himself by becoming a walking billboard
for seven cents an hour, trudging up and down Main Street
in Kansas City while people read his chest and back. "Top
of the Town, Best All-Around," both sides said. It was a
lie. Top of the Town was an overpriced mediocre restaurant
for the top hats from Society Hill who thought it was swell
to look out over their green beans and see the Kansas and
Missouri Rivers in the same view. Still, he'd felt lucky to
have the job and be able to afford a frankfurter or a pig snoot
sandwich at the Nuberg Drive-In, which he would walk to
when he got off work. The memory of his own humiliation
helped him secretly forgive the spectacle his only child was
making of himself in a sissy suit on national TV. Even after
the indictment, and the ultimate acquittal, which seemed more
like a conviction somehow, at least to Kellerman. Even then
he could forgive his son. Not now.

On the back of the postcard tacked on the schoolhouse
door the day they retired him at the capitol was a brief note.
It's always spring in Dreamland. Love, Curly. Wonderful news,
Kellerman thought. Almost as wonderful as Curly's news
seven years earlier — ten years ago now — when he quit
college and announced he was leaving Oklahoma for good
because people waste their lives here.

You mean me, Kellerman had snapped.

If the shoe fits, his only son had answered.

Except for the letter containing the picture of Marlene, the
postcards were the only communication from Curly after he
left Oklahoma. The postcards would arrive from Honolulu or
Lahaina or Hilo or somewhere else in sunny Hawaii, addressed
always to Babe until the day she died. Then the cards stopped.

Well, if you won't eat, I won't make you, he remembered
Babe shouting through the schoolhouse window as he read
the card from Curly the afternoon the state retired him. He
grimaced, picturing Babe measuring out half portions of
spiceless ham and carrots on those tiny scales. No cardboard
diabetic dinners for him that night — he tuned her out and
listened to his honeys. Their buzzing enveloped him, filled
him, as he worked. He tinkered with the valve on his
automatic air compressor and forgot about Curly and the
capitol until eight o'clock that evening, when he began to
feel weak. A few minutes later Babe was at the window with
a pitcher of orange juice.

They sat outside on the propane tank, where he could see
his five acres. *We moved out here to get away from it all anyway,*
he remembered saying. She nodded and laid her hand on his
shoulder. He looked around. To the west, the afterglow from
the sunset was fading into gray. In a few minutes the sky
would be dark enough to pick up the first pale glow of
Yukon, five miles to the south. The blacktop road in front
of the house was quiet now, the rumble of an oil-tank truck
only a faint echo. The big tankers were a rarity these days.
Beyond the road he could hear crickets and night crawlers
starting up down by the wooded creek. He turned. On the
darker eastern horizon he could make out the small ghostly
silhouettes of the Kerr-McGee Tower and the new Liberty
National Bank in Oklahoma City twenty miles away. Two
decades earlier that horizon had been little more than a flat
line above Orville Zucha's wheat fields. Another ten and the
city would be crowding them, houses burying the wheat right
up to Kellerman's fence. Yukon and its farmlands would be
swallowed whole. Kellerman stared at the distant lights and
thought about the way Curly had changed over the years.

First he wants everything from me, then nothing, he said to Babe.

Live and let be, Frank. The boy's got his own way.

Kellerman rocked back on the propane tank and looked at Babe. She had changed too, even more than Curly. Thirty years ago she had been slim and meek. Her narrow face, when he could coax her into actually *looking* at him, was pale and almost featureless, trying to hide from the light. The years had thickened her body and steadied her gaze. She looked him dead in the eye now, her thin lips stretched in a perfect horizontal line.

His own way! Kellerman snapped. *I give him everything I've got, and he tells me I'm wasting my life. Then he takes off like he's gonna save the world — and becomes a fucking game show host. I ask you — who's wasting whose life? But hell, that's all right. He's a grown man. He can do what he wants. But now that it's over and they've cancelled the show, why does he stay away? Why these stupid postcards from Hawaii every month? Is he ashamed or what? If he is, well, hell, that's good. Shows he's got a conscience, at least. But doesn't he know we'll forgive him? I forgive him.*

He doesn't want your forgiveness, Frank.

Then why won't he come home and face me once? Just one time. Why does he have to run away?

The look in Babe's eyes made him flinch even before she spoke. *Frank, you're the only one in this family who ever ran away.*

Kellerman shook his head to erase the memory. The past was past, he reminded himself. He didn't want to think about it anymore. And just before dawn this morning he had decided he didn't have to. Why should he? The past was *pain.* Nothing else. On his sixty-fifth birthday the people who had made up his past — the life he had wanted, the life he had worked so hard for — were all either gone or dead. And the present? Well, that was hardly better. What was left for him now? A nosey half-breed who brought him sugar.

A senile old woman who thought she could fly. A son four thousand miles away who had shamed him.

And his project. He looked over at the lumpy gray canvas next to the automobile frame. The hum of his honeys' beating wings made his bones tingle. He grabbed a wrench. All right. Even if it didn't matter a good goddamn to anybody but him, he could still *work*, by god — here in his sanctuary, with his honeys, where no one could bother him. Here he was and here he would stay until he was finished, no matter if the whole town of Yukon and half the dead rose against him.

2

HE HEARD THE knocking in his daydream. He dreamed they were riding in the Hudson with the ragtop down, the afternoon sun warming the left side of his face while Babe held Curly in her lap, bending forward and clutching her scarf with one hand as the wind whipped around them. He knew the road and drove confidently, aggressively; rows of ripening wheat whizzed past them like blurred spokes in a golden wheel. He was about to tell Babe how beautiful it looked when he heard the knocking. It seemed to come from somewhere behind them, but when he turned he saw only the lonely gray ribbon of asphalt receding behind the car. As he looked back, the knocking grew louder and louder until suddenly the road dissolved into the broad blank green face of a plaster wall.

"Honker!"

Kellerman blinked. The room seemed darker, but the bulb still burned overhead and a beam of daylight still shone through the peephole — at a more perpendicular angle now, striking his lap as he sat on the automobile frame. Midday, he thought. He rose, bumping slightly against one of the doorposts he'd spent most of the morning welding onto the frame. He turned completely around, slowly, taking his bearings. North wall: large auto parts — fenders, bumpers, doors. East wall: sink, toilet, cot, icebox. South wall: main hive entrance, peephole, worktable. West wall: air compressor, sacks of sugar, oak door.

Through the door an impatient voice sounded. "Honker! You in there?"

Kellerman cleared his throat. "Who is it?"

"Who do you think?"

Blanket-assed sonofabitch. "Where's the ice?"

"Right here, damn it. Open up."

Kellerman started toward the door, then caught himself. He sat down in the swivel chair by his worktable. "You alone?"

"Just me and the ice."

"Yeah? How much you got?"

"Hundred fifty pounds enough?"

He considered it. He didn't want to leave the schoolhouse until he had finished his project. There wasn't much perishable food in the old icebox, but his vial of insulin had to be kept cool. The old box was huge, but he wasn't sure it would hold that much ice. Should have taken the trouble to hook up a refrigerator. "Yeah, for now. Just leave it on the porch there."

"It'll melt."

Kellerman said nothing, then listened to the sound of Charley Bluefire's tailgate, followed by the thuds of sacks of ice dumped by the door. Kellerman counted the thuds while a bee buzzed around his nose.

"Say, Honker, you wouldn't want to sell that old GMC pickup sittin' over there under the carport?"

"What?" Kellerman fumed, losing count as he brushed

away the bee. A wild thought formed in his head: *Hell, what do I need with that old truck anymore? You can just have it. The keys are in the house.* Then he came to his senses.

"Oh, I don't know." He shook his head. He'd taught Curly how to drive in that truck when the boy was still too small to see over the dash. He'd sat in Kellerman's lap and steered. Curly couldn't pronounce "GMC." He'd called it the Jimmie Truck.

"Well, you'd still have four cars left to drive, Honker. Not counting . . . "

Kellerman stiffened. "Not counting what?"

"Never mind." Charley's voice was flat and measured. *Coy bastard.*

"Anyway, four's probably enough vehicles for a man who's got no license to drive, wouldn't you say?"

Kellerman felt his face redden.

"Looks kinda like a used car lot out here anyway, you know? Or maybe a museum. How come you want to keep so many old cars, Honker? I never figured you for a sentimental kinda guy."

Kellerman flinched. *Used car lot* was the term Curly used to use when he griped about the row of *clunkers* lined up in the carport. *Why don't you trade in all these clunkers and get yourself a decent car, Dad?*

Decent, ha!

"What the hell does he know about decent?" Kellerman said.

"What?" Charley dropped another sack by the door.

"Nothing." Kellerman took a rag and wiped his brow. "Say, your boy I used to work on that GTO for — whatever happened to him?"

"Got him a liquor store in El Reno." *Thud.*

Figures. "Does a pretty good business, does he?"

"All right, I guess. Bought him a rent house down in

Yukon, too. He's married now, you know. Got two boys of his own play on the American Legion team.''

Kellerman remembered running a compression test on the boy's GTO. The kid stood there and gawked at him, greasy black hair hanging all the way down to his sweat-stained undershirt that said DO IT across the front.

So what's the verdict, Doc? the kid had said, jabbing his cigarette butt into an empty Coors can.

Your compression's shot. You need a complete valve and ring job — at least.

Oh, wow. Wow.

Kellerman shook his head at the image, then nearly shouted through the oak door: "Mind if I ask you a personal question, Charley?"

Thud.

"Not 'less it costs me money."

"What? No. That boy of yours . . . always seemed pretty wild to me. I had him pegged for somebody who'd run off one day and never come back . . . not meaning any harm, you understand."

Kellerman paused, but Charley said nothing.

"What I'm asking is: How come him to settle down like that?"

"Takes after his daddy."

Kellerman glared at the door.

"By the way, saw Curly on the TV this morning."

Thud. A flash of heat seared Kellerman's face and neck and chest for an instant. Of course Charley had seen it. Everybody would see it sooner or later.

"I'll say one thing," Charley went on. "Curly really bounced back, didn't he? You have to give him that."

Kellerman leaned forward, propped his elbows on his worktable, held his head in his hands, and said nothing.

"You know, I was a little surprised he called it what he did," Charley went on. "I mean 'Dream Voyager' and everything. I'm surprised they let him use that name. The game-show people, I mean."

Shut up! Kellerman wanted to scream. The image came to him unwillingly: Curly, standing there cool as you please in the foreground of a panoramic view of Waikiki Beach, Diamond Head Crater, and the blue Pacific, talking to the camera in that oh-so-smooth voice of his, grinning a big shit-eating grin. And his clothes, Sweet Jesus, his *clothes*: snow white trousers, a *pink* double-breasted blazer, and a navy blue captain's cap. Kellerman had watched just enough of the commercial to realize it wasn't advertising another game show but an airline offering a special package tour called "Dream Voyager." Charley was right. It was indeed amazing that "The Dream Game" would let him use that name, or that the airline would want to. Most amazing of all, to Kellerman at least, was the fact that Curly himself would want to do this. The sheer gall of it: using the same technique, the same scam that had brought him to shame! The only thing missing was the rainbow suit. And even that, Kellerman had quickly realized, even *that* was being used. This week a pink blazer. Next week a green one. Then red, blue, yellow, and so on. All the colors of the rainbow. That's how he'd work it. Kellerman had figured it all out on his way to get the ax.

"Yep, you got to admire him for bouncing back that way." *Thud.* "You hear from Curly much these days?"

"No." Kellerman closed his eyes and remembered the last time he'd spoken with his son, almost a year ago now, the day they lowered Babe into her grave. Curly standing there next to the coffin in Turch's Funeral Home, looking like the host. At least he'd had the sense, the *decency*, to wear a dark suit. Kellerman had stared at him, then blinked.

What's happened to your eyebrows?

I had them plucked. Curly arched his brows so they formed softly curving lines the shape of seagull wings. *Smooth brown skin is what people like to see, Dad.*

Kellerman nodded. *That's terrific. You pluck your crotch too? Or do people prefer white men's crotches?*

Kellerman regretted the outburst instantly; the shock in Curly's eyes only made it worse.

When Babe died Kellerman had been stunned, then frozen with grief for three days. He hadn't been certain his telegram to Curly's old Honolulu address would reach his son at all. Curly arrived from the airport only an hour before the funeral. A tan ghost. After the burial, as the two of them walked back to the Hudson Hornet (it had been the only automobile Babe was glad he'd hung on to), Kellerman's grief erupted into rage. He tried to spare Curly, aiming his anger instead at Dr. Farber, who had maintained until the end that the complications following Babe's coronary by-pass could be brought under control.

I'll burn the bastard for malpractice, Kellerman vowed as they climbed into the old Hudson.

Curly shook his head. *There's no point.*

Kellerman gave him a look he'd been saving for years. No point? Human life, the woman he loved, the mother of his child — no point?

I'll stay around a while, Curly said.

The hell you will.

And that was that. He hadn't heard from his son since.

"Ask the fucking TV where he is," Kellerman said.

"What's that?"

Thud.

"Nothing." Kellerman took off his bifocals and rubbed his eyes.

"By the way," Charley said a moment later. "You didn't hear the Crow Woman last night, did you?"

Kellerman felt his stomach tighten. "You just got to keep mentioning her, don't you?"

"The Crow Woman?"

"Who the hell you think I mean?" Kellerman pushed his glasses back to their perch on the bridge of his nose and glared at the door.

"Sorry." Charley's voice seemed apologetic and exasperated. "I guess I just never understood why old Mabel upsets you so much. She's pretty harmless, after all."

Kellerman clenched his teeth and said nothing.

Charley was quiet for several moments. "Maybe I don't know anything about it."

"Maybe you don't."

A minute passed. Kellerman stared at the door, no longer counting the thuds.

"Well, that's all of it," Charley said finally. "Sure you don't want me to stack these inside?"

Kellerman's head jerked up alertly. "No."

"OK, I guess I'll be going then."

Kellerman said nothing.

"Oh yeah," the voice behind the door blurted. "There was one more thing. I didn't mean to, really, but I told somebody at the capitol you moved into the schoolhouse."

Kellerman hissed at the door. "I thought I told you this was between you and me. I moved in here for privacy, damn it. I only told *you* because I need supplies and Ed Hacker can't throw *your* ass in jail for driving without a license."

"Sorry."

"Sorry my ass. Who'd you tell? Not Coats, I hope! Not Popeye, that little sneak."

"I told the King of Swing."

Kellerman spit on the floor. "The King of Swing. Great. Pick one guy to tell and it has to be a 400-pound nigger junkie. Why *him* for Christsake?"

"He asked about you."

"Sure he did."

"He said to say good luck, Honker."

"Good luck with *what*? Tell him to mind his own business."

There was no reply. Kellerman squinted at the oak door and listened for the sound of Charley's pickup starting. He heard only the hum of his honeys and the shrill peal of the wind whistling beneath the shingled roof of the schoolhouse. His brow furrowed. Quietly, he stepped over to his air compressor, unwrapped the hose, then crept over by the door.

"Listen, Honker," Charley finally said. "You all right in there?"

"I'm like a spring day. Why?"

"Come out here a minute, will you? I got something I want to talk with you about, face to face."

Kellerman gripped the nozzle on the air hose. "What?"

"Come on out and I'll tell you."

"No."

Charley sighed loud enough for Kellerman to hear. "All right. Just crack the door and let me see you for a second. OK?"

Kellerman glanced at the pressure gauge on the compressor: 220 psi.

"No."

"Look, Honker, I'm worried about you is all. My old lady's been giving me hell about my part in this. The sugar, I mean — you being a diabetic and all."

"Tell her it's for the bees."

"Bees eat sugar?"

"No — they eat Indians."

"What?"

Kellerman stuck the hose into a large crack in the wall next to the door, then opened the valve. The air blasted through the space between plaster and stone. In a moment he could feel more than hear the excitement spread through the wall. His honeys were moving.

"Aiyee! No! Get away!"

Kellerman kept blasting in five-second bursts until he heard the tires of Charley's pickup squeal over the pavement out front. Then, laughing until his eyes watered, he collapsed into the swivel chair.

"I don't believe he cared for our mood, honeys."

The pale green walls roared and shook.

Half an hour later, when the roar behind the walls had faded back to a hum, he fed the bees again.

"You earned it," he said, and dipped his finger into the pan of warm sugar water to rescue a bee that had fallen in, crowded off the rim by a hundred other hungry workers.

"Don't push, honeys," he reprimanded, and let the bee fan its damp wings a moment before lifting it to the dry safety of the nearest column of boxes. He noticed the beam of daylight from the peephole was growing dim, then turned back to his project.

He stared at the gleaming automobile frame and smiled. This was the moment he'd been looking forward to for months. It was time to install the V-8 engine. Once that was done, it would take only a couple of weeks at the most to assemble the rest of the car. He had every part sorted and organized in the jumble of piles and boxes around him. Just two weeks, and he'd have a classic V-8 roadster, the one he'd wanted since he was seventeen. He had everything he needed right here. He wouldn't have to come out of the schoolhouse at all until his project was finished.

"Heads up!"

He rolled the canvas back slowly, allowing each bee to take flight before it could be trapped in the folds. Laying the canvas aside, he ran his fingers over the cold rough steel of the V-8 engine and noted the clean hard lines of the drive shaft and rear axle. He remembered it was Otis Schmidt, the master mechanic of the old West Bottoms side of Kansas City, who first explained to him the anatomy of an automobile, over half a century ago, as the two of them lay on their backs under the long black chassis of Tom Pendergast's Pierce Arrow, the one Al Capone himself had ridden in.

Feel, Schmidt had said, and lifted Kellerman's small pink hand and rubbed it along the grimy bottom of the engine block, transmission, and drive shaft. *This is her heart and soul. The engine gives her power; the drive train directs it.*

Kellerman felt a cold tingle as he remembered the sleek black Pierce Arrow gliding through the sluggish Kansas City traffic — the boss, Mr. KC himself, Tom Pendergast, riding fancy and serene in the back seat, looking out over the city with gray cat eyes.

Now, Schmidt said. *Put your hand here and feel her come to life.*

Soft palm pressed against the cold hardness of the crankcase, Kellerman felt himself tremble.

Start her up, Henry.

The first explosive turn of the crankshaft sent a shudder through Kellerman's bones into the cold cement floor beneath them.

Can you feel it? Schmidt shouted above the engine's clattering roar.

Oil — syrupy and stinging cold at first, then slowly

thinning, growing blood warm — dripped from the cracked
crankcase onto Kellerman's bare chest, forming a black pool
over his heart.

He nodded.

Kellerman, working. Thinking only about the present now
as he slipped a steel cable loop under the heavy V-8 engine.
He stretched the cable tight, then lifted the motor carefully,
guiding it inch by inch along the upper bar of the A-frame
hoist to the engine's final resting place on the carefully restored
automobile frame. Gently, he lowered the motor, lining up
the engine supports with their proper mounts. Sweat beaded his forehead as he strained to tighten the heavy mounting
bolts. The bolts had to be tight or the engine would shudder and eventually shake loose.

"No . . . ummmph . . . bucking," Kellerman vowed as
he brushed a bee away from his nose.

Faster and faster he worked: lifting, hammering, measuring, tightening. He had his rhythm now. All around him
his honeys worked too, buzzing back and forth between the
hive entrance and the pan of sugar water. The buzzing grew
louder and louder until the walls seemed to sing, the music
of a hundred thousand wings beating between stone, honeycomb, and plaster. He felt the humming song enter his skin,
felt it vibrate deep in his bones, then ripple out through the
muscles in his arms and hands, to the wrench. He felt his
head swell with the sweet intoxicating scent of fresh honey,
fanned through hundreds of tiny cracks in the humming walls.

A fine machine, Kellerman thought, and laid his palm on
the gritty surface of the clutch housing.

The itching started in his feet. First only the tips of his
toes, then the soft flesh beneath his toenails. He doused both

feet with Absorbine Jr., but the itch crawled up his ankles and soon his lower legs burned and tingled as if he were standing in salt. He paced around the automobile frame and periodically stomped on the wooden floor, trying to get the blood circulating in his legs, hoping the itch would not spread back down to the soles of his feet.

He hadn't thought about the needle since locking himself in. Hadn't thought about the itching, the cold numb feeling in his fingers, the weakness that had returned to him each day since the incredible weight loss that marked the onslaught of the disease three years ago. *It was a long shot, getting diabetes at your age, Frank,* Dr. Kiner had said. *Long shots come in,* Kellerman had replied.

He was back up to nearly 140 pounds now, but it had not been without a fight. He'd followed Dr. Kiner's instructions faithfully every day, including the day Babe died.

Now, as the itchy feeling crawled up his calves, he remembered the needle. He felt himself shrinking away, the way he used to when Babe gave him his thirty units every morning.

Hold still.

Uhhh.

Now give me your cup. Look at that now! All neg, neg, neg since lunch yesterday. You can have a dish of Sweet'n Legal tonight, if you want it.

No.

Suit yourself.

After Babe died he had to give himself the injections. In the swivel chair now, he removed the vial from his icebox, which was only slightly cool — Got to remember to bring that ice in, damn it — and prepared the syringe. He should have given himself his shot first thing this morning. When the syringe was ready he rolled up his right pant leg. He had learned to give himself the injections quickly, as if he were throwing a dart at a picture. He used his thighs most often because he hated the ugly creases insulin atrophy made on his arms.

"Uhhh."

He pushed the needle out of his mind by concentrating on a larger worry. Charley Bluefire's words still bothered him. *Takes after his daddy.* Why? He never remembered Charley and his boy being what you would call close. Charley's boy always seemed too stupid to pay much attention to anybody.

Kellerman remembered watching his own son staring curiously at the water in the deep end of the swimming pool in Spring Lake Park in Oklahoma City. Kellerman noticed how timid Curly seemed, standing well back from the edge as he looked at the big whale painted on the bottom of the deep end. Curly's first- and second-grade teachers had both remarked on how sluggish the boy was. His third-grade teacher said they were considering holding him back a year. *There might be some sort of learning dysfunction,* Mrs. Beauchamp had said.

Learning dysfunction? His son? The idea made Kellerman furious. We'll show 'em, he thought, but determined to show his son first.

Got to get wet if you want to swim, he said, and stepped up to the diving board. He bounced a couple of times, then sprang high into the air, waving to Curly just before hitting the water feet first. Kellerman did not know how to swim. He was astonished by how deep the plunge took him. When he felt his feet touch the bottom, he sprang toward the surface, frightened for an instant that he wouldn't make it. Then he broke through and splashed clumsily toward the side, kicking and windmilling to keep his head high enough to get an occasional gulp of air.

It's easy, he panted, hanging onto the gutter. He grinned at his son and glanced over at the long rescue pole standing by the bathhouse. *Try it.*

The boy looked doubtfully at the still-rippling water beneath the diving board. While his father clung to the gutter, he walked over to the shallow end and climbed down into the water by the 2½-foot sign.

"Learning dysfunction . . . my ass," Kellerman wheezed. He laid the syringe on the worktable. No, there was nothing wrong with the boy's *brain* that made him turn out the way he did. And he certainly wasn't *timid* anymore, strutting around on national TV in that faggy rainbow suit.

"No, honeys, you couldn't call the boy timid — not since he was ten years old anyway. He stood up to me more than once; I'll give him that." *Wax all those clunkers of yours? Why should I?*

Kellerman took a deep breath, then leaned over and looked through the peephole. In the hundred feet separating the house and schoolhouse stood the wide free-standing carport he'd built to house his automobiles. Babe had hated the idea. *A monument to your first and only love,* she called it. The roof was made of tin, and when it rained during the night the clattering roar kept her awake. *Car crazy,* she'd mutter, twisting fitfully in the bed. *No sane person hangs onto every car he ever owned.*

Kellerman smiled. Babe always exaggerated the point. He'd owned other cars, lots of them. The ones he'd kept over the years were special to him; he'd never bothered to explain. The way he saw it was, you live with a person long enough, you ought to be able to figure out on your own why they value what they do.

Ever since he'd built the carport, the sound of rain striking its tin roof always helped *him* sleep more soundly. "Kind of puts my mind at rest, honeys," he murmured now as he peered through the peephole at the tin structure.

The carport was wide enough for five automobiles; he could see them lined up under the canopy in the order they had come into his possession:

1. A 1929 Moon 8-80 Prince of Windsor roadster. Painted a brilliant, startling purple, the color of a lacquered Concord grape, and set up on blocks.

2. A 1951 Hudson Hornet ragtop. The "Green Hornet," Babe's favorite.

3. A faded blue 1954 GMC pickup, the one Curly called the Jimmie Truck.

4. A gleaming 1956 Studebaker Silver Hawk coupé. Kellerman's pride and shame.

5. A beat-up rusty gray Corvair sedan. Clearly out of place among the others.

He pulled away from the peephole. "Every one of them cars still runs, honeys. Every one of 'em's a piece of my life. Only one missing is my very first one."

As he said these words, a tremor passed through Kellerman's body. He took a slow, measured breath, then turned and gazed for a long moment at the dark gray steel of the V-8 engine resting on the auto frame in the center of the room.

Then his thoughts returned to Babe.

"Car crazy. First and only love." He mimicked the low accusing tone of her voice. "Well, cars *were* my first love, all right. Ever since the day I met Al Capone."

Kellerman stood up and walked over to his project. He ran his fingers gingerly over the engine block. One by one, his honeys took flight to avoid his hand, then landed on the same spot.

"Didn't know about that, did you, honeys. A lot of big boys used to hang around the West Bottoms side of Kansas City when I was growing up. Tom Pendergast, Cas Welch, Charley Clark. I sold the *Kansas City Star* on the corner of 19th and Main, right outside Pendergast's headquarters. I was hardly in long pants in them days, but I was working every afternoon just the same. Tom Pendergast always treated me good; I have to give him that. He bought every paper I had left at the end of the day and give me a shiny new quarter on top of that. If I had too many left for him to carry off, he'd take one and tell me to give the rest to the priests down in West Bottoms.

"One day it was real cold, so cold the bums were building fires in trash barrels right in front of the cops. Hell, the cops were building fires too. Tom Pendergast drove up in that big black Pierce Arrow of his, the kind that had headlights on the inside of the fender. I didn't have gloves or nothing, and when I handed him the papers my hands were shaking. 'You cold, son?' he asks me. I just stood there shivering. So then he says, 'This is your lucky day, son. Get right in here. Let's go for a ride.'

"He always had his driver and another man up front, but this time there's a man in back too. 'This is Lucky,' Pendergast says, like I was one of the boys. Then he says to me, 'This is Mr. Chi-town.' I didn't know who Mr. Chi-town was at the time, but I shook his hand when he offered it. He had on the bluest suit I ever saw, but what struck me about him was he didn't smell like a regular man. Pendergast always used perfume himself — toilet water we used to call it back in them days — but Mr. Chi-town, he must of took a bath in it every morning. He smelled, well, like he was above the rest of us, if you know what I mean. I didn't say nothing to him; I was just happy to be in that big warm car instead of out in the cold."

Kellerman licked his lips. "So off we went. The whole inside of that automobile was gold leather. Not brown or tan. Gold! Smelled just like a big brand-new pocketbook. Well, we must of gone fifty miles an hour down Main Street, right in the middle of traffic. Mr. Chi-town and Pendergast were talking about something, but I just looked out the window, hoping I'd see somebody I knew. I didn't, of course, but we rode all the way down to the Liberty Memorial south of Union Station where they had that big massacre a few years later. We pulled right up there by the monument for all the men killed in the Great War, and Mr. Chi-town shakes my hand again and says, 'Good luck to ya, Lucky.' Then he and Mr. KC — that's what I called Tom Pendergast after that — they get in another car and go off to a meeting or something. Me, I was drove all the way back downtown to the very same corner, like I had an office there or something. Mr. KC forgot to give me my quarter that time, only time he ever forgot, but I didn't care."

Kellerman sighed heavily, then smiled at a bee fanning its wings on the V-8 engine. "You can't imagine how it felt, honey: dirty black ink all over my frozen hands, riding in that big soft leather seat of that big black Pierce Arrow all by myself . . . sitting in the warm spots where Mr. KC and Mr. Chi-town had sat, smelling that rich sweet smell of a different sort of man . . ."

The smile left Kellerman's face as the bee took flight and disappeared into a crack above the skillet. Kellerman sat down in the swivel chair and stared at the wall.

"If Babe knew how that ride felt," he said slowly, his voice softening to a whisper, "she would of understood *this* too . . ." He glanced over at the V-8 engine and automobile frame. For a long moment he was silent. Then his voice rose. "The smell," he said. "I wanted to keep it with me."

The room was quiet. Kellerman sat motionless in the chair for several minutes. Then he took a deep breath, filling his lungs once again with the smell of gold leather and perfume. He leaned toward the peephole, watching the buildings on Main Street whiz by. *Beautiful*, he dreamed.

3

IN THE MORNING he awoke exhausted.

He felt the exhaustion in the stiff muted crackle of his joints as he sat up on the edge of the old army cot. He squinted at the narrow beam of daylight angling through the peephole. He was glad to see this sign of morning. The night had stolen his strength. Or something had.

He'd slept little. Something had kept waking him, long after he had finally turned out the overhead light and stumbled from his worktable to the cot, a noise he couldn't quite make out. Each time he stirred, the sound seemed to fade away as if it existed only in an unremembered dream. But the silence of the dark room unsettled him somehow, as if he expected to hear more. He lay awake for several minutes each time, listening, until the scratchy drone of crickets and night crawlers began to seep into the dark room, through the cracked stone where his honeys slept, and lulled him back to sleep.

Once, snapping awake in the darkness, he thought he recognized the sound. A ticking, a tapping, a faint rap on the window. The sound of the Crow Woman. He stared into the gloom, stomach twisting, expecting to see Mabel Zucha's carnivorous old beak pecking against the glass, her cold black eyes, eyes that truly gave her the look of a scavenger crow, watching him. Expecting to hear her other sound, the hoarse cawing sound that made him shiver as if someone were pricking him with a sliver of ice. A sound that was many sounds — a moan, a jeer, a boast, a cry of pain, and a miserable, sickening laugh: *Haaa. Haaa.*

But the sound vanished as soon as he heard it. The night was hushed. The windows were all boarded up. Only a thin ray of moonlight penetrated the dark room through the peephole. He cocked his head and listened but heard only silence. Then, gradually, the faint, monotonous whir of insects. He didn't remember drifting back to sleep.

Now the beam was hard and bright with morning, splitting the still dark room in half. He rose and switched on the overhead light. His honeys filled the room with a soaring hum, and Kellerman took a deep refreshing breath, then paced around the automobile frame. "I feel *good,* I feel *good,*" he chanted. And it was true. His strength was coming back. He had feeling in all his fingers; his toes tingled with each step.

He cooked up some canned chili on the hot plate and ate it as he started to work. The greasy gut feeling from the chili disappeared with sweat. Perspiration beaded his neck and forehead as he raised the transmission and clutch assembly onto a dolly. Now that he had the engine installed, he figured it would take no more than a week to assemble the drive train, suspension system, and basic chassis. Then another week to finish the entire car. He rubbed his chin, feeling the initial stubble of a beard. This was the morning of his second day in the schoolhouse; he'd decided to keep track just to pace himself.

"Let's go, honeys."

He used the A-frame hoist to lift the transmission off the dolly and onto a jack stand behind the engine. Unhooking the pulley, he glanced at the peephole. The beam of sunlight reassured him. "Full day ahead," he said brightly, the way he used to say it every morning when he slapped Babe on the butt and rolled out of bed to get ready to drive down to open up the garage in Yukon. "A full day for a full day's work."

Car crazy.

He nodded. Yes, that's exactly what she'd say, the grumpy hardass bitch, every morning as he tried to rouse himself to face the day with a little enthusiasm. He could manage it in those days when he still had his beloved garage and auto body shop. But that was twenty years ago.

Kellerman blinked, realizing he was just standing there, holding the pulley in his hand. He looked at the south wall — humming busily, his honeys zipping in and out of the hive — and shook his head. Again he found himself wishing he could drive the memory of Babe's voice from his mind altogether.

"Damn woman never set foot in this schoolhouse when she was alive, honeys. Now she won't stay put in the ground." He laughed aloud at the absurdity of it.

He went over to the sink and filled a glass with tap water and drank it slowly, looking over his project. "I know just what she'd say about moving in here. 'I'll swan, I'm surprised you didn't move in there before now.' That's what she'd say. Well, answer me *this*," he said, turning to the wall again. "Why shouldn't I do something just because I want to? Haven't I earned the right?"

He waited a moment, as if the wall would answer, but heard only the incessant hum. In front of the hive entrance bees landed on the rim of the pan, drinking in sugar water, then returned to the hive.

"You're right, honeys," Kellerman said. "Back to work."

Later in the morning, as he wrapped steel cable around the transmission and clutch assembly to hoist them over to the engine and frame, he began to daydream again. He tried to imagine Curly's reaction, years from now — the bees will be long gone by then, Kellerman thought, and so will I — when Curly opened the door to the musty old schoolhouse and found a shiny red Model 18 Ford Deluxe Roadster parked inside, like a ship in a bottle. What would he think?

Probably think I'm crazy, Kellerman decided. Think I built it just to show off. Kellerman shook his head, remembering how he had always tried to impress his own father. "No matter what I did, I couldn't please him, honeys."

Kellerman pictured his German immigrant father, Joseph: a grim hawk-faced man wearing heavy black boots, a dirty gray undershirt, and baggy trousers held up by red suspenders — and a long black belt. The belt had another function. During Prohibition, Joseph Kellerman mixed hops and barley malt in one of the tiny illegal brew barns on the West Bottoms side of Kansas City. At night he was a fearsome drunk.

"The bastard," Kellerman muttered. "Twelve hours a day he made beer and whiskey, honeys, then came home at night and tried to drink up every drop he'd made all day. Then he'd get after *me*, and Mom would step between us. Ten years after he was dead, you could still see lash marks on her legs." Kellerman winced as he pictured his sister Dottie cringing in a corner of the tiny living room while his mother Rose thrust herself between him and Father's lashing belt, taking ferocious licks on her own bare legs until finally Father's rage was spent and he returned to his beer.

"Drunk or not, he always did exactly what he wanted, honeys, with never a thought for the rest of us. Like when he'd do his damn trick." Kellerman bit his lip as he remembered.

Father knew only one trick. Every night, right in the middle of supper, he would push his chair back, then stand up. A thin smile creased the hawklike features of his face.

Dottie giggled and pushed her chair back away from the table. Mother glared furiously at Father for a long moment, then sighed. Kellerman held his breath.

Nobody blink, Father said, then reached down and grasped the tablecloth with one hand. Then, almost too quickly to see, he whipped the cloth out from under the supper dishes. Not a plate moved.

Yea! Dottie cried.

I swear, the first time you miss, I'll scream, Mother said.

Father's face resumed its hawklike expression. Without another word to anyone, he sat back down at the table and finished eating.

Kellerman never said anything to Father about it, but the trick always impressed him. The trick was one of the few pleasures Father took in life, the only thing that made him smile. Kellerman secretly wished he could do the trick himself and make Father proud. He'd tried it a hundred times, using rocks or books instead of plates, but never mastered it.

Then one day Sandy the carnival geek taught him something even more impressive.

Sandy was a big red-haired man with long black cat whiskers painted on his cheeks. *It's the art of it that counts, little ferret. You've got to play to your audience. When you pull that mouse out of the box, hold him up so they can see he's alive and not one of them rubber mice you can get in a gag shop. Let him move around in your fist, then squeeze him just a little bit so he'll squeak. When you're ready, hook your thumb under his jaw like this, see? So he won't bite your tongue. Then open up wide and put him in real slowlike, so they'll know you're not faking it. Now if your crowd's a little squeamish, don't forget to close your lips all the way around the head before you bite, so's you don't spray. And afterwards, have yourself a bucket or something right there to spit him out in.*

The carnival geek's eyes narrowed and he grinned, making the cat whiskers fan across his cheeks. *Now as for actually biting off the head — well, little ferret, that's strictly a matter of will power.*

He practiced the trick for a week, learning to make a clean bite and to ignore the taste of blood. Then one evening after dinner he sat down on the back porch and watched Father rock slowly in the rocker, staring into the gloom and sipping warm black beer from a copper stein. Dottie and Mother were busy in the kitchen.

After a while Father stopped rocking. *Well, what you look at me?*

Kellerman reached over the side of the porch and brought up a shoe box. *I can do something you can't do.*

Reaching into the box, he felt Father's sharp eyes watching him. It took several moments to catch the mouse, and he felt his face begin to sweat. Finally, he trapped the mouse under his palm. He knew he didn't have quite the right grip on it but pulled it out of the box anyway. Immediately he realized his mistake. The mouse's front legs were free, and it squeaked and squirmed wildly in his hand.

What the hell? Father said and rocked forward to get a closer look.

The mouse was getting loose. Desperately, he grabbed it with both hands and bit. He made a clean bite but forgot to close his lips. The blood sprayed through his teeth and hit Father in the face. He leaped up, coughing and sputtering, then reached for his belt.

Kellerman turned and ran. Somewhere in the yard he must have spit out the head.

All afternoon he worked.

He installed the transmission and clutch assembly as a single unit. "Easy," he murmured, letting out cable to lower both sections onto their supporting blocks above the frame. He aligned the driving and the driven plates, then went to work on the bolts attaching the clutch housing to the engine. The clutch was in good shape, he noted: adjustment ring tight, plenty of fiber left on the driven plate.

When the last bolt on the clutch housing was tight, he rested.

Soon his hands and feet began to itch. Nuts, he thought, and shook his head. Like the day before, he'd gotten caught up in things and forgotten to take his shot first thing in the morning.

Better watch that from now on, you damn fool.

After he had given himself the shot, and the itch was beginning to fade, he found himself staring at the needle.

He'd hated needles even before he developed diabetes. Hated them ever since the day he had saved the King of Swing's life. He could still remember the day it happened, five years ago now. He had risen to the unofficial rank of chief troubleshooter on the capitol maintenance crew by then. He was the man everybody came to when the steam pipes exploded or the governor got stuck in an elevator. He was damn good in a crisis; even Merle Coats admitted that. It was late afternoon, just before quitting time, and he was checking the master switches on the fifth floor power box when Charley Bluefire stuck his head in the door.

Honker?

Yeah.

The King of Swing wants to see you. In his perch.

Kellerman raised his eyebrows and stared at Charley. Like the other men on the crew, Kellerman had heard rumors about the King of Swing's perch, a tiny room hidden from view somewhere near the very top of the rotunda. Kellerman had never been up there.

What's he want?

The look in Charley's eyes told Kellerman he'd better see for himself. He followed Charley down the hallway.

The fifth floor was the highest level of the capitol except for the inverted saucer-shaped roof that capped the rotunda. Charley led Kellerman to a balcony overlooking the rotunda. Kellerman leaned over the balustrade and stared down through the huge stone cylinder nearly a hundred feet to the marble map of Oklahoma on the first floor where men who looked like cockroaches were busy mopping the panhandle.

Not there, Honker. Up there. Charley pointed up at the star of the Great Seal looming overhead.

Kellerman gawked. *How do we get up there?*

Charley selected a key from the chain on his belt and unlocked a door next to the balcony. Kellerman followed him inside. The room was a janitor's closet. As Kellerman watched, Charley stepped over to the opposite wall and slid open a panel in the wainscoting.

I'll be damned.

Behind the opening a narrow spiral staircase made of iron rose through a dark shaft.

How'd the King of Swing ever fit up that?

Quiet now, Charley whispered as he stepped through the opening. *This is his place.*

Climbing up the dark spiral behind Charley, Kellerman said nothing but nodded respectfully. The King of Swing was the biggest, most powerful man he had ever seen. He pictured the enormous black man Merle Coats had nicknamed for the way he handled the heavy industrial floor waxer — his thick black muscles rippling and sparkling with sweat as he swung the machine back and forth, covering the entire width of a capitol hallway with each swing: the King of Swing. He's beautiful in the way of a man, Kellerman had once admitted.

Kellerman heard only the muted plinks of their shoes on the iron steps as Charley led him up the tight spiral, winding through a hole in the ceiling — up, up, into more darkness until finally they emerged onto a curving catwalk. Kellerman was momentarily blinded by a flood of light from the leaded glass surrounding the golden disk of the Great Seal affixed to the curved roof of the rotunda. The late afternoon sunlight streamed through the leaded glass and formed a halo around the big five-point star inside the disk. The catwalk was concealed from below by the molding of the ornamental facade that surrounded the base of the curved roof of the rotunda.

This way, Charley whispered. He led Kellerman a quarter of the way around the circular catwalk until they came to a doorway filled with hanging beads. Charley pushed aside the beads and led him into a small dark room. For a moment, Kellerman saw and heard nothing. Then from the floor a black mass spoke.

I'm strung out, Honker.

Kellerman stared. As his eyes adjusted to the darkness, the King of Swing's enormous body came into focus. The King lay on his back, his powerful muscles flexing and quivering uncontrollably. He looked to Kellerman like a wounded bear caught in a trap. In the dim light from the Great Seal, the King of Swing's great black star eyes bulged and glowed around the pupils — Kellerman feared they might pop out. A thin shaft of light struck the floor in front of the trembling giant, and Kellerman saw a burned-out book of matches — and a needle.

I can't get up, Honker . . . The King of Swing clenched his teeth, waiting for a shudder to pass. Sweat covered his skin, making his great dark body flicker with each spasm. *I can't get back down the spiral, man. I can't do it* . . . *I need you to rig up something and lower me down.*

Mouth open, Kellerman said nothing.

I got to get down *from here, man! Devil comin' after me. I seen him. I seen the devil, Honker — right where you're standing now. You hear me? You the troubleshooter, Honker* . . . *You got to bring me down.*

Kellerman watched the desperate man's body glimmer in the faint light. *OK, King. I'll get you down.*

Half an hour later Kellerman had things organized. He recruited Popeye, another janitor from Yukon, to help Charley Bluefire with the lowering. Kellerman hated having Popeye help, but none of the other men on the maintenance crew would touch the job. Popeye was too terrified of the King of Swing to refuse. And he owed Kellerman for getting him his job at the capitol, just as Kellerman owed Charley Bluefire. Popeye had begged Kellerman about the job until he finally gave in and talked to Coats. In Yukon, Popeye had once driven a wrecker for Kellerman's garage, but Kellerman didn't trust him. He had hairy gray skin and stood only about five feet tall and reminded Kellerman of a cross-eyed, pie-eyed rat — the way his bulging little eyes always pointed in different directions, never looking directly at you. He gave Kellerman the creeps. Charley said Popeye had knocked his eyes out of whack when he fell off a hay truck when he was a boy. Kellerman thought he was retarded. Popeye's only virtue was that he could be frightened into doing just about anything.

I'm scared; it's too high, Popeye whined on the catwalk after Charley had dragged him up the secret staircase.

Shut up and grab that strap, Kellerman said.

Under Kellerman's direction, Popeye helped Charley strap the King of Swing onto the plank of a painter's scaffold. When the King was securely lashed to the plank, Kellerman hung two pulleys from opposite ends of an exposed iron girder that helped support the low, flat roof above the catwalk. He attached a separate rope to each end of the plank, then looped each rope through a pulley overhead. Because the balconies on every level of the rotunda were recessed, they would have to lower the King of Swing all the way to the ground floor. Charley and Popeye would handle the ropes while Kellerman supervised.

I can't do it, whined Popeye as he peered over the edge of the facade, cocking his head to aim one eye up at the Great Seal and the other down at the marble map of Oklahoma more than a hundred feet below.

Jiggle that rope one more time and I'll toss you over the edge, Kellerman said matter of factly. Lashed to the plank, the King of Swing stopped shaking enough to glare at Popeye, who instantly froze, grasping the rope like a cross-eyed manikin.

Remember, Kellerman said, *each of you's got to let out exactly the same amount of rope or the platform will tilt and he'll slide right off, straps or no straps.*

Charley and Popeye each took a deep breath. On the plank the King of Swing clenched his teeth and hissed.

The first part of the lowering went smoothly. First they pulled the slack out of the ropes and hoisted the King of

Swing above the catwalk. Then, while Charley and Popeye
held the ropes steady, Kellerman gently swung the plank over
the edge of the facade and held it there. No one looked down.

OK, very gently now, Kellerman directed. *Start letting it out.
Together now.*

Slowly, the King of Swing began to descend. *Lay still!*
Kellerman shouted as the narrow plank squeaked and groaned
under the black man's enormous weight. Lower and lower
the giant descended, past the fifth, then the fourth and
third stories.

I can't tell if he's level anymore, Kellerman said then. *Hold
him steady right there till I get down and check.*

He climbed down the spiral, then raced down the stairwell
to the third floor and stepped out onto the balcony. The King
of Swing dangled about half a story below him, his head tilted
lower than his feet.

Charley! Let out about a foot on your side! Kellerman's voice
echoed up and down the rotunda, but nothing happened.
Then suddenly the left rope quivered, and the King of Swing
was level again.

OK — hold steady till I get down on one! Kellerman yelled
and raced for the stairs.

The first floor was deserted. It was well after quitting time
now, and Merle Coats had ordered the rest of the maintenance
crew to stay out of sight until the King of Swing was down,
one way or another. Kellerman stood in the center of the
marble map of Oklahoma and looked up at the King of
Swing, who hung above him like a corpse ready to be
lowered into a grave.

OK — ease him down!

Once again the plank descended, until about twenty feet
above Kellerman's head a spasm shook the King of Swing,
rocking the platform.

Keep going!

The plank descended unevenly, jerking and twisting until finally Kellerman reached up and grabbed a corner of the board and guided it to the floor. The King of Swing came safely to rest on the southeast corner of the map, next to the town of Idabel.

He's down! Kellerman yelled, and looked down at the King of Swing. The trembling man rolled his head and looked Kellerman in the eye.

I owe you one, Honker.

That evening, as the hum of his honeys began to fade, he attached the drive shaft to the transmission. The Model 18 had a ball and socket U joint, and Kellerman was grateful this one showed no signs of wear, for he had no replacement. He worked up a good sweat as he horsed the heavy drive shaft into position.

"What goes round when you press the pedal down?" Kellerman sang softly as he completed the link. "What turns true when your life is black and blue?"

Car crazy.

"Yeah, yeah. I've heard it before." Kellerman scowled, upset that he couldn't put the mocking sound of Babe's voice out of his mind. It was like the bitch was still around somehow. Like that goddamn peperomia of hers that wouldn't die. "Goddamn road weed," Kellerman sneered.

She had brought the peperomia home in a clay pot the day after Curly left home for California. *We need more life around here,* she said.

"Life! It's life she wanted, honeys," Kellerman groaned.

That was the start of the potted plant invasion, he recalled, lining up the bolts on the U joint. Jades, ferns, African violets, a hundred other plants with names he

couldn't pronounce, much less remember, growing green and
fat on coffee tables and window sills. He remembered lying
on the living room sofa one afternoon, watching incredulously
as she watered, sprayed, and repotted, lecturing the plants
like they were children.

Now, Virginia, you perk up, she said to the peperomia.

Christ on a crutch, he growled from the sofa, but she let
it pass. He shook his head. As she spoke to the peperomia
her voice grew soft, almost lilting. Not at all the low gruff
tone he was used to hearing. He felt strangely left out. *Air.
I need air,* he said, and got up to take a walk.

He wandered across Orville Zucha's wheat fields to the
wooded area down by the creek. After a while he came to
an old willow tree growing next to a stagnant pool. He
didn't recall noticing this particular tree before, though he
had walked this way many times when he was moody. The
willow's shaggy limbs drooped so low the bottom leaves
touched the dark green water of the pool. He sat down on
an exposed root and saw that the gnarled tree trunk was
hollow. A dark crack split the bark from root to limb.

He stared up at the ancient tree and remembered another
willow he'd seen years before — in Penn Valley Park in Kansas
City where he and Babe used to go for walks after they both
got off work at the Nabisco factory. Babe had been young
then, and slim. And frightened, a scared-mouse look in her
eyes whenever she glanced at him across the conveyor belt
that carried chocolate cookies into the box stuffer. Her voice,
when he could coax her into speaking at all, sounded, in the
clanking roar of the stuffer, like a squeak.

She was different in the quiet leisure of the park. She took
off her shoes and walked barefoot over the cool grass. To
him, her walk looked more like a dance: light and springy
and joyous, the way he imagined a ballerina moved on stage.

And when she spoke, her voice was firmer, and the scared-mouse look in her eyes dissolved into a softer, more inviting expression that made him notice the curve of her body beneath the blue cotton dress. He remembered reaching for her one breezy afternoon as they neared a large drooping tree.

That's a willow, she said, and stepped lightly away from his grasp. *Willows bend with the wind, but they're strong.* She seemed to know the name of every tree and flower in that park, identifying each for him as they strolled past.

Suddenly he understood the potted plants. He got up, tripping over the root, and hurried back to the house.

Hey, he said, puffing into the living room. *I want to show you something down by the creek.*

Look at you! she replied sharply and grabbed a mop. *There's cow shit all over your shoes!*

Hell's bells, Kellerman said, and ripped off his shoes and tossed them out on the porch. So be it, he thought as he waited for Babe to bring him his slippers. I won't beg her.

The day after Babe's funeral he took a butcher knife and hacked every plant in the house to pieces. Except for the peperomia, which he shut away in a dark cabinet above the water heater. He found it again a month later, pale and wilted, but somehow still alive. He carried it out with the trash and dumped both into the cage he used as an incinerator. After spreading the *Sunday Oklahoman* throughout the cage, he set the contents on fire and watched the brown smoke trail off toward Yukon.

A month later he found a single green leaf rising out of the blackened tin cans and ashes.

All right, all right, he said. He moved his trash burner to the other side of the yard.

Kellerman, working. Into a long, exhausting night, attaching the differential and rear axles to the drive shaft. Lying stiff and sore between the jacks supporting the rear wheels. He gave each wheel a spin and watched them rotate in opposite directions.

"Atta babies."

He bolted the protective dust cap onto the differential, then reached up and ran his fingers along the drive shaft. Sixty horsepower, he thought. Sixty wild horses running down this shaft to these wheels. He switched off his extension light and squirmed out from under the frame.

"Easy," he wheezed and crawled into the swivel chair. The room was quiet. His honeys were fast asleep, huddled between stone and plaster, the sounds from the walls only a murmur. He took a moment to catch his breath, then looked over at his project.

He smiled. This was the end of his second day in the schoolhouse, and already he'd installed the engine and drive train.

"We're ahead of schedule, honeys." He said the words aloud though there were no bees left in the room to hear them.

Less than two weeks to go, he thought. Less than two weeks. As he looked over the gleaming metal of the V-8 engine and frame, his breaths grew longer, slower. His head nodded forward.

Somewhere in Kellerman's mind a key turned, and sixty wild horses galloped into the night.

4

HE AWOKE IN moonlight.

Slumped over his worktable, Kellerman lifted his head and gazed at the cold beam of moonlight streaming through the peephole. He shivered. After midnight, he guessed, lifting his head to measure the angle of the beam. Around him the room was black. He rubbed his arms to break the chill, then felt above his head for the chain that hung from the 200-watt bulb. Burned out.

"Damn."

He blinked and tried to adjust his eyes to the darkness. No good. He could see nothing beyond the beam. The worktable, cool and solid beneath his fingertips, was invisible. He rubbed his eyes and followed the beam through the darkness until a shape appeared: the skeleton of a large animal. He felt the muscles in his chest tense for an instant, then he recognized the shape of the automobile engine and frame.

Damn night. He felt around on the invisible table for the flashlight he always kept near his magnifying glass. Gone. Must have moved it. As he leaned forward into the light from the peephole, he felt a shadow cross his face.

It passed quickly, breaking the beam for only an instant. A bat, he thought, turning toward the peephole. Nothing to worry about. He started to resume his search for the flashlight, then stopped. No, the shadow was too large for a bat. A cow maybe. Or a deer.

He leaned over the table and peered through the peephole. The yard outside was gray and still. His automobiles lined up beneath the roof of the carport like a row of silent guardians. Beyond them he could see the dark silhouette of the empty house. He searched its outline carefully but saw nothing.

An animal, he thought. A deer.

He leaned back into the darkness and listened. The walls were quiet. Cautiously, he slid his chair toward the wall in front of him and pressed his ear against the cool plaster. Deep inside the wall he heard the low humming of sleepy bees huddled between stone and plaster. "Sleep tight, honeys," he whispered and started to pull away, when he heard something else.

He smashed his ear against the wall, but the sound was too faint, lost in the soft hum. He remembered the noise that had awakened him the previous night, the tapping sound of the Crow Woman knocking at his window.

Mabel, is that you? Go home, you old bat, he wanted to call out now, but did not. He pressed his ear harder against the plaster wall. The sound interrupting the droning lullaby of his honeys' wings had a regular beat but was much too faint to be someone knocking.

He leaned back in the swivel chair and stared into the darkness around him. Then, as silently as he could, he lifted himself off the chair and followed the beam of moonlight to the automobile frame. He gripped a side rail with one hand and knelt by the frame. With his free hand, he felt around for a clear space on the invisible floor. He scraped away dirt and sawdust, then pressed his ear against the bare floorboards. Through the century-old wood he felt more than heard the footsteps.

He sat up and took a series of quick shallow breaths. *Easy.* Instinctively Kellerman felt around the frame for a wrench or a hammer, but his tools had disappeared into the darkness. *Easy.* He couldn't see the oak door but knew it was bolted. And the windows — everything was secure, he reminded himself. He waited.

Nothing happened. The room was still. He could hear the distant whirring of crickets down by the creek. Nothing else. Gripping the frame, he bent down and pressed his ear once more against the cold floor. Nothing. Then a soft sound, a pat on the earth outside. Then another and another: the slow, regular pattern of footsteps. Coming no closer, moving no further away. Circling the schoolhouse, he determined. As he listened he realized the footfalls were too heavy to be a woman's. A man, walking round and round the schoolhouse in the middle of the night. Who? Why? Charley Bluefire? No, Charley wouldn't sneak around here at night. Kellerman stared in the direction of the door as he listened through the wood, trying to recognize the rhythm of the circling steps. . . .

A sudden roar burst the silence and sent him lurching back against the automobile frame, flailing his arms against the dark as the room shook with the heavy pulsing noise. Then his arms dropped to his sides and he felt the tears dripping onto his lips as he cried, then laughed. The air compressor had kicked on.

"Come on!" he cried into the overpowering sound. "I'm in here! You hear me? I'm here!"

He sat on the floor and trembled — he wasn't sure if from fear or relief or just surprise — clenching his fists in the

moonlight as the compressor continued to roar, building
up pressure, burying the night with sound. Then it kicked
off, and he could hear nothing, his ears and body numb.
He waited.

"Who's out there?" he yelled into the darkness. "What
do you want?"

No answer. He stared toward the door. Through the walls
he heard the fitful rumble of his honeys disturbed in their
sleep. Nothing else. Cautiously, he pressed his ear once again
to the floor. Nothing.

A man, Kellerman thought. Just a man. But who? He
sat up in the moonlight and waited.

Minutes, maybe hours, passed. In the darkness he couldn't
judge. He felt himself drifting off into sleep, until a word
seemed to burst through the door in front of him.

Honker!

Kellerman jumped, then turned his head and looked around.
A bright beam of daylight streamed through the peephole.

"You in there, Honker? Answer me, damn it!"

"What?" The walls were humming again. Kellerman
looked down and saw he was gripping a side rail on the
automobile frame. He let go. "Who is it?"

"Who do you think?"

Blanket-assed sonofabitch! Sneaky bastard! "How long you
been sneaking around out there?"

"What do you mean 'sneaking around'?" Charley Bluefire
answered through the door. "I've been here about two
minutes, waiting for you to find your damn voice."

Kellerman frowned and checked the angle of the light coming through the peephole. Morning. Why was the room so
dark? "Just a minute." He got up stiffly and dug around
in some boxes until he found the light bulbs. He started to

replace the burned-out bulb above his worktable, but his hands were trembling. The bulb crashed to the floor.

"What's going on in there?"

Kellerman said nothing as he screwed in a new bulb. The light made him flinch. He stepped back and blinked around the room, then took a broom and carefully swept the broken glass into a box. When he had finished, he sank into the swivel chair and looked at his hands, streaked red from gripping the auto frame. He felt tired, hungry, numb. He needed a shot but couldn't bring himself to face the needle just yet. Instead, he rose and stamped his feet to get the blood moving, then looked at the door. "All right, what do you want?"

"I warned you to let me bring that ice inside. You want me to get some more?"

"What? No. That's plenty."

"But it's . . . never mind. Look, Honker, I got something I got to tell you. But first you have to promise to hold your bees, man."

Kellerman laughed. "The hell you mean, Charley, hold my bees?"

"Don't try to shit me, Honker. I heard you start up that damn air compressor just before them bees took after me last time."

Charley's voice seemed to be moving away. Kellerman looked over at the bees gathered at the feeding pan and grinned. Blanket-assed sonofabitch won't underestimate us again, honeys!

"OK," Kellerman said, turning back to the door. "What have you got to tell me?"

"Well," Charley began uncertainly. The thing is . . . I called your son."

Kellerman eyed the door in disbelief. "You called Curly? Why?"

"I'm sorry, Honker. I had to do it. My old lady's been giving me hell — and she's right."

Kellerman gripped the edge of the nearest box. "What? What are you saying?"

"Look, it was me brought you all that stuff. All them old car parts, all that sugar. I don't know exactly what the hell you're doing in that schoolhouse, but I had to tell Curly you were in there. I had to."

"Had to my ass. What I do is my own business." Kellerman spit the words between clenched teeth. "What did he say?"

"He said for you to wait."

"Wait? Wait for what?"

"For him to get here."

Kellerman sank against the pile of boxes. "He's coming *here*? From Hawaii?"

"That's what he said."

Kellerman looked at the ceiling and took a deep breath. Curly. Coming here. He turned back to the door, the wrinkles in his brow tightening into a deep frown. "*Why* is he coming back? What did you tell him?"

"I told him you'd locked yourself in the schoolhouse and wouldn't come out. That's all."

"Nothing about the car parts? Nothing about the sugar?"

"Nope. I told him you were in there. Nothing else."

Then why the hell does he give a shit? Kellerman wanted to ask, but didn't. "I'll bet. When is he coming?"

"He didn't say. Right away, I guess."

Kellerman stared at the door. Curly, coming here. Right away.

"I'm sorry, Honker. But it was me brought you that sugar. I'm responsible."

"Responsible for *what*, damn it."

"For . . . I don't know what for. I just wanted to let
you know I called Curly."

Kellerman looked over at the automobile engine and frame
and said nothing.

"You want me to get you anything?"

"No."

"Well, I guess I'll be going then."

Kellerman said nothing. He pressed his ear against the door
and listened carefully to the sound of Charley's steps retreat-
ing. Kellerman shook his head. The rhythm was wrong —
too short, too choppy. He called out anyway: "Hey, wait
a minute!"

"Yeah?"

Kellerman tried to make his voice sound casual. "You
weren't walking around out here last night, were you?"

"Last night? No way."

Kellerman took another deep breath and glanced at the
bright morning light beaming through the peephole. "OK.
Thanks."

Charley's steps retreated once more, followed by the grind-
ing whine of the pickup starting. Kellerman listened to the
sounds of the truck: engine revving, gears clashing, tires dig-
ging into gravel, then spinning into a redundant melancholy
song on the warm asphalt, slowly fading into the distance,
until finally he could hear no more.

5

WHY?

Kellerman sat on the edge of the automobile frame, trying to figure it out. "Why would he come back now, honeys? *Now*, ten years after he walks out the door to become a big shot TV star. *Now*, one year after he watched them stick his mother in the ground. *Now*, after he's shamed all of us for the second time. Why *now?*"

Kellerman removed his glasses and wiped them with a rag. "I don't get it. What's different now? So I'm in the schoolhouse. So what? Why does he care where I am? What's changed?"

He put his glasses back on and looked around the room. Honey bees. Windows boarded up. Automobile. He shook his head. "None of this counts. Nothing's changed. The same things are between us, and we've got the same things to talk about that we always did — nothing."

Kellerman closed his eyes and remembered the last time he and Curly had tried to talk, the day of Babe's funeral. After the burial Kellerman had driven his son back to the house. They said nothing to each other for the full five miles, filling the car instead with silent grief, silent rage. Kellerman had already threatened his malpractice suit against Dr. Farber; Curly had already replied there was no point. And, even though this was the first time Kellerman had seen his son in nine years, he had rejected Curly's offer to stay a few days before flying back to Honolulu. Kellerman forgot his anger when he saw the way the rejection shocked Curly, momentarily draining the blood from his face and dissolving his perfect tropical tan into a pale, lifeless gray. By the time Kellerman pulled the Hudson into the driveway he was trying to find the words to ask his son to stay.

But Curly had one foot on the concrete even before the car stopped. In the living room he poured himself a glass of bourbon from the bottle he'd brought on the plane.

"Want one?" Curly tilted the half-empty bottle in Kellerman's direction.

Kellerman shook his head. He'd stopped drinking the day Dr. Kiner told him he had diabetes. Instead, he sat down on the sofa and took a good look at his son.

Curly was standing next to the new color TV and for a moment Kellerman was afraid he was going to turn it on. But he just stood there, tall, slim, and perfectly erect in his shiny black suit with its velvet lapels, sipping his drink and staring blankly across the room. Kellerman couldn't remember the last time he'd seen such a blank look on Curly's face. On "The Dream Game" his face was always animated, full of joy, wonder, or disappointment, depending on the stage of the game and the fate of the contestant. Kellerman had always suspected these expressions on the show were phony, masks Curly put on to show the expected emotion at the expected moment. On the TV Curly's face looked too sincere to be true. His clear blue eyes would sparkle like sapphires when he described warm sandy beaches at Monaco or Waikiki. When a contestant answered a question correctly, Curly's eyes would beam and his teeth would shine like polished ivory. Kellerman wondered if he rubbed his teeth with vasoline, like the girls in the Miss America pageant. And his hair, much blonder than Kellerman remembered it, puffed, bloomed on his head like a yellow rose. No human being had such hair. It was all part of the same gimmick, Kellerman believed, along with the rainbow suit and plucked gull wing eyebrows and the beautiful young women in cocktail dresses.

Now, as Kellerman beheld the blank look on his son's face, he wondered if he were seeing the real Curly: shocked, numbed, drained. Or was this another mask?

"What are you thinking about?" Kellerman asked.

"Mom." Curly looked down at his drink and moved the glass in a tight circle as if he were stirring the ice, though there was no ice. "I just can't believe she's gone."

Kellerman felt something surge inside him. The oh-so-smooth game show voice had vanished. This was his son. Kellerman nodded. "I know."

Curly raised his eyes and looked at Kellerman. "You know, I always thought you'd be first."

Kellerman's mouth opened but no words came out.

"I mean . . . you're older. You were always the one in bad health. I always thought in terms of taking care of Mom after you were gone. And now . . . " Curly kept his eyes on Kellerman for a moment, then looked back down at his drink.

And now you have to take care of *me*, Kellerman wanted to scream. No way. That's the last thing I need now, a caretaker.

"Don't worry about it," he said softly. "It's a natural feeling — I always expected to go first too. But you can't predict these things. Anyway, don't worry about me. I'll get along just fine.''

Curly looked up again. "I'm *supposed* to worry, aren't I?''

The urgent tone in Curly's voice made Kellerman pause. "No, you don't need to. Just go on about your business like you were. I'll be just fine.''

Kellerman thought he caught a flicker of something in Curly's eyes now. For a few moments neither man spoke. He noticed Curly was chewing his lower lip, a habit he had picked up from Kellerman. *You two read like the same book,* Babe used to say. *Every time something's bothering you, your lip disappears.* Kellerman squirmed slightly on the sofa.

"You don't need to do anything. I'll be fine.''

"How the hell can you be like this?'' Curly said.

Kellerman was baffled. "Like what?''

"Mom's dead and you act like life goes on — just like nothing's happened. You'll be fine — it doesn't phase you.''

"Doesn't *what?*'' Kellerman rose from the chair with his fists clenched.

"Don't act like you don't know what I'm talking about. You're more worried about suing the goddamn doctor than about what's going to happen to us now.''

"*Us?* When the hell in the last ten years has there been any fucking *us* to worry about? Where the hell were you when you ever thought about *us?* You think about *us* while you were cheating people out of their goddamn vacation trips?''

Curly set his glass on the TV. "I never cheated anybody. And I'm here *now,* aren't I? And you want me to get back on a plane before they've packed down the dirt on Mom's grave. You give a good goddamn about *us,* too.''

Kellerman grabbed the arm of the sofa to control the spasm that was shaking him. "Us? There's no us. There's you and

there's me. That's the way it's been for twenty fucking years
— and you can't put it all on my head.''

Curly stood there in his shiny black suit with velvet lapels,
then folded his arms — the same way, Kellerman realized
furiously, that Babe used to fold hers when they would argue.
Kellerman hissed and looked away. When he looked back
Curly was chewing his lower lip again.

"I don't want to fight, Dad.''

"Well, don't then.''

Curly took a deep breath. "I want to talk to you about
'The Dream Game.' ''

Kellerman's shoulders sagged. "No. Not now, not today.''

"When?''

"Later. In a few days — I don't know.''

Curly frowned. "A few days? I'll be gone in two hours.''

Kellerman sighed. Now was the time to ask the boy to
stay for a while. Why couldn't he say the words?

Curly looked out the window behind the TV for several
moments, then back at Kellerman. "Listen, you remember
when I was a kid and you taught me how to drive the Jimmie
Truck?''

Kellerman braced his hands on his hips. "Yeah, I remember.''

"You remember what you said about the key?''

Kellerman looked at the ceiling and tried to recall. He
remembered Curly sitting on his lap, hanging onto the big
blue steering wheel of the GMC with both hands as they
drove round and round the propane tank. What was he getting at?

"I might remember, if you give me a minute.''

Curly took a step forward. "You said only one key was
the right key. The right key was magic. It unlocked the magic
in the motor, so the motor could run.''

Kellerman felt a trap closing on him. "Yeah, so?"

"Well . . . I'm wondering how I can find the key to unlock *you*, Dad. What am I supposed to say, what am I supposed to do so we can talk?"

Kellerman started to protest that it wasn't fair, that the years of silence hadn't been all his fault, that *he* had been willing, more than willing, to talk, anytime. Kellerman opened his mouth, but again, no words came out.

"What are you going to do now, Dad?"

Kellerman frowned. The question made him feel like a helpless old man. "I told you."

"I don't mean about suing Dr. Farber. What I mean is . . . what are you going to do now that Mom's gone?"

Kellerman felt a chill on his arms and back. He sucked in a long, slow breath and exhaled before answering. "Just keep going."

"Keep going at what?"

Kellerman frowned again. "Everything. I've got plenty to do just living. I've got my work."

"That's what I mean. What work?"

Now Kellerman felt the blood in his face grow hot. The day before Babe's operation he had been doing handyman work, sharpening disc and harrow blades for Orville Zucha. "Oh, nothing that would interest a big shot game show host like you. People waste their lives in Oklahoma, remember?"

Curly chopped the air with his hand. "That's what I'm talking about. Maybe I'm like you. Maybe I've been wasting my life too."

Kellerman bit his lip. "How?"

"On 'The Dream Game.' That's all over now, you know."

"It made you rich."

"Oh for Christsake, Dad. I'm not talking about the money. The money's all gone now anyway."

"Well, what *are* you talking about?"

Curly hung his head for a moment, then raised his hand to his forehead, pushing his open palm back over the dyed blond hair, which sprang back into place. "I'm talking about the way I have to start over now, keep going, like you."

Kellerman shook his head bitterly. "It's not the same. You lost a job. I lost my wife."

Curly glared at Kellerman. "I lost her *too*, damn it."

Kellerman sighed, then nodded. "OK, OK."

Curly's voice softened. "I didn't mean it was the same for me. I just meant the situations were similar. We've both got to go on to something new. I'm not a game show host anymore."

A spark of hope flickered in Kellerman's chest. "What are you?"

Curly took a deep breath and seemed to set himself. "That's what I wanted to talk to you about. I couldn't change course completely. What I'm going to be doing is similar but different from 'The Dream Game.' I've put together a deal to tape TV commercials for airline tours to Hawaii." He paused for just an instant before Kellerman could react. "The money's not important, Dad. It's not — except that I want to use it to take care of you, just like I would have taken care of Mom."

He looked Kellerman in the eye and waited.

Kellerman glanced at the clock on the coffee table. "Don't miss your flight."

Sitting on the edge of the automobile frame, Kellerman shuddered. "He's coming back to be my caretaker, honeys. He expects to find a helpless old man."

Kellerman climbed to his feet. He didn't want to think about Curly. He *wouldn't* think about him. No, he would work.

He threw himself into his project now, sweating hard as he attached heavy metal wheels to the front axle. He fit metal to metal, pounded the kingpins into place. Faster and faster: lifting, hammering, measuring, tightening. He had his rhythm now. All around him the walls hummed, roared, louder and louder, a hundred thousand wings beating: *Hurry, hurry, time is passing.*

And in the roar he lost himself, disappearing into the throbbing sound. Parts assembled themselves. Hinges formed. Washers and rubber bushings appeared, adjusting the fit of metal to metal. Connecting joints filled up with silicone. Bolts tightened. At the end of each axle, wheels half a century old began to turn.

He noticed the pain when he tried to stand on tiptoe to reach the box of bolts for the steering column.

"Ow!"

He sat down on the auto frame and took off his left tennis shoe. The pain throbbed as he removed his sock, revealing the nickel-sized bruise just above his toes.

Damn. Must have happened last night.

Now you've done it.

He whirled around to face the voice but saw only the wall. He sighed and shook his head. "Old habits die hard, honeys."

It was true. Both the words he thought he had heard and his reaction to them were automatic. Right up to the day she died, Babe was harping at him about getting a bruise. *You get a bruise, you'll have to live with it,* she'd say. Dr. Kiner had assured him bruises were no special problem for a diabetic as long as he didn't aggravate them and kept taking his shots. Which reminded him. . . .

"OK, OK, so I forgot again."

He pulled on his sock and shoe, then limped over to the worktable and prepared the needle. He glanced at the light beaming through the peephole. Late afternoon already. Got to get going. After giving himself the shot, he stood up and reached for the box of bolts, wincing only slightly.

"Steering, honeys. Got to give this baby some guidance." Using a couple of two-by-fours, he propped up the steering column and bolted it securely to the automobile frame. Then he completed the system by connecting the left front wheel to a long steel arm attached to the steering gearbox at the base of the column.

"OK, let's see if it works." He gave the steering wheel half a turn, then smiled as both front wheels responded.

Then he took a break and cooked some macaroni and cheese on the hot plate. The cheese came in a can and tasted like glue. Better, he thought. I'm definitely feeling better. I was down for a while there, but now things are coming along. He wiggled his toes and felt no pain.

"Back to work."

Stiffly, he rose from the chair and limped over to the nearest stack of boxes. Column bolts, he thought, and dug into a box marked STEERING. A moment later his eyes seemed to grow. From deep in the box, beneath his spare worm gear and drag link, he withdrew a small blue grease-stained baseball cap. He stared at the cap for several seconds before his brow wrinkled into a frown.

"Look what happens, honeys," he said to the crack in the wall. "Curly tells Charley he's coming home — and then I come up with *this*." He waved the cap in his fist. "Well, I don't care. I'm not going to think about it."

Even as he said the words, however, he was beginning to recall what he had tried for years to forget: the first day of summer in 1961, the day Babe told him the other boys in school had been picking on Curly.

He had received the news in stunned silence, lying stiff and aching in his bed, hooked up in traction with a broken hip. Babe was sitting on the edge of the bed, repeating what Curly's fifth-grade teacher had told her on the phone the day before, just before school let out for the summer: *The other boys are picking on Curly. He runs from them, even the little ones. Yesterday he wet his pants in class. He won't go in the bathroom all day because he's afraid one of them will come in there.*

Kellerman rolled his head toward the bedroom window, and a sharp pain shot from the back of his neck down the right side of his body all the way to his big toe. Through the window he could see a golden plain of ripening winter wheat that rippled five miles to the town of Yukon. Curly stood on the edge of the backyard, hitting fly balls with the official Mickey Mantle signature Little League bat Kellerman had given him on his last birthday.

Kellerman studied the boy closely. From this distance he looked incredibly thin, his arms and legs mere sticks, his elbows and knees tiny knots. A boy made of tinker toys. He swung the bat angrily, desperately, straining to hit each ball as far as he could, but struck only weak grounders and pop flies.

Kellerman turned back to Babe. "School's over, for Christsake. Why the hell didn't you tell me about this before now?"

"Mrs. Virgil called me only yesterday."

"Then why the hell didn't you tell me *yesterday?*"

Babe folded her arms and looked at him squarely. "You were too mad to listen to me yesterday is why."

He winced. The previous evening he and Babe had had another big fight about the garage. In those days there were two garage and auto body shops in Yukon. The other belonged, of course, to Carl Vukovich, a big greasy bohunk who smelled like gasoline and cheap cigars. For the last two years he and Kellerman had battled each other to stay in business. Now, with Kellerman laid up, Vukovich had gained the upper hand. Kellerman blamed his own employees.

Mechanics — ha! They're nothing but a pack of thieves, he had complained to Babe. *I lay here helpless and they steal me blind.*

Don't blame all your troubles on them, Babe had countered. *Looper tells me the hip's your fault for working under a car with a faulty jack.*

Ed Looper's a drunk and an opportunist.

Then why did you hire him?

Who else is there? Vukovich pays fifty cents an hour more than I can afford. Yukon's just not big enough to support two garages. Half the town takes their cars to Oklahoma City. Vukovich's been waiting to get me into a spot like this. If I leave that fool Looper in charge for three months while this hip heals, we could lose everything. I don't think you appreciate how serious this is.

Babe had drawn herself up to her full height. *I appreciate it.*

Kellerman closed his eyes, then reopened them and saw Babe standing before him in the glaring light of midday, her arms still folded across her chest. "OK, last night I was mad. You still should have told me about the boy. You talk to him yet?"

"You're the one who should talk to him about it."

Kellerman looked at her. "You're right. Call him in here."

When she had gone, Kellerman automatically lifted the covers and started to swing out of bed. The pain yanked him back like a hook. "Aaah!" He sank into the pillows.

A moment later Curly stood at the foot of the bed. The boy was nervous, expecting something. He tugged the brim of his Yankee cap and chewed his lower lip. Kellerman regarded him silently at first, sizing him up. He was thin, all right, the bones in his elbows sticking way out. But look at those eyes, Kellerman thought. Smart eyes. Smarter than Babe's, smarter than mine. He'll go way beyond both of us. He's got potential.

"I hear some boys have been picking on you."

Curly's face flashed red. He looked down at his feet.

Kellerman frowned. Got to get those eyes up. "Look at me, son."

Curly glanced up, then back down at his feet.

"Who is it? Is it Eddie Hacker?"

Curly flinched, then turned slightly, shifting his weight from one side to the other like a nervous parrot on a limb. Kellerman nodded grimly. Eddie Hacker was Bill Hacker's boy. Bill Hacker once played football for the Oklahoma Sooners. Kellerman hated football because he'd been too small to play. It was no shame to be small, he had always told his son. But maybe to reach his potential Curly would have to grow in other ways.

"I'm going to tell you something," Kellerman said. "To stand up to bullies, you have to earn their respect."

Curly did not look up. "How?"

Kellerman tried to lean forward despite the pain, but the thick cast around his hips and upper legs would not let him bend. He lowered his voice slightly. "To earn anyone's respect, first you have to believe in yourself. What I mean is, you have to believe you're as good as anyone else." Curly twitched and tugged at his cap but seemed to be listening. Kellerman looked at his son's stick arms and legs. "What I think's bothering you is you're not as big as the other boys."

Curly clenched his fists. "I'm skinny," he said.

"That's right. Later on you'll learn size doesn't matter. But since it's bothering you *now*, we're going to do something about it."

Curly peeked up at Kellerman from under his cap. "What?"

Kellerman tried to make his voice sound confident. "We're going to build you up."

Curly looked down at his feet. "I'm no good at exercise and stuff."

For a moment Kellerman stared despairingly at the button on Curly's Yankee cap. Then an idea came to him. "That's what Mickey Mantle said."

The cap tilted up slightly. "When?"

"When he was your age," Kellerman lied. "He used to be a little guy like you. His old man made him work out so he could grow big and strong enough to work in the coal mines up around Commerce. You didn't know that?"

Curly looked up. Kellerman thought he saw a faint light in the boy's eyes as he chewed his lower lip.

"Let's try a few push-ups."

That was how the summer began, Curly working, Kellerman coaching. As the weeks went by, Kellerman marveled at the power in the magic words: Mickey Mantle. They were both Okies — Mickey and Curly — born on the same day, October 20, twenty years apart. Mickey Charles Mantle, two hundred pounds of raw strength and speed. Curly Francis Kellerman, seventy-nine pounds of hero worship in the year of the great quest, the race for Babe Ruth's home run record.

It was also the year of the pretend season. That first day Curly grunted and strained until he gave Kellerman ten good push-ups — and all the other exercises he called for. The next morning Curly did the same. And the morning after that. But there was more. From the bed where Kellerman lay in traction he would look out the window and watch his son work out, then play a special game.

Next to the road, Kellerman's five acres were crowded with the house, the schoolhouse, and his cars — four in those days. The back was just a flat empty lot big enough to grow wheat or play baseball. Curly had marked off a scaled-down infield in the southeast corner, old tomato crates serving as bases. The foul lines paralleled the south and east fences that separated Kellerman's land from Orville Zucha's wheat fields. Curly laid out a string fence of his own to mark the outside walls. Straight center field had a real stone wall — the schoolhouse.

The game had only one player. But it really wasn't Curly out there — it was Mantle or Mathews or Colavito. Mostly it was Mantle. The boy had the switch hitter's best swings down perfectly. The sweeping left-handed uppercut, the flatter right-handed swish. The object of the game was to rehit the home runs the stars had hit the day before, exactly the way they hit them in the actual games. Curly had never seen a real big league game and neither had Kellerman. Instead, they watched Dizzy Dean's "Game of the Week" on TV, listened to Harry Caray's play-by-play out of St. Louis on the radio, and followed the box scores in the *Daily Oklahoman*. There were plenty of home runs to rehit in 1961.

Since there was no pitcher, Curly had to toss the ball up and hit it fungo-style. He wasn't strong enough to hit a baseball the 180 feet or so to his imaginary outfield fence, so he used golf balls, which traveled much farther. Kellerman would watch him toss a tiny white ball above his head, then swing as it dropped. Bat would meet ball with a small but solid tick, then soar in a high arc over the imaginary outfield, hitting the shingle roof of the schoolhouse with an explosive *pow*. The Mick had popped another one over the center field wall at Fenway or Comiskey Park or even Yankee Stadium. "Nice hitting, slugger!" Kellerman would shout from his bed.

The only thing that bothered Kellerman was that Curly played the game alone. After all, the object of the workouts was to give Curly the confidence he'd need to get along with the other boys. Kellerman wanted to have Babe drive Curly into town to play Little League, but Curly didn't want to go. He said he didn't like the coaches or the other boys on the teams. Bull, Kellerman thought, but he didn't press the boy. By the end of summer he could work out with Curly himself. Then they'd show 'em! Besides, a curious thing happened when he watched Curly play the game; he would forget the awful stabbing pain in his hip. Watching Curly pretend to be Mickey Mantle, Kellerman felt power surge through his own blood, bone, and muscle to the bat. Mantle's power. In the evenings they pored over the sports pages together, Curly growing more excited each week.

"Mickey hit two more!"

"He did?" In bed, Kellerman leaned forward as far as he could and scanned the page, pretending not to see the headline.

"Off Shaw in Kansas City."

"Oh, yeah. Here it is: 'The second homer was a tape measure blast over the high outer wall in right field.' Must have been batting lefty."

"Yeah. That's twenty-two."

"Maris has twenty-six."

Curly's eyes narrowed. He hated Roger Maris. Maris who had been a Yankee less than two years. Maris who was challenging the Mick. "It's not fair! Maris bats in front of Mickey. Maris doesn't get as many walks."

Kellerman shrugged and pulled the bill on Curly's Yankee cap. "Mick'll beat him out in the end."

Roger Maris was to be another sore in his hip as the summer wore on. Kellerman had enough troubles of his own. The situation at the garage grew worse every day. Looper and the Simchek brothers were stealing him blind. "Business is slow," Looper said again and again. "People's taking their cars to El Reno or the city." But Popeye, the cross-eyed wrecker driver, said Looper and the Simchek boys were moonlighting, fixing cars with Kellerman's tools over at Looper's place at night.

Popeye was Kellerman's snitch. Kellerman hated having a snitch, and he especially hated Popeye, the way he slinked around the garage, never looking directly at anyone, making disgusting squeaky, sniveling sounds from the corners. Looper and the Simchek boys played tricks on Popeye, sending him out on phony wrecker calls, giving him the address of the cemetery or the sewage treatment plant. Never should have hired him in the first place, Kellerman thought. Popeye had begged for the job the day after Kellerman bought the garage. Kellerman hated beggars, but he needed someone else at the garage to keep an eye on Looper. When Popeye said Looper and the others were moonlighting, Kellerman believed him.

"Vukovich is behind this," Kellerman complained to Babe. "He put them all up to it." He pictured the big greasy bohunk pacing the floor of his own garage, puffing away on the black stump of his smelly El Verso cigar, plotting new ways to bring Kellerman to his knees. "He'll talk to the bank next."

"Since you need money, why don't you sell a couple of those cars just rusting out there under that tin roof?" Babe suggested.

"No way."

Babe rolled her eyes. "Well, then why don't you sell the garage and buy another one when you're well enough to run it?"

Sell out! The idea made Kellerman furious. He wanted to remortgage the house and five acres in order to hold on for

another three weeks, just long enough for his hip to heal.
But no, the bitch would have none of it.

"We're not going to risk our home," she said flatly.

Why, *why* did he ever put half the property in her name?

Kellerman was helpless. While his hip mended he was total-
ly dependent on Babe and hated it. When she brought him
food or sat down on the edge of the bed to talk, he found
himself snapping at her. "Leave me the hell alone," he'd
snarl if she stayed too long, or "Where the hell are you going now?" if she didn't stay long enough. The broken bone
had put him out of action in more ways than one, and looking at Babe — a wide-hipped, heavy-breasted woman in her
prime — was the biggest frustration.

"Easy! You want to break another bone?" she exclaimed
when he reached for her one evening after Curly had gone
to bed.

"Well, damn it, get over here where I can reach you."
He forced a grin to hide the pain that had begun searing his
hip when he leaned toward her.

Babe stepped back just beyond his reach and looked at him
with gray, reasonable eyes. "You don't have to grab at me
and hurt yourself. The doctor said not to exert yourself. Just
relax. You want me to do you?"

Kellerman frowned. "I don't like that."

The look in Babe's eyes softened. "OK. How should we
do it?"

Kellerman's right side stung like a raw nerve touched by
a cold wind. "I don't know. Just go away, OK?"

Babe waited several moments before replying. "You sure?"

"I'm sure."

"All right." She paused in the doorway. "Try to think
of something else."

"Right."

He did try, but trying did little good. *The problem with the brain and the body is that they're connected,* Dr. Kiner had told him.

He had known other women before Babe, and, as the summer wore on and giant red combines reaped the wheat beyond Curly's special ball park, he began to dream about those women. The day Roger Maris hit home run number thirty he was thinking of Matti Holmes, the redhead he knew just before he married Babe, when he worked for the Frisco Railroad in Fort Scott, Kansas. He was young and free in those days and had an eye for the ladies. Once a week he would hitch a ride on the Red Devil Express from Fort Scott to Afton, Oklahoma. Matti never called him Frank. She always called him Lucky. *Cause it's my lucky day when the Red Devil stops in Afton.* Babe knew about Matti. Kellerman had told Babe about her before they got married. *Well, if you don't like your life here, why don't you go back to your whore in Afton,* Babe would say when she really wanted to shut him up.

Matti was no whore. Her engineer husband had been killed during the second year of the war, when the Silver Meteor derailed outside Joplin, leaving Matti with three boys to raise. Matti claimed to be five years older than Kellerman, but she was probably more like ten. The last time he was in Afton he had given her a ring of turquoise — her favorite gem — and was astonished when she started weeping.

What's the matter? he wanted to know.

Nothing, she said and slipped on the ring. *You're my brightside man.* Then she gave her burnt-red hair a toss and smiled at him like a sunny day. Matti Holmes. Kellerman felt himself getting hard just thinking about her.

"I see you're recovering OK."

Kellerman blushed and pulled the sheet over himself as Babe entered the room and sat down on the edge of the bed. He couldn't tell if the look on her face was a smile or a smirk. He frowned.

"What's the matter?"

"Nothing." He looked at her and took a deep breath. "I think I want to try again."

Babe raised her eyebrows. "You sure?"

"I'm sure." He felt little pain as he tried to sit up this time, but the traction weight held him in place. "I'd do better if I could get out of this contraption."

Babe looked at the weight, then the sheet. "Maybe for just a few minutes."

He watched her close the window curtains, shutting off his view of the yard where Curly was doing pull-ups on the crossbar of the clothesline pole. As she lifted the weight, pain stabbed his hip like a knife. His leg bent, then kicked.

"Aaaah! Put it back!"

Gently, she rehooked the weight. "It shouldn't hurt like that unless you put pressure on it."

"Well, it does!" He groaned with the pain, then noticed he had kicked the sheet off. He was soft. He covered himself.

Babe laid her hand on his shoulder. "Relax, Frank. It's all right. Really."

"Right." He stared at the curtain.

After a minute of silence, she sat down in a chair. "Let's talk about something. You want to?"

He shrugged.

She looked around the room, then spoke. "Maybe I should get a part-time job until you're well enough to go back to the garage."

He thought it over. "Yeah, sure," he said and closed his eyes until she left.

At three o'clock the mailman delivered the *Oklahoman*. Kellerman watched Curly read the sports page carefully, checking each box score, then go outside to play his special game. He watched his son toss a ball up and lunge at it like Willie Mays. Curly's imitations of the stars were so good now that Kellerman no longer had to read the sports himself to tell who had hit home runs. Mays had hit one. And Colavito and Bill Skowron. And Maris — number thirty.

Watching Curly play the game, Kellerman began to believe the exercise program was paying off. He could swear the boy was growing, muscles beginning to stand out in his arms and neck. He was hitting the ball a little farther every day.

When the game was over, Curly came inside.

"Mickey didn't hit one yesterday," Kellerman observed.

Curly dropped his bat in the corner and slumped on the edge of the bed. "He's two behind again."

Kellerman, remembering Mantle was usually better in the second half of the season, was optimistic. "Mick'll beat him out in the end. You can count on it."

Curly shrugged, then wiggled his shoe and stared at the floor.

"What do you need, slugger?"

Curly kept his eyes on the ground. "What do I do when somebody picks on me?"

The question made Kellerman sit up as straight as he could. "Well, you fight back. But there's something else you should know. There are lots of ways to fight back — and one way is by *not* fighting. Don't play his game. Make him play yours."

Curly frowned. "How?"

"Ignore him. Walk away like he doesn't exist. No matter what he says, you keep walking."

Curly chewed his lip as he considered it. "Then what?"

"Then it's over. Unless he follows you or hits you. If he hits you, you have to fight as hard as you can."

"I don't know how to fight."

"I'll teach you, as soon as I'm up and around. But fighting's not as important as knowing how not to fight."

Kellerman bit his own lip and waited for the next question. None came.

Curly looked out the window a moment, then back at Kellerman. "OK," he said, then slid off the bed and left.

What brought that on? Kellerman wondered. With Curly home all day now, there were no bullies around to pick on him. Was he scared of what would happen when school started up again in the fall?

Kellerman didn't have much time to ponder the question because later that afternoon Clarence Schroeder of the Yukon National Bank called to inform him he was late with his loan payment. "No sweat. Check's in the mail," Kellerman lied.

Vukovich, Kellerman thought as he hung up the phone. He's starting to put the squeeze on. Kellerman tested his hip, twisting slightly. The pain was like an electrical shock. Time, he thought, sinking into the sheets. I just need more time.

But time was passing too quickly. In July the wrecker business dropped off so much he had to lay off Popeye. He had to do it by phone and listen to Popeye whine and moan and beg, with Looper snickering in the background. Kellerman couldn't bear it.

"See if you can get him a job over at the elevator," he ordered Looper.

"Anything you say, Frank."

Sure, anything I say, Kellerman repeated to himself. At least I don't have to watch the little snitch crawl on the floor.

Laying Popeye off didn't help. Regular customers continued to disappear, taking their cars to Vukovich or the city. The day Roger Maris hit home run number thirty-six, Kellerman sent Babe into Yukon to check on the garage. She found

Mike and Ollie Simchek asleep on a pile of grease rags while Christine Gimble sat in her car waiting for someone to change her spark plugs. Kellerman fired them both, which left only Looper.

"Just keep the place going, Loop," Kellerman pleaded over the phone. "Just don't *lose* any more customers."

"You got it, Frank."

But Kellerman got nothing. Babe started driving by the garage twice a day and usually found no one there except Looper, sitting in the tiny office with his feet propped on the empty cash register.

"Lord, Lord," Kellerman prayed and began to repent his sins, whatever they were, that were driving the population of Yukon into Vukovich's greasy hands.

Nothing helped. On the first of September school was only two weeks off. Roger Maris had fifty-one home runs, Mantle forty-eight, and Clarence Schroeder was threatening to call in Kellerman's note.

"Come in here and unhook this goddamn weight!" Kellerman shouted at Babe. He had tried to sit up in bed and unhook the traction apparatus himself but couldn't bend far enough with the cast. When Babe appeared in the doorway he shouted again. "Come on in here. I got to get off my butt and get to work before we're all out in the streets."

Babe stood in the doorway and folded her arms. She'd been acting contrary ever since she started answering the phone down at Turch's Funeral Home six days a week. The money helped but wasn't enough to keep the garage going. "Dr. Kiner says if you try and walk on that hip before it's healed you're looking to be lame the rest of your life."

"Lame! I'll give you lame. Unhook that goddamn weight!"

Babe shook her head. "I'm not going to be any part of this." She turned and went back into the kitchen.

Damn! Kellerman felt the blood in his neck grow hot. "I don't need you anyway!" He leaned forward and tried one more time to reach the traction weight. It was no use. Even if he could bear the pain — which he could, by God — he couldn't bend far enough. The hip cast extended from just below his rib cage to just above each knee. Only the right leg, previously broken in a railroad accident in 1949, was hooked up to the weight, but even with one leg on the floor he could do nothing. He sank back into the pillows. So this is the way a man goes to hell — strung up like a goddamn stuck pig!

Through the window came the *pow* of a ball bouncing off the schoolhouse roof.

"Curly!"

Kellerman waited. Half a minute later the boy stuck his head in the window. "Did you see that one? That was Mickey in — "

"Listen, son, come in here. I want you to do something for me. No, don't go around. Crawl right through the window here so you don't disturb your mother."

Surprised and delighted to take this forbidden route, Curly tossed his bat inside and scrambled through the window.

"OK, the first thing I want you to do is unhook that weight for me. Careful. That's it." Kellerman felt taut muscles in his leg and hip recoil as the weight was lifted. Very gently he eased toward the side of the bed, setting one foot, then the other, on the floor. Each movement brought pain, but he could bear it. "Now hand me those overalls." Overalls were the only thing he could get on over the cast.

"Where you going?" Curly asked.

Kellerman winced as he maneuvered the faded blue denim over the plaster. "To hell and back."

The first thing he was going to do was fire Looper. Then he would talk Clarence Schroeder into renegotiating his note on the garage. The prick wouldn't give in over the phone, but how could he turn down a flesh-and-blood man in a hip cast?

"Now give me your bat." Kellerman planted the fat end on the floor, then stood up, leaning on the end of the handle like a cane. When he put his weight on his right heel, pain shot through his hip. "Uhhh! OK. I'm going to borrow your bat for a while, OK?"

Curly nodded.

The better to beat the shit out of Looper with, Kellerman thought as he leaned on the bat and took a step forward.

"Well, I'll swan." In the kitchen Babe shook her head as Kellerman limped through. "Where are you going?"

"See Schroeder."

Babe folded her arms. "No remortgage."

Kellerman pushed open the screen door, then paused. "If there's one thing I've heard often enough to remember, it's 'no remortgage.' And by the way, I'd like to thank you for your wonderful support."

"This is our home, Frank. When are you coming back?"

Kellerman gave a disgusted sigh. "Coming back? If I don't get this note fixed, what's the point of coming back?" As the words escaped, he noticed Curly in the hall doorway. "Don't worry," he said to the boy, then glared at Babe and let the door slam behind him.

Four cars were parked under the carport. He decided to take the Studebaker Silver Hawk to make the best possible impression on Schroeder. Kellerman had bought the Silver Hawk new in fifty-six when he was still riding high. It also had an automatic shift. He had to move the seat all the way back to compensate for the cast. With his arms and legs almost fully extended, he could just manage to steer and brake. "Frankenstein at the wheel," he said, and started off for Yukon.

It's all right, he told himself on the way. You're back in control.

He found the garage closed, the doors and windows all locked up, the yard around the cinder-block building empty, not a car in sight. "Hello! Hello!" He banged on the door with his bat. In his hurry, he'd forgotten to grab the chain with his keys to the garage. Standing in the empty lot, he felt a sinking sensation, like the ground he was standing on was turning slowly to mud. He shook it off. "What the fucking Sam Hill's going on here?" He started to drive over to Looper's house with the idea of beating on him till he found out. Then he changed his mind. Steady boy. The bank's closer. Get over there and straighten out this loan.

"Let's not get violent, Frank," Clarence Schroeder said when he saw the bat.

"It's just a cane," Kellerman said, easing down into the big leather chair in front of Schroeder's desk. "Unless you don't want to renegotiate my note, that is."

"Mmmm," Schroeder said.

Kellerman tried to smile through the pain shooting up from his hip. He couldn't sit properly in the chair. I look like a broom propped against a barn, he thought.

"Your wife still set against a second mortgage?"

"There's no moving her on that point, no sir."

"Then I'm afraid we've reached the point of no return, Frank, unless you can come up with some additional collateral. My advice is to sell — if you can find someone to pick up your note."

The bastard. "Look, if you could just carry me another month or so — you can see I'm up and around now." Kellerman tried to cock his head to look less stiff.

"Yes, I see. That's good, Frank, but you're way overextended now."

Kellerman felt a twinge of something besides pain in his gut. "Look, don't you see? I'm back to work now. People will start bringing their cars back. The money will be coming in again, just like before."

"Frank — "

"I admit the place ain't been too well run while I was off. I left Looper in charge. That was my mistake. But that's all changed now."

"It's a matter of simple arithmetic . . . "

Kellerman looked at Clarence Schroeder's eyes. They were dull gray, eyes that didn't really look back at you. Lifeless eyes, like the eyes of a man whose brain was dead but whose body still worked as if under a spell. A zombie, Kellerman decided, like in one of those old horror movies on TV. *The problem with the brain and the body is that they're connected.* Not Clarence Schroeder's, Kellerman thought.

"So on your behalf I called some interested parties . . . "

Kellerman watched Schroeder's mouth go up and down. It was amazing. Words came out, exactly as if the face before him were alive. But these were words only a dead man could utter, said the way only a dead man would say them. As he listened to the dead voice speak, Kellerman felt something begin to happen inside himself, something fading, like a light growing dim. The face before him remained clear and sharp, but the words it spoke became garbled. No matter. Kellerman felt strangely at ease. Numb. He forgot the garage, the loan, everything, as he watched the zombie face in front of him. He felt nothing. He gazed at Schroeder's face and tried to imitate it. After a while he caught on. It really wasn't too hard. You looked, you blinked, you turned your head and smiled. It was easy when you were numb.

Then they were both standing. Kellerman saw himself shaking hands as Schroeder led him out. "It's better this way, Frank."

Better? Of course it was better to be numb. If you were numb, you couldn't feel. And if you couldn't feel, you didn't have to think, didn't have to decide about anything. If you were numb you could just drive, the way he was driving now — staring, blinking, eyes on the road ahead. The road stretched out before him in a straight line toward the distant horizon. He didn't know what road it was. He didn't care. He followed the center line, never looking left, never looking right. It was easier that way, not seeing what you passed. There must have been traffic somewhere along the way, cars and trucks and young men hitchhiking. There must have been landmarks, places and things he would have recognized, had he looked. But seeing those things would have given him a sense of distance traveled, of time passing. He would have noticed the sun slipping down behind him, the dark road ahead becoming dotted with lights. He would have noticed the moment he turned on his own lights to drive deeper into the night. He would have noticed, somewhere along that road, the point when he had gone too far to turn back.

When he finally stopped, he attached no significance to the stopping place. It was a place like any other along the road. He might have recognized it, had he tried. He might have recalled the peculiar odor of the place, the way the night air made his skin damp and tingly as he got out of the car and approached one light among many.

And when the door before him opened, he was not surprised. The face that appeared was a woman's face. In the shadowed doorway he could not see the image of himself reflected in her eyes, nor the wonder with which it was received. Had he noticed these things, he would not have been astonished by her question.

"Lucky, is it really you?"

He did not answer, for in truth he did not know. It might have been him, Lucky, standing on this dim porch — knowing, feeling nothing, waiting for whatever was to come. It might have been him. As she led him inside he noticed only one detail: the turquoise ring on her right hand.

When the morning came, he hid from it, burying himself under the blankets, refusing even to look at the breakfast of hominy and eggs she prepared for him. Instead, he lay on his back, linking his arms and raising them above his head to form a small dome of night. He coaxed her to come to him there, where no one could see. She moved on him gently, her weight a source of dark pleasure, quicker pain.

"How did you hurt yourself?"

"No questions."

"Whatever you say, Lucky." And with that, she did not speak of the past but seemed to regard him as a gift of the continuous present, a line unbroken by time or events. If he had looked deeply into her eyes he would have seen that she disbelieved the image there, that in her eyes he was really a ghost, not the flesh-and-blood man she felt beneath her. If he had thought about it, he would have remembered that this was her way and known the reason he was here. But he did not think. He felt only the moment. So that morning brought no reminders, only the comfort of her dark voice — yeah, Lucky, yeah — and the press of eager flesh.

By the afternoon he realized what he had done. The guilt he felt was like a knife of light that sliced away his covers, laying bare his nakedness before Babe and his son. He shivered under this light too bright and too cold to bear. He had to go back.

But as he started to get up, squinting into the chilling glare, he felt a warm hand on his shoulder.

"It's all right, Lucky. It's all right." And she pulled him back into the bed and pulled the covers over them both, enveloping him in the warm wrap of her body. And when he grew hot again, she coated him with moist breath and soothing words.

"It's all right, Lucky. Let me see my bright-side man!"

And he smiled stupidly, horribly — and gave in.

It was the same the next day, and the days that followed. He remained in bed, the curtains drawn tight. She left him for a while each day, and those times were the hardest. He would feel the pain in his hip then and begin to itch and sweat under the cast. He squirmed and scratched and hobbled around, never once peeking through the curtains at the light outside.

"You're getting stronger," she would tell him each evening as he pulled her into bed. It was true. He could feel new energy squeezing through the wounded flesh and bone beneath the cast. She would tap the cast playfully with her knuckles. "Anybody in there?" Then walk her fingers down to his exposed groin. "Look who's coming out to play!" Each day he could bear more of her weight and found himself pulling her toward him. "Don't break anything, honey!" He began to notice details in her face: the way her mouth curled higher on the left side when she smiled, lower when she frowned. The way her tongue would peek over her lower lip when she was thinking. She looked at him, always, in disbelief, giving her burnt red hair a periodic shake, then biting the stone in her turquoise ring to make certain *it*, at least, was real. He collected these details unwillingly, giving the image before him reluctant shape and texture, until finally one evening he said her name.

why. Why *was* it, Frank? Was there a reason? Were you mad? Scared? Bored? Horny?''

Kellerman sighed. ''Yes.''

Babe laughed bitterly. ''And why'd you come back? *What's the point?*''

He sat down across the table from her and rubbed his forehead. ''I don't know what the point is. I left. I'm back. I won't leave again — unless you want me to.''

Her face was stone. ''Where did you go?''

He felt tears welling in his eyes. ''Afton.'' She nodded slowly, then took a deep breath and stared out the window. This is it, he thought, but she gave no sign.

Later, he heard himself begin to talk again, slowly at first, then letting the words gush out, begging her forgiveness. She remained silent through it all, her back to him. ''I guess the point of it is,'' he said finally, ''I still love you.'' He waited, but she still gave no sign. Why should she? Then too exhausted to talk anymore, he gave up and went to bed. He slept for three hours before she woke him.

''Curly's still under the bed. He won't come out.''

Kellerman struggled to his feet and limped over to the schoolhouse where he kept most of his tools. With a hacksaw and pliers he removed the cast. Limping more freely, he took a plastic bucket and went outside and collected golf balls lying around the outfield of Curly's imaginary ball park. When he had a full bucket, he returned to Curly's room. Cautiously, he sat down again at the foot of the bed. He did not look under it.

''Want to talk now?''

Silence.

''Say, I've lost track. How's Mickey doing these days?''

Kellerman thought he heard something move under the bed, then silence again. He took a ball from the bucket and

''Matti.''

For a moment she did not reply, the left side of her mouth dipping slightly, the tip of her tongue flicking across her lip. ''Yeah, Lucky?''

It wasn't a case of gathering strength or will, or even of guilt. As he looked at Matti his mind was suddenly filled with other names, and the faces that went with them. Living faces: Babe. Curly.

''I've got to go.''

She took a deep breath and held it. He noticed then, the tiny lines and sagging flesh that recorded fourteen years since his days on the Frisco. It was amazing she was still here in Afton. He looked at her hair, burnt an even bolder, brighter red than in his Frisco days. But the make-up didn't work. She was older now, and, it struck him, so was he. He felt pity for them both. He leaned forward and kissed her on the forehead.

She recoiled. ''Get out.''

He limped to the car. In the front seat of the Silver Hawk was Curly's bat. He hung his head for a moment, then turned the key. In a minute he was back on the highway. The road was different this time. Instead of focusing blankly on the center line, he was conscious of certain facts. Fact: he was forty-five years old. Fact: he had abandoned his wife and son. Fact: he had no idea why.

It began to rain just outside Vinita and kept raining into the night. He drove into the storm, sheets of water pouring over the windshield like the cold sweat that covered his skin. He opened the window and let the rain spray in, soaking and chilling him through his clothes, keeping him awake, alive. He drove all night, stopping only for gas in Claremore. He spoke to no one. By morning the storm had passed and the freshly plowed fields around Yukon glimmered rusty brown in the clean light.

Pulling into the driveway, he realized he was exhausted. He had made no plans, had prepared no speeches. There was nothing to do but go in.

He entered the back way, through the kitchen. Babe was at the sink, her back to him. He stood in the doorway a moment, watching her. He noticed the tired curve of her back and the way her hips had thickened in recent years, spreading the contours of her cotton housecoat. He wondered how much of the weight she carried now was hers alone, and how much he had piled on her.

"I'm back."

She jumped, then composed herself and turned to face him. She looked him over, then spoke.

"Why?"

He saw in an instant how she had borne his absence. Her face had the hardened look of pain suffered, conquered. She looked older, stronger. He couldn't tell if she wanted him back.

"I'm sorry."

"Sorry," she repeated in a flat tone, studying his face.

He heard footsteps in the living room. Curly walked in, wearing his Yankee cap. He saw Kellerman and froze.

Kellerman bit his lip, then forced a grin. "Daddy's home, slugger!" He held out his arms.

Curly backed away, then gave a yelp and ran back through the house. Kellerman listened to his son's door slam, then turned to Babe.

"What did you tell him about me being gone?"

She looked him in the eye. "What *could* I tell him? You explained it the day you left. 'What's the point of coming back?' Isn't that how you put it?"

Kellerman took a deep breath and tried to calm himself.

"How long was I gone?"

Babe threw her rag in the sink. "You mean you don't *know*? Ask your son how long you were gone — he'll tell you! You were gone two weeks, you bastard."

Two weeks? He couldn't believe it. He looked at Babe, wanting to say something, anything, but she folded her arms and turned toward the sink. "I've got to talk to Curly," he said at last.

"Really. What about?"

He swallowed, then turned towards Curly's room.

He knocked. "It's me, son. Everything's all right. I want to talk to you." No answer. He turned the knob. The door had no lock, but wouldn't budge. "Open the door, Curly." He put his shoulder against it and pushed. It moved with a heavy scraping sound — Curly's dresser. Kellerman pushed the door open about a foot and squeezed in.

The boy was nowhere to be seen. Kellerman looked in the closet, but found only toys and clothes. He must be hiding under the bed, Kellerman thought. He knelt as best he could at the foot of the bed, but did not look beneath it.

"I want . . . I want to explain something to you, son," he began. "I went away — I *ran* away, for a while, and that was wrong." He listened for a sound under the bed, but there was nothing. "Can you hear me, son? I still love you. Will you forgive me?"

He waited, but there was no reply.

"I understand. Well, you think about it and talk to me when you're ready." He got up stiffly and closed the door.

Babe was sitting at the kitchen table, looking out the window.

"He doesn't want to talk yet," Kellerman said. "Did you tell him anything about why I left?"

Babe looked at him coldly. "*Why?* I said nothing about

rolled it under the bed. The ball hit something soft and stopped. He rolled another ball. Then another, and another. Then he stopped. Two minutes passed. Then a ball rolled back out.

"Atta boy, slugger."

Half an hour later he coaxed Curly out. They sat on opposite ends of the bed while Kellerman tried to get him to speak. "I brought back your bat. It's a little beat up, so I'll get you a new one — a Louisville Slugger. Just like Mickey's. OK?"

The boy's eyes flickered. "OK."

Kellerman wanted to reach forward and hug him, but was afraid the boy would back away. Don't push, he warned himself, and offered his hand instead. Curly looked at it, then extended his own, squeezed lightly, and withdrew. Kellerman mumbled "good," then left.

He found Babe at the kitchen table. "He's out. He's all right, I think."

Babe exhaled slowly. "That makes one of us."

Kellerman sat down and held his head in his hands. A moment later he looked up. "Wait a minute. If I was gone two weeks, then this is the middle of September."

Babe looked at him and shook her head. "That's right."

Kellerman felt his heart pounding against his ribcage as he asked the next question. "Has school started yet?"

Babe seemed to measure him as she replied. "Today's Monday. I enrolled him this morning. School starts tomorrow."

"Thank God," Kellerman said. "I'll talk to Curly tonight."

Babe put her hands on her hips. "You do that. Something else you might be interested in. While you were over in the schoolhouse, Vukovich called. He says you don't own the garage anymore."

Kellerman was only a little surprised the words didn't affect him.

"Vukovich says he owns it now."

"It figures."

"What are you going to do?"

"Anything but work for Vukovich."

Dinner that evening was silent. Babe methodically stripped the meat off a chicken wing, then ate it without once looking at Kellerman. Curly kept his eyes on his plate.

Kellerman could feel the strength of Curly's anger as he looked the boy over. The muscles in Curly's arms and neck had tone and definition now. Thank God for that, Kellerman thought. At least the summer hadn't been completely wasted.

After dinner he took Curly out onto the porch. "You've come a long way, son," he began. "You're big and strong enough to take care of yourself now."

Curly sat on the steps and stared at the propane tank by the schoolhouse, but Kellerman could tell he was listening.

Kellerman sat down beside him. "Listen. Tomorrow's a big day. A new year and a new you. I want to make sure both of you get started on the right track."

Curly looked down and poked at a beetle crawling on the step.

"Remember how I told you to handle yourself. If somebody picks on you, you ignore him. Walk away. Fight only if you have to. It'll be rough at first, but if you do like I tell you, after a while they'll leave you alone. That's a promise." Kellerman reached down and lifted Curly's chin. "Do you believe me?"

Curly's eyes met Kellerman's. "Where did you go?"

Kellerman felt a catch in his throat. He swallowed. "I just traveled. That's all."

He felt the weight of the lie begin to crush him as the

boy's eyes turned cold. With a strength Kellerman had never felt in his son before, Curly pulled out of Kellerman's grip and went into the house.

Kellerman remained on the back porch most of the evening, watching the lights from the city begin to glow. When he finally went inside, the lights were out. He tiptoed past Curly's room to his own bedroom.

The door was shut but unlocked. Babe lay under the covers, her back toward him. He could tell from the way she lay that she was still awake. He slipped into bed quietly but did not touch her. She did not move, her silence heavy as the night. After a long while he noticed her breathing slip into the slow, regular rhythm of sleep. He lay awake, watching her.

Just before sunrise she awoke. He watched her eyes flicker open and regard him. Suddenly she rolled toward him and began to stroke his chest and thighs, bringing him up from the depths as she had so many times before. He was grateful and amazed. They did not speak. Afterward, as the first light streamed through the window, he noticed an odd, disquieting calm about her. Instead of curling up against his chest as she always did afterward, she lay on her back. Not sleeping. Not restless either. She was there beside him, but seemed far away, separated from him in a way he'd never felt before. He lay awake and watched the dawn.

At breakfast he tried to sound cheerful and upbeat for Curly. "A new year, a new you," he chanted, watching the boy spoon the last of his Wheaties out of the bowl.

"Listen to your father," Babe said, and Kellerman could have hugged her, but the look in her eyes told him he didn't dare.

When the school bus picked Curly up, they stood on the porch and watched the back of the bus slowly disappear, sinking like a dirty yellow moon over the hill beyond the wheat fields.

"It's up to him now," Kellerman said.

They went back inside. A few minutes later he heard a car pull into the front driveway. Babe went into the living room, then called back: "It's Vukovich."

Kellerman sat up straight. "Let the bastard in."

Vukovich had changed too, Kellerman noticed, as his long-time competitor sat down across the table. The same greasy black cigar jutted from the corner of his mouth, but instead of puffs, the smoke streamed out in long, peaceful wisps. Vukovich's fat face had the warm glow of a man who had reached his goal in life. His voice, however, was all tears and remorse.

"Tough break, your losing the garage like that," he said, sipping the coffee Babe offered him. "I felt kind of bad taking it over, but business is business."

Kellerman nodded. "Yeah, I expect you cried all the way to the bank."

Vukovich smiled like an angel. "I suppose I deserve that, but that's not why I'm here. I've got a proposition for you, Frank."

Here it comes, Kellerman thought, sitting up straight in his chair.

"Hell, everybody knows you're the best mechanic in Yukon. I don't know what your plans are, Frank, but I'd rather have you working for me than against me. I'm offering to put you on as my chief mechanic — head man over both shops. Let's bury the past right here. What do you say?"

Kellerman started to deliver the curse he had been formulating in his head for months, but glancing at Babe, who sat grimly tracing the rim of her cup with a spoon, he felt something stream out of himself, like air out of a balloon, leaving him empty, formless.

"I'll think about it."

Kellerman watched Vukovich's eyes widen, then flicker with the light of victory. "That'll be fine, Frank. Just fine."

When he left, Vukovich gave Kellerman a smile of utter peace and fulfillment. Watching Vukovich's Oldsmobile disappear over the next hill, Kellerman was surprised the automobile didn't just keep rising, up into the clouds, then the sky and stars beyond, bearing Vukovich away, his purpose on this earth completed.

"I've hit bottom," Kellerman said to Babe. "Nothing's too low for me now."

Later that morning he found the *Sunday Oklahoman* lying on the coffee table. He flipped open the sports section and read:

MARIS HITS 47TH
AS YANKS BOW

Something about the headline made him wrinkle his brow, but he read on.

> Detroit, Sept. 16 — Roger Maris, stalled for a full week, finally regained his rhythmic stroke today and connected for his 47th homer of the year as the Yanks lost to Frank Lary and the Tigers 10–4.

Kellerman squinted at the page, shook his head, then continued.

> The blow, which could spark a belated record rush, put the Yankee slugger within 13 of Babe Ruth's 1927 mark of 60. Maris has four games remaining if he is to reach the record within the 154-game limit set by Commissioner Ford Frick.

Then Kellerman noticed it. The numerals 47 and 13 were phony. The real numbers had been erased, then 47 and 13 carefully hand-drawn in their place. Again he checked the headline, the story, and the box score. All the numbers describing Maris's home run total had been altered — first erased, then carefully sketched in with what looked like a black ballpoint pen.

"Well, I'll be goddamned," Kellerman said.

"What is it?"

He ignored her and rechecked the date. September 16. The season was coming to an end. He'd lost track but knew Maris ought to have *fifty*-some homers by now. He felt himself begin to sweat. He scanned the rest of the article quickly until he came to the last two paragraphs.

> One of the few sluggers who didn't hit a home run today was Mickey Mantle. He remained stalled at 53 for the season. After the game Mantle was ready to toss in the towel in his quest for a home run record.
>
> "I can't make it, not even in 162 games. I figure if I could have hit a couple here, I might have been able to do it. But I don't think I can do it now."

"Did Curly have this paper?" Kellerman demanded.

"He read it yesterday — why?"

It took almost an hour to destroy the special ball park. He pulled up the stakes and cut the strings Curly had used to mark the foul lines, then took a shovel and flattened the imaginary pitcher's mound. The tomato crate bases he chopped to pieces with an ax, then burned. He considered doing the same thing to the schoolhouse, but the limestone walls would survive almost anything. Home plate, the only authentic part of the ball park, he dug up and then buried in the wheat field.

Babe watched all this with amazement. "Well, I'll swan," she said when he had finished. "What's going on?"

"It's between me and the boy," Kellerman said.

At four o'clock Curly got off the bus with a black eye and a long ugly-looking scratch on his arm. Kellerman forgot about the newspaper and tried to stay calm while Babe washed Curly's arm and dabbed on the iodine.

"What happened?" Kellerman asked as softly as he could.

Curly flinched at the iodine and said nothing.

"Who was it? Was it Eddie Hacker?"

Curly stared determinedly at his feet.

Gently but firmly, Kellerman lifted Curly's chin until they were eye to eye. "Tell me what you did, son. Did you walk away from him like I told you? Did you fight back?"

Curly tried to look away, but Kellerman's grip held him in place. His lips trembled.

Babe laid the iodine aside and put her arm around Curly. "Don't force him."

Kellerman released the boy's chin. "Put a bandage on him while I call the school."

It took him fifteen minutes to get through to the principal. Then, in a matter of seconds, the color in his face turned from red to ashen.

He set the phone down gently. "Where is he?"

"I let him go play outside," Babe said from the kitchen. "What happened?"

Kellerman pushed past her and shoved open the back door.

What he saw in the back yard froze him. Except for the dusty path worn around the baseline by Curly's home run trots, not a trace remained of the special ball park. But Curly

stood, his bat in his hands, at the precise spot where Kellerman had dug up home plate. As Kellerman approached, he
saw white-hot concentration in his son's bruised eye as he
tossed a ball up and swung — a vicious, uppercutting, go-
for-broke swing. Mantle's swing. Kellerman felt more than
saw the ball sail in a long perfect arc over the roof of
the schoolhouse.

He stopped in front of Curly. "Roger Maris has *fifty*-seven
home runs," Kellerman said. "I just heard it on the news."

Curly looked past Kellerman toward the schoolhouse. "No
he doesn't. He has forty-seven. It says so in the paper."

Kellerman grabbed the bat out of Curly's hands. "Forget
this. It's over."

The boy stood rigid, his hands still raised, palms open,
fingers slightly curved, as if the bat, now invisible, remained
in his grasp.

Kellerman laid his hand on Curly's shoulder, feeling the
boy's muscles contract beneath his palm. Kellerman shivered,
then lowered his voice. "We have to talk, son. I want you
to tell me what happened with Eddie Hacker."

Curly clenched his fists and stared at the ground. "I
hit him."

Kellerman bit his lip until he tasted blood. "You mean
you hit him *first*? *Why*?"

Curly looked up, his eyes wet and burning. "I felt like
it. Why not?"

Kellerman took a deep breath and tried to calm himself.
"We're going to have to get something straight, son. I want
you to be strong. I want you to stand up for yourself. But
you *never* hit anybody first."

Curly twisted his lips into a sneer. "That's what *you* say
— and you *lie*."

Kellerman could not speak.

"You said you just traveled," the boy went on. "I know where you went. I heard you tell Mom. I heard you through the door. You're just a liar."

Kellerman's hand reached out and slapped Curly in the face. The blow knocked the boy onto his side. He lay on the dusty infield for several moments, the slap mark on his cheek beginning to glow. Then Babe came running out of the house, waving her arms and shouting.

"You don't hit your son in the face!" she screamed. "You don't do it!"

"Go back inside," Kellerman warned. "We're not through." He raised the bat.

She stopped at the spot where third base had stood. "Right, Frank." She put her hands on her hips and looked at the bat. "Who are you going to hit now?"

He dropped the bat in the dust. What was happening? He turned back to Curly. Slowly the boy climbed to his feet, the side of his face a bright pink. He did not look at Kellerman, and turned toward the house.

"Wait," Kellerman said, his voice quavering. "We're not through."

The boy did not answer as he walked slowly, deliberately, toward the house.

In the schoolhouse, lost in the drone of beating wings, Kellerman bent over a cardboard box, his shoulders heaving. Finally, he gathered himself and looked up, at each of the humming walls in turn.

"What am I supposed to do about it *now*?

He waited for a long time, but no voice from the walls answered. The light from the peephole had almost disappeared when he dropped the crumpled Yankee cap back into the box and returned to his project.

6

HE KNEW THE footsteps would return.

This time he was ready. He waited in the darkness, flashlight in one hand, claw hammer in the other. The air hose lay across his lap, the compressor already built up to 200 pounds per square inch. The walls were quiet now. They'd burst into life soon enough if there was trouble. Whoever was out there had better walk softly tonight.

He listened. Something, some*one* was there all right. He could feel a presence in the silent gloom. He leaned forward. Through the peephole he could see the moonlit yard. Beneath the roof of the carport his row of automobiles faced the road. Beyond the carport the house was black, silent. He searched the yard for movement. Nothing.

Time passed without sound. He watched the moon move across the sky.

He was beginning to feel drowsy when he heard something. Or, rather, *felt* something. Not footsteps. Not movement, exactly. A nervous, tingly sensation in his hands and feet. Then he realized what it was. He was beginning to itch. He shook his head in the darkness.

Jesus Christ, not now.

The morning itch, the insulin hangover, was beginning. It spread rapidly up his fingers and toes. Soon his head began to throb. He rubbed his forehead and looked through the peephole.

Not even midnight, most likely. I'm not due for another shot until morning. Why am I itching now?

He laid the hammer in his lap, switched on the flashlight, then turned and opened the ancient icebox next to his worktable. Beneath the bottom shelf the beam revealed the ice container which held only water. He removed the vial of insulin and pressed it to his cheek. The glass felt slightly cool. Damn. Ought to be kept colder than this. Should have brought in Charley's ice. All melted by now. Should have hooked up a goddamn refrigerator.

He turned the flashlight on the vial to check how much insulin he had left. A full vial held 10 cc's, 1000 units — at 30 units a day, enough to last over a month. Kellerman adjusted his bifocals, then stared until he could make out the level of the clear liquid.

Less than half full, he judged. But enough to last until I finish the automobile — if I finish on schedule.

He decided to have Charley Bluefire pick up a fresh batch of insulin, and more ice, tomorrow. The blanket-assed sonofabitch would be back again in the morning, sure as the night was dark. For now, he'd just have to wait. Taking an extra shot was too risky.

He made a mental note to check his urine in the morning.

"Think of something else," he whispered aloud, but felt the itch creep further up his arms, into his shoulders. He switched off the flashlight and laid it on his worktable, and, in the darkness, shook his hands and feet to get his circulation going. His left foot began to throb.

Check the color of that bruise in the morning too.

He walked gingerly around the auto frame, feeling his way through the gloom. The itch spread through his entire body now, like a wave of ants. Don't scratch. His head throbbed harder, blood pounding against his temples. His tongue tingled. Suddenly he craved something sweet.

"Don't think about it," he said aloud, and stared through the darkness toward the west wall where he knew the boxes of sugar were stacked on the air compressor.

No. He turned away. No, no, no. He licked the back of his teeth and swallowed the salty saliva beneath his tongue. Think of something, damn it. Think.

"Hey, bitch-in-the-wall! What do you say now? Got any ideas? Where's that damn know-it-all voice of yours when I need it?"

The walls were silent, his honeys fast asleep between plaster and stone. He took a couple of deep breaths to revive himself but barely felt the air drawn into his lungs. His eyelids grew heavy.

That's it. Sleep. Sleep would be the best thing. Sleep it off. Sleep away the itch, the craving.

He was beginning to close his eyes when he saw something move in the yard.

He snapped forward and stared through the peephole. Over by the carport. The row of automobiles almost disappeared beneath the black cloak of the roof as a cloud moved in front of the moon. The yard was still. He watched, waited. This time he felt no need to reach for the hammer or the flashlight. This time he was ready. But as the seconds passed he began to frown. What he had seen did not match the heavy steps he had heard the night before. What he had seen was *small*, the size of a dog or a small boy. He chewed his lower lip. Could be Charley Bluefire's boy — no, no, he's a grown man now. No kids left around here. An animal, maybe. A dog or a cat.

Quietly, Kellerman got down on his knees and pressed his ear to the wood floor. Nothing. No steps, no sound.

He climbed back to the peephole. The moon remained hidden, dissolving the yard in shadow. The house was a deeper darkness beyond. He waited.

And waited. Then, gradually, he felt himself slipping. The pain, the itch, the craving disappearing. He was growing numb. Wake up, damn it. He slapped his face, but the sting faded almost instantly. Through the peephole the yard turned darker, then black. He leaned back in the chair. Sleep. No. He took another deep breath and let it out slowly, calmly, his body relaxing against his will. He felt his heart beat slower, his breaths grow longer. As the night pressed him into a deep, exhausted sleep, he heard, somewhere along the fading edge of his consciousness, faint but somehow clear, a single unnerving sound. A sound that was both a cry of pain and a bizarre laugh. It was the hoarse caw of a crow, a caw that sounded like a word — a name — a silly, stupid name, a name that made him tremble in his sleep: *Hubert.*

It wasn't a crow he'd heard — he knew that the instant he awoke the next morning, the morning of the fourth day.

"It's *her.*" He brought his fist down on the worktable with a thump, bouncing half-a-dozen bees into the air. "Just when I get started on something, just when I think I might get a little work done in here for the first time in years — here she is."

He squinted through the peephole. The yard was a luminous gold in the morning light, and quiet. The row of automobiles parked in the carport was clearly visible now. He searched the row carefully but saw nothing out of place.

Beyond the carport the old woodframe house looked empty as usual.

"No sign of her, honeys," Kellerman reported. "But she's out there. You can bank on it. She's a stealthy old bitch." He turned away from the peephole and looked at his project. The automobile was still more than a week away from completion. He chewed his lower lip and made a vow: "I've got to keep her away from this schoolhouse."

But that was something he had never managed to do, not once in thirty years. The very first time he had seen her — peeking into the schoolhouse at him through this same window, her gray shrunken face cocked slightly, one black eye watching him like a scavenger bird eyeing a corpse — he had jumped and nearly sliced his finger on the mower blade he was sharpening. Before he could move again, she puffed her chest and made a startling noise: a hoarse moan that sounded like something dying. It shook him like an unexpected peal of thunder. By the time he got outside she had vanished.

"You hear that?" he asked Babe when he reached the house.

Her back to him at the sink, she turned slowly, cradling Curly in one arm. Curly appeared to be dozing as he sucked on a bottle.

"Hear what?" Babe asked.

"That sound a minute ago."

With her free hand, Babe removed the bottle from Curly's mouth. His lips made a smacking sound and he continued to suck but did not awake. Babe looked up at Kellerman.

"All I heard was a crow."

He called the police, as much for his own sanity as anything else. Big Bob Swanda was chief of police in those days.

"The Zuchas should have warned you about Mabel before you bought that place," Swanda said. "You'd better have yourself a talk with Orville."

Kellerman pulled the phone away from his ear and stared at the receiver. Orville Zucha had sold him the five acres, house and schoolhouse included, for two thousand dollars. Not a bad price in 1951. Kellerman had needed a good deal at the time, for even after having used all his accident settlement money from the Frisco as down payment on the garage, he already owed the Yukon National Bank more than six thousand dollars. Orville Zucha was a big square-headed wheat farmer in blue overalls and a gray striped cap. He lived half a mile east, down a narrow dirt road, in one of the shabbiest houses around. Kellerman had taken him for a dumb Polack, and at two thousand the property had seemed a steal.

"Mabel? Mabel who?" Kellerman barked into the phone. "*What* should Orville have told me?"

The voice on the phone sounded muffled, as if Bob Swanda were stifling a laugh. "Mabel Zucha," Swanda said finally. "Orville's mother. She's a sweet lady, really, 'cept for one thing. She thinks she's a bird."

Kellerman's lips parted again, and he remembered the rasping sound the old woman made at the window.

"A crow?" Kellerman said.

"What?"

"Babe thought she made a noise like a crow."

"You could say that," Swanda agreed. "Your neighbor Charley Bluefire calls her the Crow Woman."

"Christ on a crutch. Why doesn't Orville put her in a home or something?"

"He keeps her locked in the house most of the time. His wife looks out after Mabel while he's farming, but sometimes she gets out."

Kellerman sighed. "Well, fine. What's it all got to do with me?"

"Nothing, except you just bought her roost."

"Her what?"

"Her roost. The place she goes when she's on the wing, so to speak. You really don't know anything about Mabel?"

Kellerman bit the inside of his lower lip until it hurt. "I'm listening, ain't I?"

The police chief cleared his throat. "You ought to hear the whole story then. Call up Horace Loudermilk. He was there when most of it happened."

"When what happened?"

"That old schoolhouse of yours is almost a hundred years old. Used to be the Spring Creek School, only school in this part of the county. Lot of folks around here went to school there. Well, Mabel was one of them. Her maiden name's Kolar. Parents came over from Bohemia. You know, the real place in Czechoslovakia. They made the run that opened up this part of the Indian Territory in 1890. Had three boys, every one of them killed in the First World War. And Mabel. I don't know if it's true, but they say she was born on the first day of the century." Kellerman heard Swanda take a deep breath. "I don't know. Maybe Mabel would have turned out different if any of her brothers had lived to take care of her. Ask Horace. He can tell you."

Horace Loudermilk was the unofficial historian for the town of Yukon. He lived on a farm just north of the Canadian River next to Dale Robertson's horse ranch, the Rocking R.

It was me named her the Crow Woman, Horace said when Kellerman called. *It was her eyes put me in mind of a crow — round and cold black, like you could see deep inside her head if you just looked close enough. But nobody did. Look her in the face and she'd stare you down with them black eyes like a crow eyeballin' you from a tree. I don't think she meant nothin' by it, but it made us boys uneasy. So we teased her with snakes and rats and dead armadillos. It was just our meanness made us do it. She was just a little bit of a girl, and we wanted to see her bawl, wanted to see them black eyes fill up with tears. Well, we teased her and teased her till she got jumpy like a ground squirrel and wouldn't look none of us in the eye no more. But no matter what we done to her, we could never make her cry.*

Only boy let her alone was Hubert Zucha — and he was plain crazy. One day when he was twelve, he decided he was a catfish. That's right, a catfish. Jumped into the river and tried to feed right off the bottom. Took four of us to haul him up on a sand bar and pump out the mud water. Few years later, when it came time to fight the Kaiser, all us boys old enough rode over to El Reno in Luke Kastl's hay wagon to join up. Only one the army turned down was Hubert. I don't know what he did to cause it, but the sergeant said he wasn't puttin' no rifle in Hubert's hands. So Hubert stayed home for the war. 'Bout the time most of us, the lucky ones, were just gettin' back from France, Hubert and Mabel got married.

No tellin' what attracted 'em to each other. They was both out-casts, so to speak. Only passion in Hubert's life was them pigeons he raised up in the loft of his parents' barn. Had a whole flock up there: white ones, gray ones, speckled ones, you name it. You could see a hundred or more circlin' round the barn of an evening. Hubert'd be up there with the pigeons. You could see him through the loft door, lettin' birds in an' out of the cages he'd built. I swear he'd stand in the doorway and toss pigeons up in the air one by one, then point an' wave like he was directin' each bird which way to go. They say he had some of them birds trained to fly all the way to El Reno and back.

Well, I'm glad I was back in time for the weddin'. The old Church of St. Francis burned down in the winter of eighteen, so they got married in the Spring Creek School. Half the town of

Yukon was there. When the ceremony was over the two of them
came outta that schoolhouse like a couple of chickens runnin' from
a fox. Never seen a woman so scared in my life. Shakin' so bad
I thought she'd tear right outta that weddin' dress, which was blue.
First blue one I ever seen. They come down the steps all shim-
myin' and shallyin', and then a funny thing happened. Hubert,
who looked like a ghost most the time, took hisself a deep breath
and got a little color in his cheeks. Then he grabbed Mabel by
the hips and lifted her up like he was a strong man, which he
wasn't, right up into the buggy — brand new shiny black piano
box buggy he ordered special from the Studebaker Brothers. Oh,
it was a sight, I tell you: ribbed leather seats and a three-bow leather
top. Hickory cane wheels and steel tires. We still didn't have but
three or four automobiles around Yukon then, so people appreciated
a good buggy. Well, the moment Hubert set Mabel down in that
buggy she calmed down. I mean just dead quiet peaceful, sittin'
there in that buggy with her arms folded in her lap just as calm
as you please. I don't believe she ever actually looked at Hubert
the whole time, just kept her eyes shinin' on the road ahead. It
might of been the light reflectin' off the dress she was wearin',
but I swear to God when they went past, it looked to me like
them black crow eyes of hers had turned blue.

They was fixin' to go when a couple ol' boys noticed the pigeon
cages in the back of the buggy. It got quiet a moment and you
could hear 'em cooin' plain as day. Later on when we was all
talkin' about it, Ted Turch said Hubert had only his best flyers
in them cages. Well, there wasn't time to say nothin' to Hubert
about it, but just before Hubert cracked the whip over that big
roan horse of his, Luke Kastl yells out, "Where you headed?"
Hubert looks back at him an' grins the biggest grin I ever saw
an' says "We're goin to the moon."

Afterward some of us got to talkin' and Ted Turch says he
thought Hubert might of said "honeymoon." But I'm here to

tell you he said "moon" clear as a bell.

Well, nobody thought much about Hubert and Mabel for a couple of days. Then Mabel's parents got a call from the sheriff down in Sulphur. Hubert's dead, he says. Fell off a cliff above the Wildhorse River. That's what he said at first. Later on it came out Hubert had took Mabel up on that cliff and then jumped. Why, nobody knows. But a couple of miners were fishin' down on the river an' seen him up on the edge of the cliff, lettin' birds outta cages. Birds all flew around in a circle above his head like they was takin' their bearings. Then Hubert points at somethin' way up in the sky — maybe it was the moon, I don't know — and starts flappin' his arms like they was wings. He kept flappin' an' the birds kept circlin'. Then he jumped. The miners swore he flapped his arms all the way to the bottom. Birds circled around above the river for a while, then flew away. They found Mabel still sittin' in that buggy up on the cliff.

Sheriff brought Mabel home in that same buggy a couple days later. Only instead of pigeons they had Hubert in a pine box lashed on the back. We had a hell of a time gettin' Mabel outta the buggy. She hung onto the seat like death. Didn't want to leave Hubert, I guess. Just when we thought we had her calmed down, she got away from us and grabbed onto one of the buggy wheels. Took us a good five minutes to pry her off. Sheriff told her father it'd be a good idea to get rid of that buggy.

Later on you could see it was more than grief, the change in her. The shine had gone out of her eyes. They was black as a snake pit now, no life at all in 'em. She didn't stare back at nobody now and didn't act jumpy neither. Nothin' riled her now. Far as I know, she never talked to nobody about what happened on that cliff. Not to the priest or nobody. Didn't even go to the funeral. See her on the streets of Yukon after that an' she'd take no notice of you, just go on her way. It was like whatever was behind them eyes of hers died up there on that cliff. But the worst of it was,

we found out later, she was pregnant. Naturally we all thought
she'd go away somewhere before her time come, but not Mabel.
She went about her business as usual just like before until the day
Orville was born.

I don't mind tellin' you we was all scared about what kind of
mother Mabel'd be. But we was wrong. She raised that boy herself,
and, well, you can see for youself how Orville turned out. Mabel's
parents died when Orville was still little. Didn't surprise anybody
the way they both went within a few weeks of each other. They'd
lost three boys in the war and then Hubert. We worried about Mabel
an' that boy all alone on the farm. Well, we was wrong again.
Mabel hired Luke Kastl and a couple more boys to run the farm
till Orville was old enough. They did OK right through the Depres-
sion. Better'n most, anyway. Looked like things was going to turn
out all right for Mabel after all.

Then the next war came and Orville stayed home to run the
farm. The two of 'em come through that OK too. Then one day
not long after VJ Day it got real hot, so hot the locusts was crawlin'
out of their skins. Right in the heat of the day, Mabel disappeared.
Orville finally found her standin' in the sun outside the old Spring
Creek School, starin' into a window. They'd closed up the school
before the war, and Orville'd bought up the five acres around it
from the township and built the house you're livin' in now. He
had in mind to tear that old schoolhouse down, I believe. Anyway
when he called to Mabel she appeared to take no notice of him.
Just kept starin' real intentlike into that window like she was lookin'
for somethin'. Place was empty then. Wasn't nothing in there to
see. Well, before Orville could catch up to her, she turned away
from the window an' run off down to the creek. Sight of her runnin' kind of froze him, I guess. He'd never seen her move fast
like that before. By the time he got after her she'd disappeared in
the trees. He looked and looked — an' then he saw her. Up on
one of them gully cliffs above the creek. Starin' up into the sky

and tremblin' all over like she'd spotted somethin' up there that scared her. But there wasn't nothin' in the sky but the sun. No clouds, no birds, not even a moon. From where he was down by the creek, Orville couldn't see her eyes, but they had to be burnin' from starin' up into that bright sun. Then you know what she did? Hooked her thumbs under her armpits an' started flappin' her arms like they was wings. Flappin' an flappin' like she was gonna jump right off that cliff and fly away. Hot as it was, Orville froze like a icicle. Then she opened her mouth and made that sound . . .

Kellerman sat on the automobile frame and wiped his glasses. "Why'd she have to come back *now*, just when I've started something, just when Curly's coming home?" He put his glasses back on and looked around the room, halting his gaze on the beam of light through the peephole. It was already midmorning, but he made no move to get back to work.

He clenched his fist. "I can't work with her out there, honeys. I'll never finish. I've got to do something." He stood up, hoping the motion would carry him into action. But he stopped almost immediately. What could he actually do, here in the schoolhouse? He looked around the room again, his glance falling on the ax propped against the door. "Chop her damn head off like a turkey, way I should of done years ago."

He smiled at the thought, then sighed and sat down in the swivel chair.

"If Bob Swanda was still chief, I could just call the cops and have them haul her away till I've finished my project," he mused. "Swanda'd understand. But Swanda's dead, like everybody worth a damn in this town.

"Know who's chief now, honeys? Eddie Hacker, the grown-up Nazi that took away my license for runnin' Ed

Looper off the road, that punk that used to beat up my boy.
Fat lot of good it would do to call *him*."

Let the poor woman be.

He didn't turn around, just stared straight ahead at the
blank wall. "Yeah, I know, I know. That was your fucking advice from the start. You and the boy wanted me to
treat her like she was some kind of poor dumb bird fell out
of the sky. Well, she ain't!"

He bared his teeth and remembered the day when he'd
gone looking for Curly down by the creek. It was two weeks
after he'd returned from Afton. Two weeks after Vukovich
had offered him a job in his own garage. Two weeks after
he'd destroyed Curly's pretend ball park and slapped him in
the face.

The boy had barely spoken to him since that day, staying
away from the house for hours whenever Kellerman was
around. He wondered where the boy went off to, but stopped
himself from asking. The pattern of his own life was changing then, slipping further and further out of his control. He
hadn't accepted Vukovich's offer. Instead, Charley Bluefire
got him a job on the maintenance crew at the capitol. It was
Charley who told him where Curly went off to. *Whenever
I go hunting I usually see him roaming around down by the creek.*
That's as good a place as any, Kellerman thought.

Then one evening Curly was late for dinner, and Babe sent
Kellerman out to find him. Careful, Kellerman thought as
he started off. You've blown it once with the boy. If he's
found a secret place, let him have it.

Nearing the creek, he began calling Curly's name. He
wanted to give the boy a chance to come out without revealing his secret spot, if there was one. Kellerman heard his own
voice echo along the banks but received no answer. It was
early October and the creek was dry. He looked along the

wooded part first, past the sycamore and redbud trees, then wandered up the deep gully cut out by flash floods during the spring tornado season. From above, the gully looked like an exposed wound, the living earth sliced open to reveal its tender red flesh. From below, on the dry creekbed where he walked, the earth looked long dead, the red wall of the gully turning slowly brown, chipping and flaking away in the hot sun. Sweating dizzily, he had almost forgotten about Curly when he rounded a bend and looked up.

Fifteen feet above on the edge of a gully cliff he saw the Crow Woman. She stood in silence, staring up into the empty sky. She wore a long dress of faded indistinguishable color that reached all the way to the ground. Despite the heat, a gray shawl was wrapped around her shoulders like the furled wings of a bat. Kellerman stepped back out of sight, then peeked around the bend of the gully and watched.

For a long time she didn't move. Then her mouth opened a little and worked up and down, silently, as if she were whispering something too softly to hear. Then she opened her arms, extending them to each side, slowly, until they were parallel with the edge of the cliff, the shawl spreading open like wings.

Kellerman was afraid she was going to jump. No! he wanted to shout, but his mouth made no sound. A breeze came up, lifting the shawl, making the fringe flutter beneath her arms. Kellerman forced himself to look away, then spotted another figure silently watching the Crow Woman from the bend at the far end of the gully. Curly. The look in his eyes intent, enraptured, the same look he'd always had when he played the pretend ball game.

"Curly!"

The boy jumped, then stumbled onto his knees, in full view. He looked up at Kellerman, then leaped to his feet and turned and ran, disappearing behind the red wall. Kellerman started to call after him, then swallowed his breath. When he looked up the Crow Woman had vanished.

Back at the house, Babe and Curly were already eating supper. "Yours is in the oven," Babe said. Kellerman ignored her and sat down across from Curly, who mashed his meatloaf with a fork and did not look up.

"I want you to leave that old woman alone, son. I don't even want you to watch her."

Curly piled his potatoes on top of his meatloaf and said nothing.

"What old woman?" Babe asked.

"Stay out of this," Kellerman said and took the fork away from Curly. "I'm not saying this to be mean, son. Something happened to Mrs. Zucha a long time ago, and it made her . . . different. There's nothing you or me can do about it. Orville's had the best doctors in the world look at her and there's nothing they can do. You just make it worse on her by watching. So the best thing to do is just leave her alone. OK?"

The boy squinted at Kellerman, then bit his lip.

He doesn't know if he can trust me, Kellerman thought. "I'm right, son. Everybody leaves Mrs. Zucha alone."

Curly looked at Babe, then back down at his plate. "OK."

"Good," Kellerman said, trying to hide the joy in his voice, and handed Curly back his fork.

After dinner, when Curly had gone to his room, Kellerman told Babe about what had happened on the cliff. "This is getting out of hand," he said. "It's bad enough she pokes her damn beak into the schoolhouse every time I turn my back. Now she damn near killed herself in front of my boy. Well, that's it. If Orville can't keep his bird-brained old lady locked up at home, then I'm going to have her put someplace they will."

Then Babe said it. "Let the poor woman be. What's she hurting?"

Kellerman's jaw dropped. "What's she *hurting*? You didn't see her spreading her wings like a buzzard up on that cliff. You didn't see Curly watching her."

"He just feels sorry for her is all."

"Sorry my ass. You didn't see it. That woman's spooky. I want her away from my boy. If Zucha won't have her committed, I will."

Orville Zucha was sympathetic but unmoved. "I'm sorry Mama scared your boy, Frank. I really am," Orville said when Kellerman confronted him the next day. "But I can't put Mama in a home. I just can't."

"It'd be for her own good," Kellerman reasoned. "You're damn lucky she ain't killed herself already."

"I'll keep her shut in the house," Orville promised. "I'll have Mary Lou watch her close."

Three days later Kellerman looked up from the pipe he was welding to see Mabel eyeballing him like a vulture through the window above his worktable.

"That's it! I'm going to have that woman put away," he vowed after he chased her off.

And so the battle began. Kellerman went to Bob Swanda first, but the police chief told him it was a matter for the Canadian County Board of Mental Health. Kellerman called and put in a complaint, but the board told him to go through the courts. He filed a petition in the district court in El Reno. But Orville Zucha had a lot of government friends left over from his Victory Crop days when the War Department gave him a medal for growing so much wheat to support the allied effort in Europe and the Pacific. Orville wore his medal every year in the Czech Festival Parade. Kellerman's petition went nowhere.

"War hero," Kellerman snapped when he saw Orville in the Yukon National Bank. "Never left the fucking county while I was nearly getting my ass blown off on Iwo Jima."

"You leave my mama alone," Orville warned.

"Watch out she don't fly over and shit on your head, war hero," Kellerman countered. Orville's square face turned red. He shoved his fists into his overall pockets and stomped out. Kellerman laughed. He could always get Orville's goat, but the old woman continued to run free. Orville tried putting padlocks on all his windows and doors, but about once a week Kellerman would look up from his worktable in the schoolhouse and see Mabel's sharp beaklike nose pecking against the glass or hear her hoarse crow laugh, a laugh that was both a jeer and a cry of pain: *Haaa! Haaa!*

"I swear I'm going to get me a shotgun and put both of them out of my misery," Kellerman said to Babe.

"Why don't you try talking to Orville again instead of taking him to court all the time," Babe suggested.

"Good idea. I'll send him a message he can understand."

The next day Kellerman made a scarecrow and faced it toward the Zuchas' house half a mile down the road.

"That's supposed to be funny, I guess," Orville observed as he drove by on his tractor.

"Not to a crow," Kellerman answered.

And so it went. Orville managed to keep the old woman locked up for a time after that, but Kellerman knew it wouldn't last. He dreamed about putting an electric fence around his five acres. Let her fly over *that*.

Unnoticed, in the middle of all this, was the change in Curly. Kellerman discovered it one evening as he laid a plate in the kitchen sink and glanced out the window into the back yard.

"Babe, I want you to come look at this. Your son is

talking to a skunk.''

Boy and skunk faced each other about a yard apart. Curly sat cross-legged on the ground, holding out a piece of raw bacon. The skunk was twisted into a U with both ends facing Curly — nose sniffing cautiously at the meat, tail pointing straight up, ready to spray. *Don't let him touch that thing,* Babe whispered hoarsely when she saw them. Kellerman told her to calm down. The boy knew all about skunks. If he was fool enough to get close enough to one to get sprayed, then maybe this was the best way to learn.

But despite its menacingly erect tail, the skunk seemed to Kellerman to be more intrigued than angry, and the animal was definitely edging closer to the meat. Curly's lips were moving, as if he were whispering something soothing, the way one would speak to a frightened puppy. The skunk moved closer, to within a yard or so of the bacon. It was then Kellerman realized the boy might be bitten.

"Hey!" He banged on the window as he yelled.

The skunk jumped, sprayed Curly, and ran into the field. Curly gagged and struck wildly at his face. Kellerman gasped, then ran to his son.

"You stupid, stupid," Babe stammered a few minutes later, and struck Kellerman several times on the back as they rubbed Curly's face with wet soapy towels. The stench choked off the boy's sobs and made Kellerman's nose and eyes burn as if he'd been sniffing gasoline. He held his breath and tried to convince himself it would have been far worse if the skunk had gotten close enough to bite Curly.

"I'm sorry," Kellerman moaned, but couldn't tell if the boy even heard him.

It took days to wash the stink off. Kellerman winced whenever he saw Curly's raw red face, the dead chafed skin peeling off in patches like a first-degree burn. Their roles had

been reversed, Kellerman realized in shame. He was now afraid
to look his son in the eye. Babe's unforgiving stare was almost
as difficult to bear.

What are you going to do about this? her eyes asked.

He had no idea.

Curly hardly even acknowledged Kellerman's existence
now. And when the boy did take note of him, it was with
suspicion, as if there were always another angle, another shade
of meaning in every word, movement, gesture. Kellerman
chewed his lip and tried to think. He needed a lever, a point
of common interest, like the baseball game, to reach the boy.
The Saturday after the skunk sprayed Curly he came up with
an idea.

"Get in. We're going to town," he ordered and held open
the door to the old GMC pickup.

"What for?" Babe asked as she climbed into the cab.

"We'll know when we get there," Kellerman answered
and held the door open for Curly to climb in between them.
The boy remained where he was, standing about six feet away,
frowning at the truck. Kellerman waited. He had deliberately
chosen the GMC because it was Curly's favorite.

"Hop in," Kellerman said brightly. The boy glanced at
Babe sitting quietly in the cab, then raced past Kellerman
and climbed into the back of the pickup, settling down in
the corner next to the spare tire.

The ride to Yukon was silent. They stopped in front of
Kroeger's Pet Shop. Babe looked over at Kellerman and
sighed. "I appreciate what you're doing, but I don't think
it'll work."

Probably right, Kellerman thought as they went in. He
had tried this tactic once before when Curly was eight, bringing home a slobbering German Shepherd pup named Fritz.
What kind of a boy doesn't like dogs? he reasoned. But

Curly would have nothing to do with the pup, who wet the rug five times before Kellerman decided to keep him strictly in the garage. *I'd rather have a rat,* Curly said and refused to feed the pup. *You're forcing it on the boy,* Babe said. *You should let him pick out his own pets.* Kellerman was bitter. *My old man wouldn't even let me have a dog,* he said. He was sure Curly would learn to love the pup in time, but after only a week Fritz had been run over by a hay truck.

Maybe Babe was right, Kellerman conceded as they gawked at the newspaper-lined cages of howling, hissing, whimpering, pissing dogs, cats, turtles, geese, hamsters, and other stinking animals.

Got any skunks or rats? Kellerman almost asked old man Kroeger, but thought better of it. If the boy sees something he likes, fine. If not, I ain't saying a word. All the animals seemed to bore Curly, especially the yowling, scratching dogs. He passed cage after cage, barely glancing at the wet eager noses pressed against the wire. At the end of the row was a single cage. Curly stopped in front of it and stared inside.

Casually, Kellerman moved over to the next aisle and began examining boxes of bird seed. Out of the corner of his eye he peered back at the cage. Inside was a lump of brown fur. Kellerman pretended to read the back of a box of Hartz Mountain parakeet seed, waiting for Curly to move on. He didn't.

"What's in that last cage over there?" Kellerman whispered to old man Kroeger at the register. Babe was looking out the window, but he could tell she was listening.

Kroeger was a tan wrinkled old man with a face like a dried mud pie. "Golden basset hound," he said tonelessly.

"Dog?" Kellerman asked, lifting his eyebrows.

"Practically purebred." Kroeger was peeling 75¢ price tags off plastic bowls and sticking on tags that said $1.98.

"Dead or alive?" Kellerman said, looking back at the motionless lump in the cage.

"You couldn't afford a dead one," Kroeger said.

Kellerman walked back to where Curly was still standing in front of the cage. "You like that dog?" he asked hopefully.

Curly shrugged. "OK."

Kellerman looked down at the dog, who lay in a wrinkled heap with one eye open, watching a bug crawl along the rim of an empty water dish. "This here dog chase cars?" Kellerman shouted back at Kroeger.

"Guaranteed not to. Legs too short."

"Yeah, well what *does* he do?"

"Drinks beer. He prefers Budweiser, but he'll drink Coors."

Kellerman glanced back down at the dog, who lifted its head and gave him a droopy-eared look, like one of the winos in the alley next to the Athenium Hotel.

"You sure this is the one you want, son?"

Curly curled his fingers around the wire of the cage and nodded.

A beer hound. Curly named him Boozer.

The fence around the acreage consisted of only three wires stretched between posts, so the first thing Curly did was teach Boozer never to cross the road in front of the house alone. Kellerman watched him spend hours training the dog to be walked across. Curly would grab a magazine, then walk Boozer right up to the fence, then stop. The first several times, the dog would bound merrily ahead, and would have gone right under the bottom wire if Curly hadn't grabbed his collar.

"No!" Curly would say, then whack Boozer on the butt with the rolled-up magazine.

Now that's sense, Kellerman thought as he watched. Eventually Boozer learned to stop at the fence.

At night they gave Boozer a pail of Budweiser with his Kennel Ration. "Sonofabitchin' dog drinks like my old man used to," Kellerman remarked the first time the dog lapped up an entire pail without coming up for air. When he was finished, Boozer raised his head and licked the foam off his nose. Fifteen minutes later he lay on his back on the dry grass, making gurgling noises and moving his legs back and forth like he was trying to walk upside down. Then he fell asleep.

"Well, I'll swan," Babe said, laughing on the back porch.

"Not exactly Rin Tin Tin," Kellerman observed.

"He's better," Curly said.

Curly loved Boozer from the start. Kellerman noted this with satisfaction and hope. Satisfaction that he had finally given the boy something he liked, hope that the dog would somehow get them back on the right track.

As the days passed, however, Kellerman was careful not to appear to take advantage of whatever feelings the dog might have awakened in Curly. For his part, Curly remained distant, never inviting Kellerman to join in the games of chase and tug of war he played with Boozer.

The third week of October a cool wind blew from the north for a few days, the first whiff of autumn. One afternoon just as Kellerman arrived home from work, he saw Curly coming out the back door of the house with a Daisy air rifle propped on his shoulder. Kellerman was surprised and encouraged, for until this moment the BB gun had been another one of Kellerman's gifts that didn't work. He had given it to Curly not long after school started. *I never had such a thing when I was growing up,* Kellerman had said the day he handed the shiny black rifle to his son. But Curly had stared blankly at the barrel. *I don't like to shoot things,* he said and put the rifle away in a dark corner of his closet.

Where are you going? Kellerman called out as Curly marched off the back porch with the rifle propped on his shoulder.

Hunting, Curly answered. Then Boozer ran up to him, woofing and sniffing merrily. And boy and dog rounded the corner of the house, then crossed the road to Orville Zucha's freshly plowed wheat fields, then headed toward the creek.

Well, I'll be damned, Kellerman thought, and smiled.

His elation soon faded, however, for in the days that followed a pattern developed. Every afternoon, as soon as Curly stepped off the bus, he would take Boozer and the BB gun and disappear. They would be gone before Kellerman got home from work. *Just once I'd like to come home to my family when my family's here,* Kellerman complained. One evening he could stand it no longer and went out to look for them.

As he crossed the plowed field to the wooded area down by the creek he began to have second thoughts. So the boy has his own private time with his dog. What's wrong with that? Now you're going to horn in on it. Why? Because he doesn't include *you.*

He had almost talked himself into going back when he spotted them. They were just ahead, moving through the dry brush around the redbud trees, nearing the creek. Without thinking any more about it, he decided to follow them.

He crept along about fifty yards behind Curly as Boozer led the way, sniffing and scratching through the brush. That dog's probably buried his empty Budweiser cans down here, Kellerman thought, as he peeked through the redbud trees. Curly was close behind Boozer, air rifle braced against his chest, trying to move quietly through the brush, but snapping twigs and catching limbs across his face with every other step. As hunters, they were a pathetic pair, Kellerman decided. Birds, rabbits, and chipmunks would hear Boozer thrashing long before he became aware of them. And when Boozer did manage to catch a scent, he would rear up and bellow, scaring off everything within a hundred yards. As for Curly, Kellerman watched the boy spot numerous sparrows in the branches of the redbud trees. Each time, Curly would line up the shot but never fire. Kellerman began to wonder if the BB gun was even loaded.

He lost them when the dry gullies leading into the creek began to branch out into the pasture beyond. He started to turn back when he heard Boozer woofing and baying at something further up. Beerbelly's finally cornered something, he thought, and hurried up the gully to see. He rounded a bend and saw the Crow Woman on the edge of a cliff.

Kellerman froze. Curly was on the cliff with her, only a few feet away. The two were facing each other, squatting about six feet from the edge, flapping their arms and making laughing, crowlike sounds. Boozer trotted nervously around them, barking and howling and trying to join in. Kellerman had no idea how long he stood on the dry creek bed looking up at the sight above him. He saw, felt, perceived only the image before him: the idiot woman and his son, facing each other, two gross mockeries of birds, flapping their arms like wings, cawing, staring into each other's eyes and seeing God knows what, while the howling dog bounded around and around them. Then, in a flash that nearly knocked him flat, Kellerman recognized what was taking place: Curly spread his arms wide and held them steady like the wings of a hawk gliding above a field. The Crow Woman spread her own arms an instant later, her gray shawl lifting with the breeze. *She was imitating him.*

"Curly!"

The cry was involuntary. He had yelled without thinking, without meaning to. If he had been thinking, he would have kept silent. The sound of his voice startled the woman more than the boy. She jumped, took a couple of flapping hops, trying to right herself . . . and stepped over the edge. Her long dress caught the wind like lifting wings, holding her a moment in midair, like a great bird beginning to soar. Then the dress blew over her head and she dropped like a sky diver whose chute had failed. The cliff was about twenty feet high at the point she fell, and Kellerman felt the smack of her brittle body on the sandy floor of the gully.

The impact flattened her into a splotch of indistinguishable color on the sand. She lay silent, unmoving, the dress covering her like a shroud.

Kellerman raised his eyes to the cliff. Curly stood looking down at the Crow Woman, his own eyes glazed over, seeing and not seeing the image before him, like the blind clerk Kellerman had once seen drop a porcelain statuette of Will Rogers on the marble floor in front of the Bureau of the Handicapped booth in the capitol. The statuette had shattered with the explosive pop of a light bulb. The blind man remained standing over the spot of impact, arms still extended, clenching and unclenching his fists, as if time could somehow be reversed, as if he could find again in the empty space before him the fragile object that had slipped through his grasp. On the cliff above Kellerman now, Curly's hands dangled helplessly at his sides, fingers quivering in faint electrical spasms. Next to him Boozer peered over the edge, ears half-lifted, half-drooping, in futile attention to the mute figure lying on the sand. He wrinkled his nose and sniffed the air, then began to whine.

"She's OK," Kellerman yelled suddenly. Even before Curly's stunned eyes turned toward him, Kellerman knew what he had done. "She's OK," he repeated, as if saying the words could make them true. He moved toward her with a will that was not will, a hope that was not hope. The air around him was thick and heavy, resisting him like water.

He had never seen her close up. When finally he stood breathless and trembling over her still body, the first thing he noticed was insignificant, ridiculous. The dress she wore was blue. Or once had been blue. Age had left only a hint, a memory, of the color. He didn't wonder about it, for lying there in a rippled splatter on the sand, she looked chillingly birdlike. Like a chicken hawk dashed to earth, knocked out of the clear sky by a farmer's shotgun. He saw no blood, but the profile of her bird face displayed the rigid contortions and contradictory slackness of death: her eyes pinched shut from opposing pressures of earth and twisted shoulders; her beaklike mouth opened slightly allowing a gray tongue to spill out, coated with speckles of sand. She must have weighed all of eighty pounds, a wreckage of hollow broken bones.

Then she moved. The head twisted upward and the eyes cracked open, looking up at Kellerman with a cold black gaze. In the eerie suspense of the moment her stirring did not really surprise him. What he saw in her eyes did. He had expected only the dumb stricken look of a wild bird brought to earth. But as she looked up at him, the impenetrable blackness in her eyes seemed to dissolve for a moment into a soft blue. And something else — a look he did not expect and could not explain, could *never* explain, not in the twenty years that had passed since that day — a look that startled, perplexed, and finally terrified him: a soft blue look of intimacy . . . of trust. Then a single word issued faint, but unmistakable, from her cracked lips:

"Hubert."

The name shook Kellerman to his bones.

But before he could say anything, the soft blue look in her eyes vanished. Her eyes returned to black, and she was unconscious.

Still trembling, Kellerman glanced up at the cliff. The boy and dog had disappeared.

He couldn't remember much of what happened the rest of that evening. He must have returned to the house to call Baptist Memorial in Oklahoma City for an ambulance, must have led the paramedics back down the gully to her motionless form, must have watched them lift her limp body, gathering the dangling broken limbs onto the stretcher. He must have watched them drive off, sirens wailing. And he must have called Orville, must have found words to describe what happened. He remembered none of it, only Babe's dark voice murmuring *It's not your fault* (to him or to Curly?), her voice and his own, asking where Curly was. *He's out back with Boozer.* He remembered wanting to say something to his son, something important. Remembered going to the window and seeing the two of them, boy and dog, playing a silent game of tug of war with a rag. The silent fury of the boy's tugging made him pause, and he realized the game was not a game but a release. He did not interrupt.

The next day was Saturday. Orville Zucha drove up in his International pickup just as Kellerman stepped out onto the front porch. "She'll live," Orville said, leaning out the window of the cab, and drove on.

Kellerman heaved a strange sigh of relief and went inside. Babe was helping Curly clean up his room.

"She's OK," Kellerman said. "I mean — she's going to live."

"Thank God," Babe said. She put her arm around Curly. "Did you hear your father? Your friend is going to be all right." *Your friend.* Kellerman almost flinched at the phrase but said nothing, waiting for Curly to respond. Curly looked out the window with a blank face.

I've got to talk to him, Kellerman thought grimly. But not now, not when I'm upset. Not when I'm likely to blurt something stupid. Tonight. After I've figured out what needs to be said.

After dinner he was still sorting things out. *Idiot. Just tell the boy what you want him to know.* But what was that? That his father still loved him after running away, after destroying his special game, after lying, after what happened in the gully. It was true. Why was it so hard to say?

The three of them sat on the back porch watching Boozer lap up his pail of beer, foam bubbling up his snout. Kellerman smiled, though he'd seen this sight many times before. Babe and Curly were smiling too, watching the dog, and Kellerman was grateful — grateful for this rare moment when each of them felt the same way about something. A few minutes later they were all laughing out loud as Boozer staggered around the back yard on three, then two, legs, dragging his butt over the grass. Curly tried to help him keep his balance, by lifting his rear end. It was no use. "Nice try, Rin Tin," Kellerman said when Boozer finally gave up and rolled over on his back to sleep. It was the dumb dog's own fault, Kellerman would say later, but he didn't really believe it. Boozer always slept for at least an hour after taking his brew. As the sky darkened, Curly went inside to watch television while Babe started the dishes. Kellerman remained on the porch, watching the lights of Oklahoma City begin to glow on the eastern horizon, feeling more content than he had in weeks. He didn't notice Boozer roll groggily to his feet and head for the road.

The Coca Cola truck wound up in the ditch, bottles stuck in the earth like stubby knives. "I swerved to miss him," the driver swore. "But he came right at me."

"I'll bet, you blind bastard." Only the absurd knowledge that it was the *dog* who had been drunk kept Kellerman from grabbing the driver by the throat. Curly did not cry. In the deepening darkness he buried Boozer in the southeast corner of the five acres where home plate had been.

Kellerman waited for him on the porch. "We'll get another dog. You can pick one out tomorrow."

The boy did not answer. In fact, he did not speak to Kellerman for three months.

7

"SO HERE SHE is again, just when I'm going good on my project, just when Curly's coming home." Kellerman was speaking to the crack in the south wall, where bees appeared and disappeared like tiny commuters in and out of a subway entrance. On those occasions when he took time to observe his honeys closely, Kellerman thought they looked like little golden-robed angels, the way their yellow legs and torsos drooped as they hovered, passing back and forth between heaven and what Father Jaworski — whose chanting, softly righteous voice he had feared as a boy — used to call the netherworld. But Kellerman wasn't observing now.

"I've got to do something. He paused, as if waiting for a response to issue from the crack. For years, whenever he cursed the Crow Woman's name, Babe had felt compelled to defend her. *Let the poor woman be. She hurts no one.*

"No one?" Kellerman bellowed at the crack. "What about me? What about the way my fucking skin crawls every time she laughs her goddamn crow laugh outside my window? You thought it was just a goddamn laugh. Goddamn *haaa,*

haaa. You never heard what she was really saying, she never looked *you* in the eye and called you *Hubert* . . .''

A loud knock startled Kellerman into silence.

''Frank, are you in there?'' It was Orville Zucha's voice.

Kellerman took a few moments to calm down before answering. Why hadn't he heard Orville approach? He looked over at the peephole and the beam of morning light, still the morning of his fourth day in the schoolhouse. Or was it? He frowned.

''Yeah, what do you want?''

''I want to talk to you is all.''

''Go ahead. I ain't stopping you.''

''Man have to shout through a door to speak to you these days?''

''Only if he wants to make himself heard.'' Kellerman pictured Orville Zucha pulling his green John Deere cap down tight over his big square head, then folding his arms like an Indian.

''All right, it's your castle,'' Orville said a moment later. ''What are all these bags of water against the door?''

Kellerman glanced over at the icebox containing his insulin, then made a fist. ''That all you wanted to ask me about?''

''No, that ain't it. You got somebody in there with you, Frank?''

''Sure, I got me a whole battalion of hookers from El Reno Junior College in here. What's it to you?''

''Not a thing to me. I'm lookin' for Mama. Charley Bluefire said he thought he maybe saw her out here around your place this morning.''

Kellerman grabbed the corner of his worktable. ''Was that blanket-assed sonofabitch out here last night?''

Orville's voice sounded confused. ''Last *night?* I don't know if he's been here at all. He can see your place from his. All he said to me was he thought he saw Mama out here early this morning.''

Kellerman snorted. "Right. Well, she ain't here.''

Orville paused. "Well, has she *been* here? Was she here last night?''

Kellerman took a deep breath to control his anger. "Yeah, I heard her cawing at the moon last night. You listen here, Orville. Curly's coming home anytime now, and I've got some work I need to get finished before he gets here. I want you to keep that loony bird mother of yours away from my property. I mean it this time.''

"That's what I'm trying to *do*, Frank. Damn you, what are you doing all locked up in this goddamn beehive anyhow?''

Kellerman smiled as the answer came to him. "Thought I'd build me a crow cage.'' A pause. He pictured Orville hitching up his trousers the way he would when he didn't know what to say next.

"That's not funny, Frank, no matter what you think of Mama. Looky here now, I'm worried. Mama's been gone a whole day. Always found her after an hour or two before, but this time I can't.''

Kellerman blew a deep sigh through his nose. "All right, all right. You check the creek?''

"Yep.''

"The cliff?''

Another pause. "Yep.''

"Then I don't know where she is.''

Kellerman heard Orville's sigh through the oak. "I'm going to look down by the creek again. Look, if she goes anywhere else, it's probably going to be right here, Frank. You know how she loves this old schoolhouse.''

"I'm not responsible for that.''

"I know you're not responsible!" Orville's voice was full of fury now. "Who ever accused you of being responsible for anything?"

Kellerman stared bewildered at the door.

Orville's voice softened. "Look, if you see her — if you even *hear* her, call me, will you? I'll come pick her up."

I've got no phone in here, Kellerman started to say, then reconsidered. "Sure."

Orville sighed again. "Thanks. I mean it. Well, I better get going again. I don't want to call the police, but it looks like I better. I don't know how long she'll last outside by herself."

She's lasted thirty years like this, Kellerman wanted to say, but didn't. He waited for the sound of footsteps trailing off toward the creek, but Orville didn't leave just yet.

"So Curly's coming home, hey?" Orville's tone had changed again, from urgent to curious.

Kellerman's stomach tightened. "Yeah, he's coming home."

"He still livin' over in Hawaii?"

He knows, the bastard. "Yeah."

"Thought so. Saw him on the TV again just yesterday. Looked pretty good in that shiny suit."

Kellerman wanted to crawl under the stack of boxes and hide.

"What's the new deal he's got now, 'Dream Tours'?"

"I don't know anything about it."

"Looked like a pretty fancy deal, not for the likes of me. Well, you wish him good luck for me." Orville paused a moment, then continued. "You know, I'm sorry we never talked more over the years, Frank. I always did like your boy. Really. Mama did too."

"Just keep her away from here," Kellerman said.

Orville's voice sounded more disappointed than angry. "Sure, Frank. And you call me if she comes by here before I find her." Kellerman heard a couple of footsteps before Orville stopped and spoke again, his voice slightly fainter. "You know, you might have been right all along, Frank. About putting Mama in a home, I mean."

You hear that, bitch-in-the-wall? Kellerman wanted to shout but didn't.

A moment later he put his ear to the door and listened to Orville's slow, heel-dragging steps fade off toward the creek. He turned and faced the room pulsing with the beat of a hundred thousand tiny wings.

"No, honeys. Not our man."

He could tell by the diagonal beam of light through the peephole that it was late afternoon. The afternoon of the fourth day. He'd had his reviving shot hours ago — thirty units. But still he sat motionless on the automobile frame, his set of transverse springs and other suspension parts spread neatly before him. He ignored them. It was time to decide what to do about the Crow Woman.

He chewed his lower lip as he thought. He couldn't count on Orville to keep her away. He couldn't just call the police or the loony squad either. Orville had every town and county official in his hip pocket.

No, the only human being Kellerman could expect help from was himself. Too bad he hadn't been building a crow cage in here . . .

Kellerman snapped erect, then began to tremble with excitement as the thought came to him. *Why not?*

"That's it!" He stood, unable to contain the energy that pumped through his veins now. "I'll cage the old bird myself. I'll lock her up right in here. Just until I can talk Orville or

Eddie Hacker or somebody into locking her away for good.''

He paced around the automobile frame and chewed his lip. "If I can stand it, that is. If I can stand to listen to that damn crow laugh in the same room with me. If I can stand to look at that goddamn crow face, those goddamn black eyes. Or worse, those *blue* eyes that think I'm Hubert. *Hubert*, for Christsake! What a stupid name.''

Kellerman stopped pacing and stared blankly at the wall. The Crow Woman had called him Hubert only once, as she lay battered and dizzy at the bottom of the gully, with that blue look in her eyes. *Hubert.* With the name and the look, Kellerman had felt the old woman lay a strange, unreasonable claim on him, felt her call in a loan he had never asked for and had no idea how to repay.

He had never mentioned that part of the incident to Babe. What would have been the point? He wasn't Hubert. He didn't even look like Hubert. This he knew from the picture old man Loudermilk had shown him, the picture of Hubert and Mabel on their wedding day. They were taking off in the buggy. Hubert had raised the whip above his head. The photograph was in black and white, but you could see that Mabel's eyes were lighter then, at least on that day, as she stared straight at the road ahead. The picture clearly showed Hubert Zucha to be a sallow, straw-haired boy with a nose like a knife.

By the time of the accident in the gully, Kellerman was already wearing glasses, was almost completely bald, and had a fat "Roman" nose, as Babe called it, a nose three times broken. They looked nothing alike, he and Hubert.

Kellerman walked around the automobile frame to the toilet by the sink. He raised the lid and peered down into the water. Reflecting up at him was the gray silhouette of a bald head and jowly face. The image reminded him of a rotten egg.

He turned away from the toilet and chewed on his lip and rubbed the four days' growth of beard on his face. Then he took a deep breath.

"I can do it, honeys. If I can trap her and keep her in here for just a few hours, she'll get her fill of me and this place. Orville won't like the idea of his mama bein' locked up in here with us, honeys. He'll keep her away for sure after this." He paused. "After this, she won't *want* to come back."

Kellerman thought he heard a pulse, a rise and fall of volume in the hum. He looked at each wall.

"I know, I know," he said finally. "Let the poor woman be." He listened then, but the walls made no reply.

He began to pace around the auto frame again as his thoughts turned to the new task. It wouldn't be all that easy to coax Mabel into the schoolhouse, though she clearly wanted in, and was never very far away. She was frightened of the bees, for one thing. Except at night, when his honeys were asleep. Then she'd sneak up to the window above his work-table and peek in. Over the years he'd spotted her several times from his bedroom window across the yard, on nights when the moon was full. But he'd never been able to get close enough to catch her. By the time he slipped on his trousers and reached the back door, she was gone. So it was clear he wouldn't be able to just spot her and chase her down outside the schoolhouse tonight. He would have to set a trap.

And Kellerman knew about traps. He'd trapped rats and mice for Sandy the Rat Biter back in Kansas City. He'd trapped rabbits in Babe's garden after Boozer had been run over by the Coke truck. Once, he'd been caught in a trap himself, on the island of Iwo Jima during the Pacific war. He'd been climbing a hill of volcanic rock and ash with a platoon of green troops when the Japanese opened up on them from all sides. The hill was supposed to have been secure. The Marines had stormed it twenty-four hours earlier, using flamethrowers to burn the last snipers out of their caves and cracks in the rock. But as Kellerman's platoon made its way up the slope, rifles suddenly protruded from the earth all around them.

Kaplan, the Jewish haberdasher from Chicago, caught the first bullet right between the eyes. An instant later Kellerman flattened out on the gray rock. Ash exploded in tiny puffs all around his head. The only cover to be had was Kaplan's body. He rolled towards it. Years later he would laugh about the lesson this move taught him. Never trust a dead Jew, he'd say. For when he rolled next to Kaplan, the earth opened beneath them.

When he awoke, pain throbbing in his temples, he opened his eyes and beheld the bloody face of a monster. He lurched back in horror, thinking he had fallen into hell. Then he realized the face was Kaplan's. The dead man lay directly beneath him, a twelve-inch wooden spike sticking through his neck, another through his arm. Kellerman removed his own helmet and placed it over Kaplan's face. The thundering, twanging sounds of battle reached Kellerman's ears then, and he looked up to see a slice of blue sky about six feet above his head. He turned away from the sky and lay quietly on Kaplan's body until the shooting stopped.

Driskell, the platoon sergeant, hauled him out with a rope. *Kaplan must have fallen right on the edge of the crevice when he was shot*, Driskell explained. *When you rolled up next to him, you both fell in. Kaplan first. Now I see why they call you* Lucky.

In the schoolhouse, Kellerman grabbed his circular saw and plugged it in next to the outlet by the door. He had learned something from Kaplan. Not about luck or life or death, but about traps. In a way, human behavior was simple. People behaved either by instinct or by reason. Instinct had made him drop to the ground after the first shot echoed over the rock hill that day. His training at Fort Riley had helped him reason against moving toward the obvious cover, the booby-trapped rocks. It was the fact that he knew Kaplan, had drunk out of the same tin cup with Kaplan, that made him roll toward the dead man's body — and the real trap. This, he now understood, was the secret of successful snares. Not greed or pride, the way they showed it in the movies, but the false security that leads to a wrong step.

To coax Mabel into the schoolhouse he would have to use something familiar, something she would recognize. He knew just the thing: a flap door like the one he had put in the garage for Boozer.

Mabel Zucha knew all about that flap door. He remembered seeing her hiding in the wheat field, watching Boozer go in and out of the garage. Curly like to crawl through that flap too. She must have been looking for Curly the day Kellerman caught her pushing open the flap with her beaklike nose. After that he put a bolt on the flap and kept it locked at night.

The flap door in the garage had been locked almost twenty years now. Boozer had been dead that long. But once or twice a year Kellerman still caught Mabel Zucha pecking at the flap, trying to sneak into the garage.

"I'll build one just like it right here," Kellerman said, tapping the bottom of the big oak door he'd bolted shut on his birthday. "She wants in this schoolhouse bad, honeys, and I know why. She thinks she'll find her long lost love bird *Hubert* in here. Well, I ain't Hubert, and that's for sure. But I've kept the old gal out of here for thirty years, and it's about time she saw the improvements we've made."

He dug around in some boxes by the sink until he found a carpenter's square, a pencil, and two metal hinges. About

1½ feet by 1½ feet, he figured, and drew a square for the flap at the bottom center of the schoolhouse door. The whine of the circular saw made the bees near him take flight, but they returned as soon as he had finished, drawn to the scent and pollenlike texture of the fresh sawdust. He finished off the corners with a keyhole saw.

In a few minutes he removed the square of oak from the door and planed it down to make a flap. Before installing the hinges he painted the outer side of the flap a bright red. It had to be red because that was the color of the flap door he'd put in the garage for Boozer.

"She'll recognize this, honeys," he said as he screwed the hinges onto the flap. "She'll know what this is — or think she does."

As he knelt to fit the flap back into the hole in the door, he glanced through the opening and saw the dull red sphere of the sun sinking toward the hazy horizon beyond the highway. Almost evening, the evening of his fourth day in the schoolhouse. He hesitated a moment at the opening, smelling the fresh, yet oddly musty, scent of wheat ripening in Orville Zucha's fields. He took a deep, invigorating breath — forgetting for a moment where he was, what he was doing — then noticed the ten bags of melted ice by the door.

"Old fool," he muttered and went back to work.

After attaching the last screw, he tapped the flap and watched it swing. Perfect. He opened a small tool cabinet next to his worktable and pulled out a metal mechanism about the size of a pack of cigarettes. He examined it under the bulb for a moment, then knelt by the door.

"Know what a rube latch is, honeys? It lets you *in* — but not *out*."

Using a keyhole saw, he cut a notch one inch square in the oak next to the upper left side of the flap. A minute later he had the latch installed. He raised the flap inward. When it was nearly parallel to the floor, high enough to admit a large object, the rube latch clicked. Kellerman released the flap and watched it swing back down until the latch clicked again, locking the flap shut.

Kellerman giggled like a girl, then reached down and stuck his index finger into the mechanism and wiggled it until he heard another click. "Now anyone can unlock a rube latch — *if* he knows where the trigger is."

To complete the trap, he padlocked the bolt on the main door and stuck the key in his pocket.

When he was finished, he sat down in the swivel chair. He stared down at the flap door and tried to figure the odds. No trap was perfect. This one might work, and it might not. He would have to wait and see.

8

SHORTLY AFTER SUNDOWN he turned out the light. He watched the room turn slowly darker, the shaft of light through the peephole growing more luminous by contrast, though the light outside was fading.

The throbbing, deafening hum from the walls faded with the light until finally he began to hear the softer scratch and whir of night creatures waking up outside the stone walls. He sat in the swivel chair at his worktable, a claw hammer in one hand, a flashlight in the other. He felt strange and foolish holding the hammer. I won't need this for an old woman, he told himself, and started to put it down. His hand never moved, however, and in a moment he realized why. He'd built the flap door trap in an afternoon of euphoric anticipation: after thirty years of frustration he was finally going to cage the loony bird for good. Even Orville had admitted the old bat belonged in a home. He would make sure Orville got a chance to put her there.

That was his plan. But it had one flaw, the knowledge which made Kellerman's grip tighten on the hammer. It was the Crow Woman he had heard last night, her *Hubert* laugh mocking him in the darkness. He had no doubt about that. But the heavy, ominous steps he had heard the night before — those belonged to someone else. He still didn't know who. But whoever it was now had a way into the schoolhouse.

"Idiot," he whispered in the dark and the word seemed to echo through a thousand hidden corridors in the stone.

Late into the night he strained to stay awake, rocking back and forth on the bare wood floor, listening, hearing only the ticking, whirring noise of insects, the whistling, gushing wind, an occasional big truck groaning up the highway. Still later in the night, the sounds began to blend, then fade. The beam through the peephole disappeared, and he was dreaming: hanging onto the pocket of Dottie's dress as they climbed a dark stairway behind the deep shadow of their father. Feeling Dottie's larger hand grip his own, lifting him over the big steps as they followed the *clump, clump* of Father's heavy boots up the steps.

Then up into light. Into the clamor of horns, bells, and sirens. Into air filled with red, green, and blue balloons, and clouds of paper snowflakes. Father stood above it all at the edge of the roof.

Come here.

He gripped Dottie's dress as they inched toward the edge of the roof. Father's huge hands grabbed him, lifted him up into the cool wind. He clung to wide shoulders, afraid to look down at the noise below.

Look.

Peeking over Father's strong shoulders, he spied a thousand, a million people on the street below, cheering, waving straw hats. White horses marched down the street. On their backs rode golden-haired women covered with diamonds. Black dogs jumped through flaming hoops, and men with baggy pants and painted faces bounced in the air and juggled plates. Giant cats with black and orange stripes paced back and forth in cages.

Look, Father said again, and pointed toward the end of the street. He looked where Father pointed — then gasped.

Above the crowd a mighty giant rose, dressed in leopard skins. Floating above the street, he grew bigger and bigger. Tiny men with long ropes tried to hold him, but he grew swiftly bigger, closer.

Scared. He shut his eyes and turned away, clinging to wide shoulders. Strong hands understood, held him tighter.

Look at him now. He smiles at you. Wave to him.

Feeling strong shoulders and big hands that held him safe and tight. Believing the voice.

He looked up at the giant and waved.

He awoke in the morning, stretched out on the floor in front of the flap door, his body blocking the flap. The hammer lay beside him. He almost rolled over to get up — then remembered just in time to run his hands along his legs and torso for bees.

Something was wrong. His body was numb and his head felt dull and thick and fuzzy, as if he'd been holding his breath under water. He stood and tried to shake off the cobwebs with a good stretch — and felt the pain in his foot.

"Ow! Ahhh."

He sat on the automobile frame and pulled off his shoe and sock. The bruise had grown to the size of a half dollar and had turned a deeper purple ringed with green. Kellerman felt a cold flash at the base of his throat.

I warned you.

The voice seemed to come from the south wall, near the hive entrance. Kellerman glanced at the crack as his honeys buzzed in and out.

"Warned me is right," he said. "Warned me so god-damn many times it put my head to sleep. Well, I'm awake now, so shut up!"

He hopped on one foot over to his worktable and dug through the clutter until he found a bottle of alcohol. He sat in the swivel chair and applied the alcohol gently with a rag. The lightest touch made his foot throb and tingle. He opened the icebox and took out the vial of insulin.

"Morning of the fifth day, honeys." He paused, eyeing the bruise, then the vial, and tried to determine if he still had enough insulin to last until he finished his project. The vial looked less than a third full. He would be cutting it close. Then he wondered if the lack of refrigeration might be caus-ing the insulin to spoil. Before filling the syringe, he sniffed the vial. A useless gesture. He knew insulin was odorless. He adjusted his bifocals, then squinted until he could make out some of the larger print on the vial:

U-100 N
Isophane Insulin Suspension

The expiration date was nearly two years off, he noted with some relief. Then he read the less comforting words:

KEEP IN A COLD PLACE. AVOID FREEZING.

As he gave himself the injection, he realized Charley Blue-fire hadn't come by yesterday. Had he finally frightened off the blanket-assed snoop? If so, who'd pick up his insulin when he needed more?

The aftereffects of the shot felt different this time. Instead of quelling an itch, the insulin seemed to send a prickly sen-

sation straight to his sluggish heart, which started to pound.
From there the feeling spread in a tingling wave through
the rest of his body. For several moments he trembled uncontrollably, like the time he grabbed the live electrical wire
in the generator room at the capitol. That shock had knocked him out. This time he grabbed the edge of his worktable
and hung on till the spasm passed. When it was over he sank
back into the swivel chair, panting and sweating until his
clothes were soaked.

When he finally caught his breath, he leaned forward on
his elbows and tried to think about something else. He
wondered when Curly would come home. Or would he?
Maybe Charley was wrong. Maybe Curly wasn't coming
home at all. Why should he?

A sharp sound made Kellerman's head jerk up: the unmistakable slam of a car door.

He moved quickly to the peephole to check his automobiles.
Next to the carport, on the edge of his field of vision, was
a sleek silver Mercedes 450SL. Kellerman's heart began to
thump quickly again, his breaths coming in short, shallow
gulps, as he picked up the softer sound of footsteps approaching the schoolhouse. Steps he vaguely recognized from
somewhere, steps that sent a sharp electrical burst of hope
through his chest — until he heard the voice.

"Frank? Are you in there, Frank?"

It was Carl Vukovich's voice.

"I'd like to speak to you, Frank." He was knocking, too,
but Kellerman heard only the voice, the sugary, self-fulfilled
voice of the man who had stolen his soul twenty years ago.
Stolen his garage, his ambition, his future.

"Have I come at a bad time?"

Kellerman detected a vaguely sour note, the slightest agita-
tion, in the sugary voice. He said nothing.

"Really no point in keeping me waiting, Frank."

Kellerman pictured the greasy bohunk standing there in his too-expensive, too-tight, three-piece suit, the same shit-eating grin on his fat face, the rotten stump of a burnt-out El Verso cigar sticking out of the corner of his crooked mouth. Kellerman could already smell the stench of them both, the cigar and the man, wafting through the cracks around the door.

"Well, Carl. I thought you were a patient man."

"Patient but busy, Frank. Normally I'd send another man out on a matter like this, but I figured since we've known each other thirty years, I'd come out here myself."

Vukovich paused. Kellerman smiled and said nothing, holding the upper hand for the first time in years.

"Frank, this schoolhouse is full of *bees*."

Kellerman laughed. "Just my honeys."

"Well . . . how about stepping out here so we can talk face to face." Vukovich's voice conveyed new respect.

"No, I like the sound of your voice through oak, Carl. Gives it a nice woody tone."

"I'll come right to the point, Frank." The sicky-sweet quality in Vukovich's voice had all but disappeared. "Looper tells me you've had that Indian janitor Charley Bluefire all over the county buying up parts for a '32 Model 18."

"Looper? Now there's a reliable source."

"Looper's a good man . . . if you keep a proper eye on him. I know you and him had some problems back when he worked for you, but that's neither here nor there. The point is, Frank, what am I to think when I hear you've been collecting parts for a Model 18 right after my very best antique V-8 — the only original Model 18 engine in Oklahoma, I'll wager — disappears out of my storage barn?"

"If I was you, I'd think about a new security system."

"That's another thing. I don't know how you got past that electric fence, but Nicholas and Napoleon have been in awful poor spirits for three weeks now. Won't go anywhere near the fence or strangers neither one. That's low-down, Frank, frightening innocent dogs. Why, Napoleon's just a shadow of himself. He's got a delicate nature, in his way."

Kellerman clapped a hand over his mouth to keep from laughing out loud. "Couldn't of been something nasty they bit into in that auto graveyard of yours, could it?"

"Nothing that belonged there, that's for sure. I want that engine back, Frank. I was thinking of donating it to the Classic Car Museum in Tulsa. I don't want it damaged, and I sure as hell don't want it stuck in no junkmobile. I figure you've got it locked up in your garage over there, fixin' to stick it in some burned-out hulk. Now I don't know whether you're planning to sell it to a collector or just add to your used car lot here . . ."

Used car lot! Kellerman reached for the air hose.

". . . but whatever it is, it's not going to work." Vukovich's voice had risen to a strident pitch. Kellerman heard a deep, determined sigh. A moment later Vukovich's voice was calm again, a trace of sweetness returning. "You and me go back years, Frank. I see no need to be vindictive about this. I'm just here to claim what's mine. So if you'll agree to give that engine back, we'll just forget about the whole thing. I'll even send Looper out to pick it up. You won't have to lift a finger. What do you say?"

Kellerman chewed his lower lip for a moment, then lay the air hose gently back on the compressor. "I say you're in fine voice today, Carl. Nice to hear from you again."

Vukovich's reply was flat, toneless. "I'll have what's mine, Frank."

Kellerman's words tasted like the honey packed inside the

walls around him: "I'm sure you will."

A full minute of silence followed. Then Kellerman heard Vukovich turn to go. Kellerman couldn't resist a parting shot: "One more thing before you go, Carl — that cigar of yours *still* smells like a dog-shit pie."

"Cigar? Your nose is full of beeswax, Frank. I gave up smoking ten years ago."

Lying bastard, Kellerman thought, but raised his eyebrows all the same. He almost forgot to press his ear to the door as Vukovich's steps retreated toward the car. When the silky purr of the Mercedes had finally faded, Kellerman turned to face his honeys.

He shook his head and said nothing.

9

FOR A LONG TIME after Vukovich left, Kellerman sat in the swivel chair, gazing through the peephole. The return of Vukovich had started something up inside him, *re*started it, like a cold engine cranking stiffly back to life. His mind swept back to another time — six, no seven months ago, five months after Babe had been buried, a moment when he sat in this same chair next to his worktable, gazing not through a peephole but an entire window, the sunlight flooding in, filling the musty room with a brilliance his weak eyes could hardly bear. He remembered squinting at the row of ancient automobiles parked beneath the tin roof of his carport, wondering why his life had gone the way it had.

Staring at the row of automobiles on that cold gray November morning, he realized for the first time his true reason for building the carport over Babe's objections, and why he had hung onto these five particular automobiles, and no others. Squinting at the purple Moon 8-80 Prince of Windsor sitting up on blocks, the green Hudson Hornet, the Jimmie Truck, the Studebaker Silver Hawk, and the battered Corvair all lined up beneath the canopy, he understood why he had parked them in that order, in perfect view from the window above his worktable. The reason was so obvious he had overlooked it all these years. Yet there it was, right in front of him. Each automobile represented an unmistakable stage in his life. By lining them up in the order they had come into his possession, he had assembled his automotive history.

"They're all there, honeys," he said, peering through the peephole now. "Every damn one of 'em, except the very first one."

He leaned back into the swivel chair and appeared to stare right through the south wall. "There's something magic about a man's first car, honeys. Or maybe I should say, a boy's. 'Cause that's what I was, if you want to know the truth."

It took a boy to believe in magic, he thought. To a boy, a car was magic because it could take you anywhere you wanted to go. It could take you away from where you were. Away from home. Away from your father. If you had a car, you could escape.

Kellerman's expression suddenly changed, growing grim, his brow wrinkling into a sharp V above squinting eyes as if a hard bright light suddenly shone on him. "You have to know my old man, honeys, the kind of man he was, to appreciate what he did to that car and to me." He paused. "He was cold-eyed, like a hawk."

Kellerman closed his eyes and pictured his father Joseph standing over him like a grim giant in black leather boots and baggy trousers held up by red suspenders. "He wore a belt too, but that was for *my* benefit." He thought again of his mother Rose throwing herself between them, taking the licks on her own bare legs until his father wore himself out swinging and went back to his beer.

"All day the bastard made that West Bottoms moonshine in Clyde McCulley's warehouse, then come home and tried to drink up every drop he'd made. I'm just lucky it finally killed him." Kellerman winced as he remembered seeing the same strap marks, grayer, but still prominent on his mother's legs ten years after Joseph Kellerman was dead. It was the last and only time he saw her after she moved to Denver with his sister Dottie and her husband the druggist. *Just send the check and let Mama brag on about her loving son in Oklahoma,* Dottie snapped when he called. *My sweet big sister with the heart of gold,* he replied and addressed his letter to Rose Kellerman, though his mother could not read.

He remembered them all sitting in Dottie's living room while Curly played outside beneath the mountain looming in the picture window. *Can you hear me, Mom?* In the flowered chair, a living ghost — Rose Kellerman sleeping with her eyes open, looking directly at her son as she snored out of the sides of her mouth. Kellerman watched the rosary in her lap fall to the floor. *I should have killed him myself,* he whispered to Babe as they both gaped at the marks on the old woman's legs. *You don't mean it,* Babe said softly and laid her hand on his knee. He felt the muscles in his jaw tighten as he stared, remembering. *The hell I don't.*

Kellerman leaned forward in the swivel chair, then took a rag and wiped a layer of sweat off the top of his head.

"I was his personal slave, honeys. Whatever he wanted done, I did. When I was ten years old he had me carry a thirty-pound sack of coal up Mulligan's Bluff from the rail-yard every day just so we would cook and keep warm.

Kellerman stared at the crack in the wall, remembering the way the rails trembled beneath his feet as the Burlington freights rumbled by the coal pit. A glaze came over his eyes as he saw himself walking through the railyard again, iron lines marking his path as he stepped gingerly over the loose gravel beside the rails, stopping occasionally to adjust the piece of cardboard in his shoe. He carried the empty gunny sack over his shoulder, black coal dust staining his shirt underneath. His eyes opened wide, watching the huge gray engines belch black smoke as they chugged along the switching tracks. The heat rising from the yard made the more distant trains shimmer as they passed under the 23rd Street Bridge, where the Kansas & Berger streetcar, small and serene, glided by overhead. He imagined himself controlling it all, guiding the long trains through the haze like paper boats on a pond.

Controlling it, until he heard the whistle of Engine 909, chugging into the yard with a train of A & P icebox cars. Now the pattern of the yard, so clear from the top of the bluff, fell apart. He felt himself shrinking smaller and smaller as the big locomotive approached, clouds of white, iron-smelling steam hissing from the pistons. Screeching and puffing, the train stopped by the coal pit. Above the steam he recognized the engineer who once let him blow the whistle — a giant of a man in gray overalls and a blue Burlington cap.

"Hey bub, what do you say? Hungry today?"

Nodding, he shrank away, hearing another voice that seemed to come from deep inside the boiler of Engine 909. Father's voice: *Stay away from the trainmen.*

But the engineer climbed down and took his hand. "This way, bub." He resisted, but the engineer was too big, too strong, pulling him past the icebox cars to the red caboose at the end of the train.

"What you got there, Homer?" a short, red-faced man in a blue Burlington cap asked. "Looks like a trash-eatin' hobo to me."

"Could be. Or it could be a Jewboy in disguise."

"Jewboy? Why, Jewboys know better than to show their little kike faces around here." He looked down at Kellerman, who bit his lip. "Mmmm. Way we can tell for sure. Jewboys always squirm a little at our table. We'll see."

Feeling confused, dazzled, he watched the red door of the caboose open into a dark room containing a table piled high with food, more food than he had ever seen, ever imagined. Slices of ham and beef and salami and other kinds of meat he didn't recognize; blocks of Swiss cheese and cheddar; whole loaves of black bread and white; with butter, oranges, and fresh milk. He felt himself grow faint.

"Who's this one?" Two dark men with black beards and blue Burlington caps leaned forward on wooden crates marked A&P DAIRY-FRESH TO YOU. *Stay away from the trainmen.*

"Could be a Jewboy."

The bearded men looked at each other and nodded. The red-faced man closed the curtains and lit a kerosene lamp.

He looked at the food again — fresh pink meat and white milk — feeling empty and itchy inside as the first bearded man reached under his seat and set a small black crock on the table.

"Hungry now, bub?" the engineer asked and pushed away all the meat except the plate of ham. "You are? Well, this could be your lucky day."

Eager, frightened, he felt their eyes watching as the bearded man pushed the crock toward him and opened the lid. The stench hit him in the face like a club. He jerked his head back to get a breath, thinking of the day his father made him crawl under the house to look for the dead rat.

"Yessir, this could be your lucky day," the engineer continued. "Mmmm! Don't that smell fine! Tastes as good as it smells, too." He took a knife and sliced off a piece of black bread. "Now the nice thing about limburger is its texture." He dipped the knife into the crock and spread a yellowish glob over the bread. "Just like fresh warm butter. Course, no sandwich is complete without a nice big slice of *ham*, right, bub? You can eat *ham* now, can't you, son?"

The faces in the car were dark and silent as the engineer carefully laid the ham on top and handed him the sandwich. Sweating, he held his breath and pretended the yellow smear underneath was butter. The odor penetrated his nostrils as he took the first bite, making his eyes tear. He ate quickly, trying not to taste the fumes in his mouth.

"Don't act like no Jewboy to me," the red-faced man said. Then the other voices, warm and congratulating:

"A sight, that one!"

"Your lucky day, bub."

"Lucky is right."

"You never had it so lucky, Lucky!"

They piled the food in front of him, breads and meats and cheeses. His taste quickly returned as he bit into spicy-hot smoked salami and sweet apple pie. Amazed and unbelieving, he ate.

"Like a blowfly on a shit pile." They laughed.

"Like a Chinaman climbing Rice Mountain."

He ate until he could eat no more, held back by the strange new *full* feeling. Then he sat, too weak and stuffed to move, and listened to men in blue caps tell stories of the railroad. Their words were strange — payloads and trunk lines and cities with faraway names: Black Hawk, Chi-Town, Onalaska, Maiden Rock. And through each town roared great engines with names stranger still: Mikado, Zephyr, Silver Streak. Closing his eyes, he tried to imagine the sight.

Then everyone was saying goodbye.

"Have to open up a dining car for this one!"

"Next time bring your appetite!"

"Mum's the word on where you got all this stuff, Lucky," the engineer whispered in the doorway and handed him the gunny sack — filled not with coal but with bread and meat and cheese wrapped up in newspaper. "Remember, mum's the word."

Elated, he ran all the way across the loading yards to the bluff. Then climbed, proud, up the trail, taking the longer, secret way — no tough kids to steal his prize — through the bramble bushes and papaw trees, into the backyard where he saw Father rocking on the dark porch, sipping beer from a copper stein.

He slowed to a walk and gripped the sack tightly.

Father leaned forward. "Well, what?"

"I got this." He handed over the sack, studying Father's expression, his grim hawk face leaning into the light as he emptied the contents of the sack into his lap. The grim face did not change as he unwrapped first the meat, then the cheese, sniffing both.

Your lucky day. Eyes on Father, he waited, out of breath, remembering the other two times he had brought things home. The time he borrowed Eddie Magril's Red Rider wagon and hauled home the big catfish he'd caught in a muddy tide pool by the Kaw River — the surprise and delight in Father's eyes when he saw the huge black fish, head and tail hanging over each end of the wagon.

Rose, Rose, Father had called out. They built a bonfire in the middle of Fairmont and shared catfish steaks with the rest of the neighborhood.

My boy catch, he remembered Father saying to Uncle Ludwig. And the other time — the swift anger in Father's eyes when he found three bottles of sacramental wine from Sacred

Heart Church hidden under the house. *Altar boy* was all Father said as he unstrapped his belt. Mother was at the A & P. An hour later Father Jaworski lectured him that pain and confession were good for the soul.

"Where you get this?"

The accusing tone of Father's voice brought back the engineer's warning: *Mum's the word, Lucky.*

"Well?"

"Down at the loading yards . . . it was give to me."

Father shook his head. "The trainmen are thieves. They steal from the boxcars." He rewrapped the cheese and meat. "You give to Father Jaworski all this food, then bring back *two* sacks of coal." He paused for emphasis. "Stay away from the trainmen."

Weakness. The sack hung heavy over his shoulder as he started off for the church. Fading behind him, the squeaking sound of his father rocking on the dark porch.

He took the long way, along the edge of the bluff. At the lookout he paused, seeing again the pattern of the loading yards — hundreds of boxcars dividing into long rows as they disappeared beneath the 23rd Street Bridge. He listened for the familiar whistle of Engine 909 speeding away toward cities with faraway names . . .

"It was magic, I tell you," Kellerman said, bringing his fist down on the worktable. "Looking out at those trains, wondering where they were going, knowing I could go too, if I just got on one. It was like when Tom Pendergast gave me a ride in his Pierce Arrow. I had it, *inside me,* until the day I showed my old man that car I built with my own two hands in Miller's barn."

Kellerman closed his eyes and pictured himself approaching the splintered double doors of the old unpainted barn on the Sunday morning of the unveiling. He was seventeen and still living at home and wanted to inspect his finished creation one more time before showing it to Father.

Even before he swung open the heavy barn doors, a sharp stinging smell reached his nose, making his nostrils quiver, his eyes water. Wafting through the bitter air he thought he caught the scent of fresh strawberries.

He swung open the double doors, the scent washing over him like a wave of liquid perfume, and let in the light. The luminous shaft struck the only object in the barn and seemed to set it aglow from within, like the golden chalice on the altar of the Church of the Sacred Heart on Sunday morning, when rainbow beams struck it after passing through the stained glass figure of Saint Christopher in the round window above the balcony. But in the barn Kellerman saw only a blaze of red. *It's fire engine red,* he had said to old man Miller the night before as he stood back and eyeballed his work after applying the last brushstroke to the last louver on the driver's side of the hood. *Just like the hook and ladder at the Summit Street Station.*

Old man Miller had squinted at the gleaming red metal and rubbed the gray stubble on his chin. *Looks more the color of strawberries to me.*

Now, as the morning light flooded through the open barn doors, Kellerman looked at the finished automobile before him and tasted the bittersweet tang of red paint and fresh strawberries. The headlights of the Model 18 Deluxe Roadster stared back at him like the pleading eyes of a thoroughbred, ready to run. *It's mine. I made this.* He stepped up to the driver's side and touched the red hood. It was dry. *I can drive it now.* The cloth top was down, folded neatly between the front seat and the trunk lid containing the rumble seat, and suddenly he could smell the richer, softer scent of new, brown ribbed leather. But he made no move to climb into the driver's seat that Buster the upholstery man had helped him restore. Instead, he ran his right hand along the length of the strawberry hood, feeling its smoothness in his fingertips, then ran his left hand over the equally smooth curve of the jet black fender above the white-spoked wheel. *Beautiful.*

Kellerman opened his eyes and looked down at a bee crawling on his thumb. "Took me a whole year to build that first Model 18, honey. A full year from the day Harley towed it into the junkyard next to Otis's garage. I had to build it on the sly cause of the old man's rule: as long as we lived in that house, all the money Dottie and me earned was supposed to go to *him*, for the family. So I had Otis hold a little bit out of my check every week. I wanted to surprise the old man when I had that automobile all finished."

Kellerman shook his head, remembering that it turned out to be much easier to fool the old man than he had expected. He formed careful excuses at first — late studying at Eddie Magril's house, overtime work at Otis's garage. On the back porch, Father would look up from his copper beer stein and nod silently, seldom questioning Kellerman the way he had in the old days. The hawk look in his eyes was beginning to dim.

"I already knew he wasn't the same man, honey. He was pushing sixty by then, working ten hours a day in the Muehlebach brewery. It was wearing him out."

Kellerman watched the bee crawl down his thumb into his palm. "Me, I was on the way up then, honey. I couldn't believe I'd actually rebuilt a whole automobile, almost completely by myself. I figured a man who could do that, well, that man could do just about anything."

He took a deep breath. "So I brought the old man to the barn to show him what I'd done."

Kellerman bit his lip, remembering the way he practically had to lead Father down the hill, Father's once firm, heavy

steps now tentative, almost frail. And when they finally stood
in the barn before the Model 18, its strawberry metal glow-
ing like dawn, Father's eyes seemed cloudy. Kellerman
wondered if he even saw the automobile.

I made this, Dad. By myself.

Father blinked. He looked at Kellerman, then back at the
strawberry roadster. Kellerman watched Father's eyes: light
began to shine behind the murky gray.

Suddenly Father turned toward him. *You never ask me can
you make this.*

Kellerman drew himself erect. *I know. But I done it on my
own time. With my own money.*

Father's eyes flickered. His hands moved quickly to his
waist for his belt. But it was Sunday, and Father was wearing his good gray trousers with the black suspenders. The
purposeful look on his face dissolved, as if he had suddenly
forgotten where he was. Kellerman felt something inside
himself begin to deflate as he watched Father fade.

Then, without warning, something else began to happen
inside Father. He pulled back his shoulders and straightened
his spine. He looked at Kellerman and his eyes flickered once
more. *You wait here.*

Without another word, he turned and strode out of the
barn, his step brisk and firm.

Kellerman stood beside the strawberry roadster and began
to tremble. *He's gone to get his belt. He thinks I'm gonna wait
right here for a licking.* Kellerman felt his throat begin to con-
strict as if something were choking him.

He stared through the open doorway. Father was already
out of sight around the corner of the barn. Kellerman sucked
in a deep breath. *No. I'm not gonna run from him. And
I'm not gonna take a licking. Not this time. This time I'll
fight him.*

The sound of footsteps approached from the north side of the barn. Kellerman bit his lip and took a fighting stance, feet spread, left foot forward. But something was wrong. *He couldn't have gone all the way home and back by now.*

Then Father stood in the doorway, silhouetted by the morning sun. His shadowed figure was tall and straight. Somehow Kellerman could see Father's eyes staring out of his shadowed face as if they shone of their own light. Then Kellerman's own eyes fell to Father's hands, which held, not a belt, but a double-edged ax.

No.

Father strode past Kellerman to the automobile.

Kellerman could not move. He stood frozen in his fighting stance. *No,* he pleaded. *Don't.*

Father raised the ax above the hood of the strawberry roadster. *I teach you now,* he said. *One last time.*

In the swivel chair Kellerman leaned forward, his eyes refocusing on the automobile frame in front of him. He exhaled deeply and looked down at the hard, white-knuckled fist in his lap. He unclenched it. In his palm was a dead bee.

10

THE MEMORY rejuvenated him. By midday, his fifth day in the schoolhouse, he was back to work, installing the suspension system of the Model 18. The voice in the wall was mercifully silent, and he worked swiftly, efficiently, like a professional with a deadline to meet.

"For a while there I forgot what we were doing in here, honeys. No time to waste now."

The Ford Model 18 was equipped with transverse springs, semielliptical springs mounted parallel to each axle. The shackle ends of each spring were attached to the axle, the center of the spring to a supporting crossbar that spanned the frame. When all bolts were secure, Kellerman attached radius rods to brace each axle at right angles to the frame. The rods would allow the springs to absorb only the up-and-down motion of the axle, preventing front-to-back axle movement.

When the radius rods were in place, Kellerman grabbed the hub end of each axle and tried to move it forward, then backward. Both axles held firm.

"Atta babies!"

He crawled out from under the automobile and took a deep breath, pleased with his progress. "We're back on track, honeys." He ran his fingers over the cold rough steel of the freshly painted engine. "This is the original Ford V-8, honeys. Not more than half a dozen of these babies in the whole Southwest, I'll wager. Pretty nice and convenient of Vukovich to have one in mint condition just waiting for me in his storage barn."

Convenient was not a word he would have used to describe his trip to pick up the mint V-8 engine from Vukovich's barn. There was another, better word to describe the mood that gripped him like a dream as he wheeled the Jimmie Truck out onto the empty highway into Yukon shortly after midnight. A full moon laced the edges of the asphalt and the branches of trees with silver. As he topped the last dark hill above the Canadian River, the town of Yukon spread before him in a necklace of shimmering lights. He glided unobserved through the empty streets to the gap between the giant twin walls of the grain elevator and flour mill. His skin tingled as he slipped through the gap, coasting with his lights and motor off, down to the small cinder-block building that had once been his life's dream.

In the years since Kellerman had lost the garage, Vukovich had expanded the wrecker service into a large and profitable salvage business. Behind the original building a narrow junkyard had arisen, a graveyard for dead automobiles. Whenever Kellerman drove by the strip of land that was once his pride and joy, the sight of Vukovich's men picking through the smashed and rusted hulks sickened him.

And now, two decades later, he had returned. Not to steal, but to take back something that rightfully belonged to him. A thing that had been lost or stolen (it didn't matter which now) so many years ago. He thought it had died inside him, but he was wrong. It was *here*, in this place, and he would get it back.

Only two obstacles stood in his way: a ten-foot electric fence and Vukovich's two purebred Doberman pinscher guard dogs, Nicholas and Napoleon. Kellerman had read the article on them in the *Yukon Review*, complete with photographs of the two black beasts straining against their leashes, eyes wild and vicious, teeth bared at the camera. "Man's Best Friends?" the caption asked. The dogs had to be dealt with first since they could raise the alarm.

He hadn't really expected to be able to sneak up on the Dobermans, but as he stepped down from the cab no challenging bark issued from the shadows behind the fence. They might be playing possum. Guard dogs were like that sometimes, quiet until they were ready to spring. He approached the fence practically on tiptoe, careful not to crinkle the paper sack held under his arm. So far so good. About a yard from the fence he set the sack on the ground and opened it. Inside were half a dozen tissue-wrapped balls of strong pepper. The first dog will be easy, he cautioned himself. The second one's the one to watch out for.

He touched the chain link fence lightly with the back of his hand. The shock snapped his hand into a fist. He shook the sting out of it and bit his lip, reflecting on Vukovich's cruelty — and strategy — in allowing the dogs to run free behind the electric fence. They gave the fence a wide berth most of the time but were too hot-blooded to control themselves when a stranger approached. From a distance Kellerman had seen them try to drive their snarling muzzles through the links only to spring back an instant later, howling and whining, the fur on their back pricking up as the charge dissipated. The punishing shock of the fence and their uncontrollable desire to penetrate it kept the Dobermans in a constant state of neurotic rage — and made them ideal as guard dogs. There was no soothing them, but he was not here to soothe.

Kellerman gave a low whistle. A snarl answered from the darkness, then quickly, more quickly than he had believed possible, two black shapes leaped out of the shadows and hurled themselves against the fence, bared teeth gleaming with rage. Kellerman took an involuntary step backward, then took out the first pepper bomb. He stepped up within a foot of the fence. The closer dog, which he recognized as the smaller one, Napoleon, leaped high against the fence, going for his throat. Kellerman thrust the bomb forward at the same moment, smashing and splitting the package against the dog's nose. The pepper gushed out, stinging Kellerman's own eyes.

By the time Kellerman could see again, Napoleon was rolling on the ground in a sneezing, howling fit. The stricken dog pawed madly at his eyes and nose, while Nicholas raced round and round him, barking viciously at Kellerman. Then Napoleon lurched upright and ran howling off into the shadows of the auto graveyard.

To Kellerman's surprise, the larger dog, Nicholas, remained. The Doberman faced Kellerman and suddenly ceased barking, emitting instead only a low, businesslike growl.

Kellerman was impressed. "Know better than to desert your post, even for an injured comrade, eh, boy? Well, let's see how you handle temptation."

With that, Kellerman got down on his hands and knees right next to the fence and growled back at the dog. This was too much for Nicholas, who rushed at Kellerman but stopped a full two feet from the fence. The Doberman barked and snarled and rocked and lunged but came no closer to the fence.

"Smart boy, eh?"

I'm going to have to take a burn, Kellerman decided. He squeezed the second pepper bomb lightly in his fist, then thrust it through the chain links. The current flashed through his entire body, making his own hair prick up on his arms, back, and neck.

In the same instant, Nicholas leaped forward and snapped his jaws around Kellerman's fist. The pepper bomb split in a tiny burst that Kellerman somehow felt through the pain.

The next moment was all reflex. Kellerman sprang backward, yanking his hand back through the fence. He rolled in the dust while the muscles in his arm jerked and twitched in machine-gun spasms. By the time the twitching began to subside, and he managed to look up again, Nicholas had disappeared. Kellerman could hear both dogs howling and whining in fury and pain in a far corner of the huge salvage yard. Kellerman wrapped his bleeding hand in a rag, then climbed to his feet.

Shorting out the fence was easy. A bucket of water, and some wire, and he was free to saw the gate lock. Once through the gate, he risked using his headlights as he drove the Jimmie Truck down the crooked aisles between columns of wrecked automobiles piled on each side. His destination was the corrugated metal storage barn in the center of the junkyard where Vukovich kept the vehicles and parts too valuable to be left out in the open lot.

Before getting out of the truck Kellerman listened for the sneezing, whimpering sounds of the stricken dogs echoing among the wrecks. They would be in no shape to bother anyone for a while. From the bed of the pickup he unloaded a rented mobile winch.

It took only a crowbar to break into the barn. Inside, his flashlight revealed a collector's treasury. In the far left corner was a 1933 LaSalle in the final stages of restoration,

freshly coated with primer, newspapers plastered over the windows and grill. Next to the LaSalle was a classic '55 Chevy
Bel Air. In the center of the barn were two heavyweights:
a white '49 Packard Clipper 8 and a black '38 Cadillac 60
Special. On the right side, a '36 Chrysler Airflow C-9 Sedan
and a beautifully ugly green Edsel convertible. Kellerman felt
an eerie tingle spread through his body as he took it all in.

He thought of a day half a century ago when a man from
Detroit drove a brand new Lincoln V-8 Sport Phaeton into
Otis Schmidt's garage for a lube job. The man was a sales
representative for Lincoln and had a distant glimmer in his
eyes, as if he were looking out over the ocean. Kellerman
noticed the look as he raised the Lincoln on the hydraulic
lift. He wasn't surprised when the man spoke to him. *You're
a lucky boy,* he said. *Working right here in this garage, you're
a witness to history. The history of the automobile is the history
of this country, sonny. The search for the fountain of youth, the
opening of the West.*

Kellerman had looked up at the twelve-foot wheelbase of
the big Lincoln and knew it was true.

The rest of Vukovich's barn was filled with engines,
fenders, bumpers, and other parts in various stages of restoration. For a moment as he scanned Vukovich's riches, he was
afraid it wasn't here, that Charley Bluefire's report had been
inaccurate. A tiny panic pricked his stomach like a needle.

Then he saw it. Right beside him, next to the door,
mounted on two jack stands like a dead — or maybe just
sleeping — king on a double throne. He reached out to touch
it, fingers trembling, and the word came to him, a word
he almost never used — for he didn't believe in it or hadn't
for almost half a century — a word he found once again on
his lips, fifty years later, in his schoolhouse workshop amid
the rising drone of bees, as he touched his fingertips to the

cool black steel of the mint V-8 engine mounted above the glistening automobile frame, a word he could no longer keep from saying:

"Magic."

11

THIS TIME HE did not hear any footsteps, only the knock at the door.

Kellerman looked up from the yellow legal tablet he was scribbling on. He was busy taking inventory of the major body parts — structural supports, angle iron pieces, doors, rear quarter panel, firewall — ready to be assembled on the chassis. She's ready to take shape now, honeys, he was about to say when he heard the knocking.

"Who the hell is it?"

"It's me."

Kellerman almost dropped the tablet. He couldn't believe his ears. "Me *who*?"

"Come on, Dad. It's me, Curly."

Curly *who*? Kellerman almost shouted. Instead, he laid the tablet on his worktable and stood trembling in front of the door.

"Dad?"

Kellerman stared into, through the oak. He saw an image, blurred and shapeless at first, but slowly assuming the figure of a man — or was it a boy?

"Can you *hear* me, Dad?"

He tried to place the voice. He recalled the eager birdlike voice of a boy in a Yankee cap, calling to him from home plate in an imaginary ball park, the words flying through the open window to the bed where he lay watching.

"Dad, why don't you open the door?"

This was a different voice. A voice less eager, less certain than that of the boy in the Yankee cap. Kellerman tried to fit this new voice with another image taking shape in his mind, the image of a young man with sapphire eyes and teeth that gleamed like polished ivory. Hair puffed out like a blossoming flower, blooming in blond swirls all over his head. A man whose eyes seemed to look right through you to something more distant, more beautiful. A man Kellerman had seen on TV only a few days ago.

Kellerman looked wildly around for his ax.

"Dad!"

Kellerman shook his head and slapped himself on the cheek.

"Hey!"

"Wha, uh," Kellerman stuttered. "What are you doing here?"

"*Doing* here?" the voice outside cried. "There must be a thousand bees flying around out here. What are *you* doing in that schoolhouse?"

Kellerman said nothing.

"Open the goddamn door, Dad. Talk to me."

The haze in Kellerman's mind began to clear. Here we are, he thought. Right where we were before. "Never mind what I'm doing in here," he said. "What are *you* doing here?"

"Come off it, Dad. You know why I'm here. What are all these bags of water by the door? They look like melted ice."

Kellerman folded his arms. "Never mind that — and I *don't* know why you're here."

"Do I have to talk to you through the goddamn door, Dad? What's this flap door for? Do you have a dog in there?"

Kellerman remained steady. "I asked you what you're doing home."

"I want to *talk* to you, for Christsake."

"Right. About what?"

The voice outside the door sighed. "I don't believe this — I fly four thousand miles and I'm supposed to talk through a fucking door? This is stupid, even for you."

Kellerman shook the remark off. "I didn't ask you to come."

"Don't give me that," Curly snapped. "You knew I'd come, you *wanted* me here. Now what's it all about?"

A wave of dizziness passed over Kellerman. "What do you mean I *knew* you'd come?"

"Come on. You know Charley Bluefire called me. What was I supposed to do — send you a postcard?"

"That was always good enough before!" Kellerman cried. He took a deep breath. "What'd the blanket-assed sonofabitch tell you?"

"He told me you'd moved into the schoolhouse with the goddamned bees, that's what he told me."

"What else?"

"Nothing else. What else is there? Why'd you lock yourself in there? That's what I'm supposed to find out, right? That's why I flew four thousand miles. What is this, some sort of a game?"

Kellerman grabbed the corner of his worktable to lean on. "Game! *You're* the one who plays fucking games. Well, this ain't TV, and I ain't interested. You can turn right around and fly back to your grass shack or whatever the hell it is. I don't give a shit."

"Oh, sure. Now that you've got me here, of course I'm going to turn around and fly back without finding out a thing. You've got this all pretty well mapped out, Dad, whatever it is. I'll give you that."

"Mapped out?" Kellerman sank into the swivel chair. "What mapped out?"

"Come on, Dad. It worked; I'm here. We never got along, so I don't know why you wanted me home — but obviously you knew how to get me here. Well, it worked. I'm scared."

Kellerman could hear the faint thumping of his heart, like a distant echo, like it came from somewhere else. "Scared of what?"

"What do you think? Scared of you being in that schoolhouse with those bees. Scared of what Charley Bluefire said."

Kellerman leaned forward in the chair. "That blanket-assed bastard — I knew he told you something else. What'd he say?"

"Come off it, Dad. You know what he said."

"I don't know!"

Curly seemed to pause and take a deep breath. "He told me you'd moved into the schoolhouse, locked yourself in. He wouldn't say why or what you were doing — but whatever it was, it reminded him of the Crow Woman."

Kellerman gripped the arms of the chair. "What? How?"

Curly's voice softened for the first time. "Dad, we both know you've been alone here for a year now . . ."

Kellerman lurched forward, then scrambled to his feet. "You think I'm going to do something *crazy* in here. You think —"

Curly's voice resumed its combative tone. "Is this part of the game, Dad? I'm supposed to point out the obvious now, right? OK, I'll say it. We all know Mabel lives in her own little world inside her head. She can fly like a bird there. And we all know this schoolhouse has always been *your* special place, your own little world, right Dad? Now you've locked yourself inside it, just like Mabel's locked inside hers. Of course, Mabel can't come out."

Kellerman made two fists. "I can come out of here any damn time I please."

"Oh really? Prove it to me, Dad. Open the door."

Kellerman stood staring at the heavy latch bolt. He did not move.

12

HE LISTENED TO the sound of the engine slowly build up rpm's as it strained to accelerate the car, pulling it up the first hill toward Yukon, carrying his son away.

He hadn't gotten a look at the car the boy was driving, hadn't looked through the peephole at all, even when Curly crossed the yard to enter the empty house, looking for "clues."

Now that you've got me here, I'm supposed to find out what you're doing in the schoolhouse, right? Curly had shouted through the door after Kellerman had refused to come out. The tone of his son's voice, sarcastic, almost vicious, astounded Kellerman. *Are you hiding something from me in there?* Curly demanded. *Or am I just supposed to keep trying to coax you out? Is that the game?*

Kellerman had said nothing in reply. He was numb.

Well, if you won't open the goddamn door and you won't tell me what you're doing in there, I'm going to search the house. Maybe there's a clue in there to tell me what the hell you're doing locked up in a goddamn beehive.

Kellerman had sunk down onto the auto frame and waited.

Game? Why would I be playing a game?

He looked around the room: bees, boxes, sugar, automobile — and chewed his lip. Curly's steps returned about half an hour later. They were quick, businesslike steps, just like his own.

What happened to the TV? Curly shouted through the oak. *Looks like you blew it up.*

Kellerman winced. He'd forgotten about the TV. He glanced at the ax leaning next to the door and said nothing.

A smashed TV, a flap door, bags of melted ice, a man locked inside a schoolhouse filled with bees. Is it a riddle, Dad? Am I supposed to figure it out?

Kellerman stared blankly at the floor.

Oh, I see, Curly continued a moment later. *Now you're not talking at all. Just like old times, hey? I'm supposed to feel guilty or something, right? It's my fault. Huh? This is stupid, Dad. What about your diabetes? How are you taking care of it in there? I guess I'm supposed to break down the door now and rescue your ass. I thought you wanted me to leave you alone!*

Kellerman put a hand over his eyes.

When I was a kid you told me to leave the Crow Woman alone because she was nuts. Somebody might get hurt, you said. Now you're acting just like her. What am I supposed to do?

Kellerman wasn't sure, but the boy's last words seemed softer, almost pleading. Kellerman opened his mouth to speak, but no words came out.

All right, Curly had said, his voice hardening again. *Here's what I'm going to do. I'm going to leave now. I'm going to go talk with Charley Bluefire and Merle Coats and Vukovich and old man Loudermilk and anybody else I can think of. Somebody'll know what the hell you're doing in there. I'll make them tell me. And then, after I've found out all I can, I'm going to come back here and get that fucking door open, if I have to break it down. You hear me?*

He paused, but Kellerman did not reply.

Is this the way it's supposed to go, Dad? I can't read your mind.

Kellerman had tried to force words — any words — out of his mouth then. He'd managed only a dry, grating sound, like a rusty gate swinging open. Curly must not have heard it. A few moments later Kellerman heard a car engine start.

Long after Curly had left, Kellerman remained sitting on the automobile frame. From the peephole, the beam, barely visible now as the evening light faded, stretched across the room to the east wall.

A game. He thinks I'm playing a game.

He frowned and tried to rise but remained exactly where he was. A thick fog seemed to settle in his brain, blurring everything. Then another thought flashed through the cloud like a streak of lightning. Crazy. He thinks I'm crazy. Like the Crow Woman, like Hubert.

He turned and stared at the flap door, the Crow Woman's bait — and trap. A moment later he was on his knees, crawling toward the door, lifting the flap until the rube latch clicked, then letting it down until the latch clicked a second time, sealing off the trap, locking the flap door shut.

He had no idea how long he sat with his back against the door, thinking about what he had just done. Something had turned around inside him. Sitting there with his back against the oak, he felt it moving, a cold prickly feeling deep in his chest, spreading into his arms, his legs, his neck. Not until it had spread throughout his body, making him shiver like a naked man in the snow, could he give the feeling a name.

"I'll be damned," he said aloud, amazed by fear.

Fear of what? The Crow Woman was afraid of *him,* afraid of his honeys, always had been. She gave him the creeps, sure, with her black-eyed stare and her *Hubert, Hubert* laugh.

But whenever she saw him, or heard the powerful hum of his honeys swell to an angry roar when he used the air hose, she always turned and ran, hopping awkwardly over the grass like a wounded bird. And yet here he was, with his back pressed against the door, shutting off the trap, locking her out.

He shook his head. It was silly to be scared of a senile old woman. He'd even promised Orville he'd help find her, and a promise was a promise. He took off his glasses and rubbed his eyes with the heels of his palms and remembered what Orville had shouted through the door when he was looking for Mabel: *Who ever accused you of being responsible for anything?* Babe had said practically the same thing when they used to argue about what he should do about the Crow Woman. *If you won't let the poor woman be, you should do something to help her.*

Kellerman stared grimly at the crack in the south wall.

"All right, all right!" he snapped a moment later. He turned around on his knees and unlocked the rube latch, resetting the trap. "Fear or no fear, back to Plan A. Can't help her and can't get rid of her either if she's still on the loose." He climbed to his feet and, in an afterthought, shouted through the door: "Goddamn it, I can be in here and be responsible too!"

He turned away from the door. "I didn't move in here to hide, honeys. And I sure as hell didn't move in here to play games. I moved in here to *work.*"

He looked at his project: chassis, engine, drive train, steering, suspension all assembled. "Bones, muscles, vital organs all in place. All we need now is skin."

Well, not quite. He still had to weld on the structural supports for the cab. Then the doors, hood, fenders, and the rest of the outer body could be attached.

He began to work bolting the upright body supports to the cross members in the frame, thinking not about the job at hand but about his son. The sarcasm in Curly's voice — *I'm supposed to feel guilty or something, right?* — had shocked him, the way the boy's voice had so many times over the years. Like the time he overheard Curly and Charley Bluefire's boy talking about sex. Curly was sixteen, but Kellerman had never heard him bring up the subject. Kellerman had assumed the boy had the same ignorant, romantic ideas about it that he'd had at the same age. Kellerman had told him the basics three or four years before. He would have said more, any time, if only the boy had asked or shown any interest at all.

Then one weekend Kellerman was lying under the Corvair, working on a stripped plug bolt, trying to change the oil. He heard the powerful rumble of Curly's Corvette pulling into the drive. The boy had bought and paid for the used car himself, with the money he earned working at the post office in Oklahoma City after school. Kellerman was pleased the boy was working. It showed independence and initiative. He was embarrassed by the car Curly had picked out — a metallic blue monster that looked like the hydroplanes juvenile delinquents raced on Lake Texoma. It had a 427-cubic-inch V-8 with a supercharger. Kellerman couldn't even guess how much horsepower it produced. He thought the car was ugly, almost obscene, but pretended to like it, not forgetting what his own father had done to the Model 18.

The Corvette pulled up next to Kellerman's Corvair and stopped. From their angle in the sports car the boys evidently could not see him. He didn't mean to eavesdrop; he thought they would get right out and come in for a coke or something. Instead, they sat in the car and talked while Kellerman worked away on the stripped bolt. He paid little attention until something Charley Bluefire's boy said caught his ear:

I heard you made it with Lila last night.

Kellerman stopped breathing. No sound issued from the Corvette. It was several seconds before he realized Curly's silence meant yes.

Then he heard the Bluefire boy's voice again:

Well, how was it?

The voice that answered was Curly's voice, but a voice Kellerman had never heard.

Well, there were no haunches or wrap-arounds.

Kellerman's chest collapsed like a tent. What shocked him were not the mysterious words (what was a wrap-around?), but their *tone*: flat, cool, objective. *Experienced.* That his son could have such experience, so much experience, left him open-mouthed. After he had thought about it (and he thought about almost nothing else for the next several days) he would add another, more depressing word to describe his son's tone: cynical.

Kellerman heard none of their conversation after that. Curly and the Bluefire boy eventually entered the house, never noticing him stretched like a corpse under the Corvair. It was a full week before he could bring himself to discuss the incident with Curly.

That's not the way I think of women, he stammered, trying to convey the disappointment he felt.

And you're an expert on women.

Kellerman was shocked again. *No. No, I can't say that. I just — this is* wrong, *son.*

Grow up, Dad.

Curly sat there on the sofa, flipping through the TV guide, case dismissed. Kellerman had thought, had almost hoped, the boy would fly into a rage, stomp out of the house and into the ugly Corvette, revving its oversized engine to a furious howl before disappearing over the hill toward Yukon.

At least that would show the boy still had some feelings on the matter. But there he sat, flipping through the TV guide. Kellerman had no words to say to him.

Now, as he finished bolting the last upright body support onto the frame, Kellerman tried to figure out the real reason his son had come home. He gave the last bolt a final twist, then looked up at a bee crawling on the upright.

We both know you've been alone a year now. "That's what the boy said, honey. He thinks that's why I moved in here — and maybe he's right. Except it's not being alone so much as all the *time* I've got."

The bee flew away, but Kellerman continued, a distant look on his face. "When a man has a whole year alone to think, some things begin to come clear."

Kellerman got up from his project and sat down in the swivel chair. He squinted through the peephole, across the yard at the row of automobiles under the roof of the car-port. On the left, first in line, was the purple Moon Prince of Windsor roadster up on blocks. Kellerman began to speak in a low voice, the words tumbling softly out of his mouth. "When my old man chopped up that Model 18, he cut me free, honeys. I never set foot in his house again."

The day Kellerman left home he also quit high school. It was the autumn of 1933. He moved in with Otis Schmidt, in the apartment above Otis's garage.

You got permission to do this, Lucky? Otis asked when Kellerman announced his intentions. *I ain't no foster parent.*

I'm legal age now, Otis, Kellerman lied. *I'm my own man. From now on, I want you to call me Frank.*

The master mechanic stared at him for a long moment, and Kellerman began to wonder where he could go, what he could do, if Otis said no. Eddie Magril had a part-time job after school in a shoe factory on the Kansas side. His other two buddies, Ninny and Yanny Yorkovich, had quit school long ago. They were bone breakers now, collecting gambling debts for Willie the Mouse.

Then Otis spoke. *We'll try it for a while and see how it goes, Frank.*

Kellerman lived with Otis for six months, then found himself an apartment within walking distance of the garage. He never returned to Miller's barn, but paid old man Miller eight dollars to have the Model 18 hauled away to a junkyard somewhere far outside the city. Kellerman didn't want to know where. Then, when he was eighteen, he got his second car.

"One day I was changing the plugs on a Hupmobile," Kellerman said, staring through the peephole. "And the cops towed in a white Moon coupe somebody'd rolled halfway down Mulligan's Bluff. An 8-80 Prince of Windsor. It was a total wreck, but I could see what a beautiful automobile it'd been. I bought it for ten dollars as junk. Straightened out the frame, knocked out all the dents, chopped off the cab and made it into a convertible. Then I painted the whole thing bright purple."

Kellerman smiled as he gazed at the shining purple auto beneath the roof of the carport. "Anybody who wasn't trash could of told you purple wasn't no color for a Prince of Windsor. But I didn't care. I was like Curly and his fancy Corvette in them days. I wanted something bright and gaudy with a lot of speed. That Prince of Windsor had a four-speed straight-8. I cut the windshield down two inches so it'd look jaunty." He paused and rubbed his chin. "Yeah, I thought I was hot shit in them days."

Kellerman closed his eyes and pictured himself wheeling the Prince of Windsor into the Nuberg Drive-In on Wyandotte Avenue. He pulled the purple car into a stall in the center island and gave the horn a toot. When a pair of long tan legs and pink Hollywood short-shorts appeared, he settled back into the seat and propped his elbow, as casually as he could manage, on the edge of the door.

Lucky! Where'd you get this?

He turned his head and looked up in feigned surprise. *Oh, Bonnie. How've you been?*

Bonnie Parscales seemed not to hear him. Her round brown eyes, the ones he could see so clearly when he closed his own, were sweeping back and forth, checking out the sleek convertible from bumper to bumper.

Is this yours, Lucky?

He smiled and looked through the windshield at the purple hood, then gave the wheel a pat. *All mine.* Then, in an afterthought, he added: *Call me Frank.*

Still staring straight ahead, he felt her round brown eyes focus on him for the first time. He tried to hold his chin at exactly the right height: not too proud, not too shy. He wished he could make his fat, misshapen nose smaller somehow. Very slowly, he inhaled, expanding his tubelike chest to its full capacity beneath his white starched shirt. He started to flex his left bicep and make a knot in his skinny upper arm just below the short sleeve, then thought better of it.

So where are the jailbird twins?

He looked up and found the brown eyes staring into his own. For a moment he could say nothing, as she was leaning over the driver's door now and the musky scent of her perfume drifted into his nostrils and made his head feel light.

I haven't seen Ninny and Yanny for a long time now, he said finally.

She cocked her head and lifted one dark eyebrow. *Stepping up in class now, are you?*

He smiled again. *You might say that.* Her long raven-colored hair was pulled in a tight bun tucked beneath her pink carhop's cap. He imagined the dark tresses suddenly unbound, cascading over her bare tan shoulders like black water flowing over copper. *What time do you get off?*

Bonnie took a step backward and stood erect on her long copper legs. She regarded Kellerman in silence for several moments, and he felt himself being measured. He matched her gaze and tried to breathe without contracting his chest.

Then her lips, exactly the same shade of pink as her Hollywood shorts and carhop cap, crinkled upward at the corners. *I'm off right now.*

They drove out 25th Street toward Muehlebach Field. He made a point of winding out the gears after every stoplight. He could feel the power of the straight-8 through the pedals at his feet and the strength of his own intentions in the wheel he gripped with both fists. Bonnie sat close beside him and traced the curving line of the dash with a long pink fingernail. When they pulled out of the Nuberg she had unpinned her hair, and now, as the wind rushed over the open cab of the Prince of Windsor, long tresses lifted on each side of her head like raven's wings. Neither of them spoke until finally Muehlebach Field came into view.

Kellerman pointed at the left field scoreboard, just visible above the stands. *When I was a kid I saw Hal Trosky hit a ball over the very top of that scoreboard.*

Who?

A musk-scented lock of hair blew across his chin as they pulled into the ballpark lot.

He opened the door for her but was careful not to touch any part of her as she stepped onto the gravel. When she stood next to him he saw that, even in flat shoes, she was at least an inch taller than he was.

Well, are we going in? she asked.

Sure. Right now.

The further they got from the Prince of Windsor, the less certain he became. He squared his shoulders and walked erect like a soldier beside her, but felt his confidence vanishing like the crowd disappearing into the tunnels beneath the stands ahead.

Then, as they moved through the turnstile, she turned toward him and winked. *Maybe we'll see somebody we know.*

And suddenly his confidence came rushing back. She wanted to be seen with *him*. As they made their way beneath the stands, he beamed. His step was light and springy, and he dared to lay his palm on the small of her back as he guided her around a hot dog vendor's cart. His eyes swept the moving crowd ahead, looking for familiar faces. He hadn't been to a single ball game all season. He'd been too busy restoring the Prince of Windsor. But they were heading toward the entrance to the left field bleachers, where he and Eddie Magril and the Yorkovich twins used to sit on summer afternoons, game or no game, sipping moonshine from a bottle in a brown paper bag with the No-Neck Girls from Sacred Heart School. Now he was here with Miss Hollywood Shorts herself.

He was picturing the stunned faces of the No-Neck Girls when, in the shadows beneath the bleachers, he bumped into something rock hard.

Bonnie!

Kellerman hadn't even regained his balance when he saw her brown eyes gaze brightly on the tall, immovable figure of Bud Schaefer, the blond-haired basketball player for Manual Vo-Tech.

Well, hi there, Bud. Bonnie's voice was light and full of mischief, Kellerman thought. He felt something inside himself begin to sink.

e heated some canned beef stew on the hot plate. But
ead of recharging his batteries, the food gave rise to another
e — the tingling under his tongue, the desire for some-
g sweet. He looked over at the sacks of sugar stacked
the air compressor and began to itch.

No, no, no." He wrenched his eyes away from the sugar.
itch spread rapidly through his arms and legs. Soon the
on his chest seemed to tingle. He looked at the syringe
g on his worktable. "No. It's not time. I'm too weak."
hen his skin began to burn, but he did not sweat. "No,"
issed, then grabbed the syringe and began to prepare a
: forty units, ten more than his prescribed dosage. He
himself the injection before he had time to think.

Minutes later, as the itch was beginning to fade, he real-
what he had done. "This is still the fifth day," he
, blinking.

eventy units in one day, more than twice his normal
age. Dr. Kiner had warned him never to vary the dosage
ss told to. Too little insulin made his blood sugar level
spectacularly; too much made it drop. If it dropped too
he could slip into a coma.

'Eat more, eat more," he chanted and opened up another
of beef stew. Eating would help keep his blood sugar
l up. Once again he reminded himself to test his urine
he morning. No point in testing now, after two shots.
As he downed the stew, he squinted at the vial of insulin.
ppeared to be less than a quarter full now. Maybe a week's
rth left. Maybe not. Might not last until he finished
project.

Better have Charley pick up more.

"I'm OK, I'm OK," Kellerman assured himself as he
lped the stew. The second meal brought another corner
his brain back to life.

What the hell are you doing here? Schaefer demanded.

Bonnie smiled shyly. *We're here for the game, Bud. You know
what a fan I am.*

Schaefer gave her a furious look, then turned toward Kellerman. *And who's this runt?*

Kellerman thrust himself between them then and drew
himself up to his full height. He stared up at Schaefer, his
nose about three inches below Schaefer's chin. *My name's
Kellerman. And she's with me.*

For about three seconds Schaefer gazed down at him with
what appeared to Kellerman to be surprise, even uncertain-
ty. Then Schaefer's square face turned businesslike. *Better stay
away from women till you grow up, runt. Now get on out of
here. Move.*

Kellerman stood his ground.

Now, Bud, Bonnie said.

Suddenly the underside of the bleachers spun out of sight.
It was dark for a moment, then colored lights flickered all
around, like Christmas Eve. Then darkness again, followed
by a dim glow that slowly assumed the square shape of Bud
Schaefer's frowning face. Kellerman tried to turn away from
the sight, then realized he was lying on his back.

He's coming around. He's all right.

For goodness sake, Bud, Kellerman heard Bonnie say. *Why'd
you have to hit him there?*

Kellerman rolled his eyes toward her voice and spotted Bonnie bending over him. Her brown eyes were fixed on his,
the brows above them furrowed, and her pink lips were
twisted in an expression halfway between horror and delight.

Then he felt the pain in his nose. A burning coal, melting
through his face. He touched the pain with his fingertips
and found his hand covered with red.

I'll get you, Schaefer.

The blond athlete smiled. *Sure, runt. Anytime.*

Kellerman tried to rise as Schaefer took Bonnie's arm and led her back toward the exit, her raven hair swish, swishing behind her shoulders. When he lifted his head, a rush of light and heat and noise swirled all around him, and he collapsed flat on his back. He closed his eyes and lay motionless until finally the spinning stopped.

When he reopened his eyes, he thought Schaefer's fist had made him suffer double vision: two identical pairs of pinched gray, close-set eyes stared back down at him.

Lucky, one pair of eyes said. *Long time no see.*

That evening, Kellerman drove the Prince of Windsor up the long hill on Summit Street to The Rendezvous tavern. Ninny and Yanny Yorkovich were waiting in the shadows outside.

I can handle my own goose, Kellerman, his nose wrapped in thick gauze, protested.

Sure you can, Lucky, Ninny agreed.

We just want to watch, Yanny added.

The door to The Rendezvous opened and two figures stepped out, a tall man and a dark-haired woman clinging to his side.

Kellerman started to step out into the light when four strong hands shoved him back into the shadows. He tumbled into a row of garbage crates and broke one open, landing flat on his face in a pile of rotten vegetables. His nose exploded with pain. Then he heard Bonnie Parscales scream and looked up in time to see Ninny and Yanny drag Bud Schaefer into the deeper dark of the opposite alley across the street.

In the schoolhouse Kellerman removed his glasses and felt the hardened hump of his nose.

"I never was much of a fighter, honeys. But in them days I didn't really have to be. There was always enough tough

guys around to do my fighting for me. It that stage in my life. All through the De war, and even three or four years after th what I was doing. There was a word Cu from school one day that describes it: *C* that stage of my life was. Wasn't till I me began to change."

He looked over at the hive entrance were slowing down for the evening, only ing around the crack. The voice from t quiet for a long time now. Kellerman sh sneered. Just like her to dummy up on start happening.

"Hey, bitch-in-the-wall, the boy's back of me being in here — what do you thi

He stared at the crack in the wall, but th The hum, so constant, so powerful throug fading. The last few bees floated across t motion before disappearing into the crack. his body — the blood in his veins, the n along the nerves between muscle and brain with his honeys. Weariness wrapped him li He fought it, taking deep breaths, trying stretch himself to get the blood flowing

No. Not now, not yet.

He lurched, stumbled, fell. On the floor no pain, not even the pressure of the floor remembered the bruise on his foot and a t shot through the center of his chest. He be He sat up on the floor and slapped himself until he could feel his face stinging. His sto fold and fold again, and it dawned on him eaten all day.

"OK, honeys, back to work."

As the words came out, he realized there were no bees
left in the room. The walls were silent. He laid the empty
bowl on his worktable and cocked his head to listen for other
noises coming through the stone and plaster. Nothing. The
peephole was a black spot.

Night. Already.

He reached up and pulled the chain, switching off the
overhead light. In the darkness the beam reappeared, a silver
thread spun from the full moon. He saw the moon itself when
he placed his eye next to the hole. In the moonlight the yard
looked cold and dead, the row of automobiles as still as stone.

Where was Curly tonight? Kellerman wondered. Who
was he talking to? Charley wouldn't tell him about the car
— and what if he did? What difference would it make?

"In his eyes I'm crazy either way."

He reached up and turned the light back on. The glare
made him squint. Around him the cluttered room, with its
piles of boxes, tools, parts, the skeleton of an automobile,
looked frozen, lifeless. Like a picture of a room. He shook
his head and glanced at the south wall, where the crack gaped
at him.

Then a sound broke the silence. It came not from the crack
but through the ceiling, the roof. A tapping sound, like fingers
drumming on the roof.

"Rain," Kellerman whispered, and leaned back in the
chair. Slowly the rain increased. He heard it pound the tin
roof of the carport across the yard, sending a metallic vibra-
tion through the stone walls of the schoolhouse.

He turned out the light and tried to relax and let the drumming roar of water striking tin dampen his senses and numb
him to sleep. But it was no use. His eyes popped open in
the darkness, the way they had on another rainy night a

quarter century ago, when the sudden ring of the hall phone made him bolt upright in bed. Babe was already up; the clatter on the tin roof had driven her from bed half an hour earlier. She reached the phone before it could ring a second time and wake Curly in the next room. Kellerman sat on the edge of the bed and looked out the window where a shaft of lightning penetrated the thunderheads to light the carport roof in silver.

It's Dottie, Babe said.

Kellerman got up and went to the phone. He must have said something to Dottie. A few words — hello, goodbye, and something in between — before he hung up. He had no memory of his own words, nor even of Dottie's, though her message was unforgettable.

He returned to the bedroom. *The old man's dead.*

Babe was watching the rain. She turned and came to him and slipped her arm around his waist. He looked past her to the window.

After a few minutes she spoke. *Are you all right?*

Yeah.

But he was not all right. Not because his father was dead, but because of the thought that had formed in his mind when Dottie had told him the news.

At last, he had thought. At last.

He could admit it now, twenty-five years later. The relief he had felt at that moment. The old man's death had freed him somehow, lifted a weight off his shoulders.

Or so he had thought. For Kellerman now realized his father had *not* died. Not then, not since. He had come back again and again in the years that followed, in various forms. In memories Kellerman had long tried to forget. In the footsteps he had heard circling the schoolhouse at night. In the ax he always kept close by, the one he had used to chop his color TV to pieces. The old man just kept coming back — and he wasn't the only one. Babe came back, too. In the peperomia that wouldn't die. In the bitchy voice in the wall, who spoke to him still, whenever it was her pleasure to speak.

Kellerman looked over at the crack, then spoke aloud to his honeys, asleep behind the still walls.

"The trouble with this life, honeys, is that things don't really die. They live on, just to kill you. Bit by bit, every day."

Kellerman stared at the crack and clenched his teeth. He felt a chill then and discovered he was trembling. He grabbed the edge of the worktable and hung on, but the trembling did not stop.

13

THE TREMBLING did not stop until the first beam of dawn, the dawn of his sixth day in the schoolhouse, angled through the peephole, waking up the walls, restoring the hum, the beat, the rhythm of his workshop.

Kellerman watched his honeys emerge one by one from the crack. A yawning flutter of wings, then off to work, buzzing straight to the feeding stations, sucking up sweet water, bringing it home. Or fanning out over the room, searching for sawdust they must have thought was pollen, landing on the floor beneath the vise on his worktable, where he'd cut his cedar planks to board off the windows. He'd deliberately chosen cedar because his honeys preferred the sharper, sweeter scent of its sawdust. Sometimes he would sprinkle the grains with sugar water to give them a special treat. Now he watched them crawl over the dusty mound on the floor, collecting grains on the barbed backs of their legs before returning to the hive.

As the trembling in his sore muscles faded, he pushed the swivel chair right up next to the crack where he could watch his honeys closely, observe their sense of purpose, feel their buzzing energy, their strength. The first few years he had shared the workshop with them, before he began to observe them so closely, he had believed their movements around the hive were all gracefully coordinated, choreographed, like a dance. Closer study showed this was not true. When he positioned his magnifying glass just above the crack, just out of their flight path, he discovered their movements were clumsy, almost reckless. They flew poorly, laboring in the air like hot air balloons on a windy day, and their landings on the rim of the crack were often more like crashes. They bumped frequently, knocking one another out of the air and off the wall as they crowded in and out of the hive. Close up, their movements seemed chaotic.

And yet, when he looked even closer, something *was* orchestrating their movements. Something he observed in the motions of a few individual workers returning from the feeding stations and mounds of sawdust. Most disappeared quickly into the crack, but occasionally one would touch down on the wall beside the crack and begin to crawl round and round in a tight circle. The other bees gave room, backing away until an audience of bees formed a ring around the first one. Round and round the first bee turned, until the other bees began to fan their wings and fly away. Kellerman would sometimes follow these other bees, who always flew straight to a feeding station or a pile of sawdust. He had witnessed this phenomenon many times, and it fascinated him. One afternoon he called up the same beekeeper he had once hired to steal the queen.

"It's the round dance," the beekeeper declared after listening to Kellerman's description. "It means food is near — close by the hive. The dance tells the other bees where to find it. Now if the food was farther away, say a hundred yards, they'd dance the wag-tail dance. Now *that's* a sight to see."

Kellerman nodded into the phone, thinking yes, yes, that must be.

"You're lucky just to see the round dance," the beekeeper went on. "Usually only professional keepers ever get to see it. Bees are supposed to dance only inside the hive, on the honeycomb. But every once in a while one'll start to dance as soon as he lands."

The thought of his honeys dancing round and round on the hidden honeycomb made Kellerman's heart leap. He wanted to ask the beekeeper to describe the wag-tail dance but decided not to, thinking perhaps one day he'd get to see it for himself.

Kellerman leaned back in the swivel chair and tried to relax. He touched his forehead and discovered he was sweating again. And yet the room seemed cool enough. Strange — it was the middle of June, but he couldn't recall feeling the usual blistering Oklahoma heat. Must be getting up in the nineties afternoons by now. He reached across his worktable and turned on the fan. Dry the sweat off anyway, he reasoned.

He looked through the peephole. The yard was bright under a cloudless sky, the shaggy, uncut grass starting to bleach a grayish brown in the sun. Looks like it's going to be a real scorcher out there, Kellerman thought, but felt only the stale breeze from the fan.

His gaze rested on the Hudson Hornet, second in line beneath the carport. Late last night, as he was hanging on to the worktable to keep from shaking, he thought he had seen something, some*one*, moving around the Hudson. He saw it only an instant: a flitting shadow, too small for a man, too quick for an old woman like Mabel Zucha. He'd seen nor heard nothing else all night.

Tired, probably imagined it, Kellerman told himself. But

he had seen the same shadow once before.

Staring at the Hornet now, he tried to recall details, anything that could give form to the shadow he had seen. Nothing came. The Hornet offered no clue, its mouthlike grill expressionless, neither a grin nor a sneer. The Hornet was the third automobile, counting the first Model 18, in his history. And it was his favorite. His favorite automobile and the favorite time in his life. The best time, the time when everything started to fall into place for him, for Babe, for the whole family. He'd driven the two of them from Kansas City to their new home in Oklahoma in the Hornet. Mother and son, Babe wide-eyed and cooing, Curly wrapped up snug in a baby blue blanket. The best time of his life — and all, he remembered now, because of the accident when Bigfoot Pete Yuri had saved his life.

Jobs had been scarce after the war, even for vets. Kellerman had counted himself lucky to catch on as an electrician at the Nabisco factory in Kansas City right after he mustered out. After two years he quit and went to work for the Frisco Railroad in Fort Scott, Kansas, first as a gandy dancer, then as a mechanic on the new diesels they brought into Fort Scott for servicing.

On the day of the accident he'd climbed into the dining car on the Indian Nations Express, where Hondo the cook always slipped him a sandwich made from whatever was left in the kitchen. He was just climbing down again when the train started without warning. The engineer was supposed to wait for the all clear signal from the brakeman, but the Indian Nations was twenty minutes behind schedule and the engineer had a nineteen-year-old Italian girlfriend waiting for him in Oklahoma City. The first lurch threw Kellerman against the side rail, where he hit his head. The blow stunned him. The second lurch threw him forward, off the

train, but a loop in his overalls caught on the assist handle
and flipped him back under the train, just behind the back
wheels of the dining car. The loop held as the train began
to drag him, battered and unconscious, over the tracks.

Pete Yuri, the diesel foreman, was standing in the middle
of the maintenance yard when the Indian Nations started up.
While the brakeman screamed and waved at the engineer,
Yuri ran toward the dining car. He grabbed Kellerman's right
arm, breaking it just behind the wrist as he planted his feet
and yanked. The loop snapped and Kellerman was free.

An hour later he regained consciousness in St. Mary's
Hospital in Fort Scott. Standing over him, palms clasped like
a praying priest, was Pete Yuri. Kellerman tried to speak,
tried to ask what had happened, but pain struck the words
out of his mouth. His right arm, right leg, and seven ribs
were broken. And his nose, for the third time. His neck was
braced for whiplash. Helpless and bewildered, he looked up
at Yuri. The diesel mechanic leaned closer and whispered in
Kellerman's ear the best advice he would ever receive.

"Sue the railroad," Yuri said.

He did. The Frisco doctors sent him to a back specialist
in Oklahoma City. Lying in traction, watching them stick
pins in his toes (the feeling in his lower leg came back gradually, along with more pain), he realized this was his chance,
the one he'd been looking for most of his life. He was thirty-
three years old and had fifty-two dollars in the bank. Nobody
got rich working for the Frisco. When the Jew lawyer he
hired told him he could expect some money for the accident,
he began to think seriously, for the first time in his life, about
getting married.

"There was Matti Holmes in Afton, honeys," Kellerman
said, rocking back in the swivel chair and staring again at
the hive. "And there was Babe."

Kellerman's eyes glazed as he rocked further back and stared up at the ceiling, recalling the day he first met Babe.

The cookie lines in the Nabisco factory consisted of a row of parallel conveyor belts in a room big enough to build airplanes. Along each belt ten to twenty women in gray caps and aprons operated machines that squirted chocolate or vanilla or butterscotch icing on freshly baked cookies before stuffing them into boxes. Kellerman was poised on a stepladder, replacing the big 400-watt bulb hanging from the ceiling above one of the middle belts, when he spotted a slim girl with mousey brown hair. She was running the stuffer.

That throw any light on the subject? he shouted down through the clattering roar of the machinery after replacing the bulb. Eyes fixed on the belt, the girl appeared not to hear. Kellerman descended three steps on the ladder, low enough to reach down and tap her on the shoulder.

Her scream pierced the machine roar. Startled, Kellerman had to grab onto the ladder to keep from falling. The burnt-out bulb slipped out of his hand and fell into the stuffer.

Christ on a crutch! Kellerman shouted at the girl. *You almost made* me *fall into that thing!*

At that instant an alarm bell rang, and Kellerman looked up at the catwalk and saw Waldo, the line supervisor, curse and yank a lever to shut off the belt. Along the belt the machines shuddered and whined to a halt.

Recovered, Kellerman reached for the last box of Chocolate Marvels to come out of the stuffer.

Always wondered why Mom never bought these things, he said, grinning, and removed a cookie laced with broken glass.

The look in the girl's eyes froze him. Shock, embarrassment, anger — all these expressions he expected. But he recognized something else in her eyes, remembered feeling it himself as a boy, when he returned the stolen sacramental wine and Father Jaworski lectured him about the path of the soul to heaven.

It's not your fault, he said to the girl.

All right, what's all this? Waldo, wearing a visor and a white shirt with a gray circle of sweat under each arm, now hurried up the line toward them. The girl shrank back as he approached.

My fault, Waldo, Kellerman said, heading him off. *I scared her. Told her she won the company lottery, and the prize was a date with you.*

Kellerman felt the girl's eyes flash at him for just an instant.

Smartass, Waldo said, his face reddening. *Clean out the stuffer. And for Christsake make sure you get every piece of glass.*

Later, on the loading docks, Kellerman asked Buddy Harcorn about the girl running the stuffer.

The jumpy one? Martha Greychek. Wakes up in a new world every day.

Kellerman nodded. Like a newborn babe, he thought. Probably a sharecropper's daughter or something.

At the end of the day he followed her home.

Name's Kellerman. I'd like to speak to your daughter.

Keller-who? Behind the screen door Anton Graychek pulled up his trousers and eyed the stranger suspiciously.

*Keller*man. *Frank, as in* Frankenstein. *I work at Nabisco with your daughter.*

Anton Graycheck cocked his head and sized Kellerman up from head to toe. *Janitor?*

Kellerman drew himself up to his full height. *Right now I'm an electrician, but I've got an option to buy a piece of the Muehlebach Hotel from William Powell.*

Anton Graycheck scratched his chin. *William Powell, he owns the Muehlebach?*

Just a small percentage. He was a few years ahead of me at Sacred Heart. Soon's I can get the money together, I'm going to buy him out.

From the dark hallway behind her father, Martha Graychek spoke her first words to Kellerman. *Well, I'll swan*, she said. *I'll swan*.

In the schoolhouse Kellerman got up from the swivel chair and stepped over to his project. "At first she'd believe *anything*, honeys. William Powell, the Muehlebach, shooting craps with Al Capone and Babyface Nelson."

He grabbed a file and began to fix a rust spot beneath the latch hole on the left doorpost.

"She was only twenty-two," he murmured. "Wouldn't even look me in the eye in those days. She had the face of a mouse trying to hide from the light, like the world was just too big and scary for her to look at it direct." His eyebrows knitted into a frown. "Not that she was *dumb* or anything." He winced, remembering the jokes Eddie Magril used to make: *Hey, Lucky! How many Graycheks does it take to screw in a lightbulb?*

"Not dumb," Kellerman repeated. "Just shy and ignorant. When I quit Nabisco and went to work for the Frisco down in Fort Scott, I believe she thought she'd never see me again. Seventy miles was like crossing the Atlantic Ocean to her. But I couldn't leave her all alone for long. We was actually planning for her to move down to Fort Scott just before we'd get married. Then the accident fouled everything up."

Kellerman shook his head and kicked the side of the auto frame to emphasize the point. A bee tried to land on his ear. He waved it away unconsciously.

His claim against the Frisco dragged through the courts for two years, during which time Kellerman recovered enough to move back to Kansas City and go to work as an automotive mechanic for Zeke Grabowski, who had bought Otis Schmidt's garage in 1943, after another mechanic, a 4-F'er, had opened up the big doors one Monday morning and found

Otis lying flat on his back, his fingers curled stiff around a socket wrench, beneath the chassis of a Packard 115 coupé. Babe was still working at Nabisco and was relieved to have Kellerman back in town, no matter where he worked.

Finally, in the summer of 1951, the Frisco settled with Kellerman for seven thousand dollars, half of which went to his lawyer. By that time Kellerman had a wife, a baby boy, and a plan for the future. Pete Yuri's brother, Cecil, had a garage and auto body shop for sale in a little town west of Oklahoma City called Yukon. The day after the settlement check arrived, Kellerman drove down alone to take a look at the garage. He fell in love with it at once. The next morning he found the house and five acres north of town. By the end of his second day in Yukon he had been to the bank twice and was eight thousand dollars in debt. But he had one more item to buy before returning to Kansas City for Babe and Curly.

Kellerman sat back down in the swivel chair and rocked back and forth. "Believe it or not, I was still driving that old Prince of Windsor in 1951, honeys. I wanted a new car for my new start, something really *special*. So I drove over to Coogan's Motors in Bethany and bought a brand new Hudson Hornet. English racing green, the Green Hornet. Step-down body, rear wheels inside the chassis, independent front suspension — nothing like it on the road. I had everything going for me the day I drove that Hornet back up to Kansas City to pick up Babe and Curly. That car, that time, well, there's just one word for it — *hope*."

Kellerman leaned forward to gaze through the peephole at his favorite automobile, then jerked back in astonishment. Instead of the green Hudson Hornet he saw a blue and white police car.

A sharp rap on the door made him jump a second time. "Who is it?" he cried, shocked that he hadn't heard the car or any footsteps.

"City of Yukon Police, Frank. We'd like to talk to you a minute. Out here."

Kellerman sat right where he was. He knew that voice. The voice of Ed "Eddie" Hacker, the punk who had beaten up on Curly in the fifth grade, the grown-up man who had taken away Frank Kellerman's license to drive an automobile.

In the four or five seconds that passed between Hacker's words and Kellerman's reply, Kellerman felt a sudden rush of energy, as if somewhere inside him a tiny hand had thrown a switch and all circuits were now complete. He knew what Hacker was here for; he'd anticipated this move by Vukovich, who had the police chief and half the town of Yukon in his hip pocket.

"Yeah, well, go ahead and talk to me, Eddie. I can hear you just fine from here."

"It'd be better for everyone if you came out here."

Kellerman laughed. No doubt Vukovich had warned Hacker about the bees. He could tell this from the sound of Hacker's voice: a voice always a bit too loud, too sure of itself. But then Ed Hacker was a klutz, beef on the hoof, a small-town bully grown up to be police chief. A muscle-bound linebacker who failed to make the grade with the Oklahoma Sooners like his ham bone of an old man. Now he wore a baby blue uniform that would never fit, handing out parking tickets to bowlegged bohunk farmers in pickup trucks. Kellerman pictured Hacker's fat red face sweating in the June heat, droplets clinging like salty pearls to the pimply pink flesh of his eighteen-inch neck.

"I don't believe I care to, Eddie."

Hacker's voice went up an octave. "I got a complaint from Carl Vukovich, says you stole an antique V-8 engine out of his salvage yard."

"Now how did I do that?"

"We'll get around to that, if we have to. Carl doesn't want any trouble. All he wants is his engine back."

Kellerman chewed his lip. "Mmm-hmm. What's the temperature out there?"

"It's getting hotter all the time, Frank. Listen, I've got another officer out here with me — speak up, Dennis — "

"Yeah, right. I, we —"

"Maybe you'd prefer to discuss the matter with Officer Robinson," Hacker broke in. "I'm agreeable, just so we get this thing settled."

Kellerman grinned and winked at the bees buzzing around the oak door. "Oh now, 'Eddie.' What you *really* need to do is come in here and inspect the place, don't you? See if I'm hiding any V-8's amongst all the McGuffy Readers in this old schoolhouse, right? Tell you what, the big door's stuck shut, but that little red flap's open — you could crawl right in. Just *you*, Eddie. Not Officer Harelip there."

Kellerman heard the muffled sound of low voices. He smiled. Then after a minute Hacker spoke again. "I'm not crawling anywhere. You come out here."

Kellerman grinned. "Let me make it easy for you, Eddie. You got a search warrant?"

"I can get one if I have to."

Kellerman continued to grin. Hacker's voice had sounded relieved, almost grateful. "Why don't you do that — if you want to look around inside here, that is."

Behind the door the low voices started up again, louder this time. It sounded like they were arguing. Kellerman rocked back and forth in the chair, beaming.

"Say, Frank," Hacker said finally. His voice seemed softer, probing. "Guess who I talked to this morning."

Kellerman stopped rocking.

"Curly. Hadn't seen him since the funeral."

Kellerman sat up straight in the chair. "You don't say," he replied, trying to sound disinterested.

"Yeah," Hacker went on. "Seems he's going all over town asking about you. I guess he's worried about you being in there or something."

"Well, next time you see him, you can tell him for me I'm just fine." Kellerman began to chew his lip.

"Yeah, whole town's talking about Curly and you. Big TV star comes home and finds his old man locked up in a room full of bees." Hacker paused. "Be lucky if the news people don't get hold of it."

Kellerman flinched, then quickly replied. "Well, you tell 'em all to come right on out and bring plenty of film. I want the old place to show up nice on TV."

He waited as the voices outside were muffled once more. Kellerman felt himself begin to sweat.

"Let me get this straight," Hacker said a minute later. Kellerman noticed with relief that Hacker's voice had resumed its stiff, professional tone. "You say you don't know anything about a stolen engine, right?"

"I say I'm busy in here. My honeys and me, we've got work to do." Kellerman bit his lip and waited.

"I'm going to look into this matter further, Frank," Hacker said finally. "Next time I come out here I'll have a warrant. I'm just telling you now, in case you want to think it over and maybe settle this thing without any trouble."

"Well, that's sure white of you, Eddie. Say hi to Carl for me."

"OK, if that's the way you want it."

Kellerman waited until he heard them turn to go. "Oh, say, Eddie!"

"Yeah?"

"Make sure you come out yourself now. Don't send an Indian to do the Chief's job!"

Kellerman threw back his head and laughed. He forgot to press his ear to the oak and check the sound of their footsteps fading into the summer heat.

Not long after Hacker and his partner had left, Kellerman noticed he was tiring again. His head felt fuzzy and weightless, like he had risen too quickly after a long sleep. Why these sudden shifts? he wondered. It wasn't time for another shot — he'd just had one, a big one, just last night. In a mild panic, he glanced at the beam through the peephole to make sure it was still morning. The beam struck his worktable at a forty-five degree angle. Midmorning.

He relaxed a little, but continued to stare at the beam that stretched like an arm of luminous flesh through the paler artificial light of the overhead bulb. The bulb gave everything in the room a sickly yellow-gray color. I need more light in here, he thought. Real light.

He grabbed his crowbar and started to pry loose the top cedar plank covering the window, then realized what he was doing.

The crowbar dropped to the floor with a clang, scattering the bees around their feeding stations. He sat down on the auto frame and tried to sort things out. He was facing a threat now — Vukovich was serious — and had to be prepared. But other things were happening, too. He was having trouble keeping it all clear in his head: Curly, Vukovich, the car, the things he'd seen and heard around the schoolhouse, the way he felt from moment to moment, his metabolism racing, slowing down, racing again. Right now he felt himself getting worked up again, his blood surging. He had to keep it all under control somehow. What was Curly doing talking to everyone in Yukon? What did he really want? Why did he come home — to offer me his goddamn money again, be my caretaker? Kellerman shook his head. And what about the Crow Woman? Why hadn't she fallen into the trap? He looked over at the flap door. Where was she? He hadn't heard her awful laugh in days now. And what about the footsteps and the shadows he'd seen around the cars? *Who was out there?*

Around him his honeys worked steadily. Hive to pan, pan to hive. Hum, beat, flutter, buzz. He didn't mean to start working again, didn't mean to grab his wrench and begin bolting the windshield posts to the cowl supports. He did it without thinking, without knowing, checking and rechecking the upper framework for fit and strength. Measuring, adjusting, going with the flow. The floorboards were next; he'd cut brand new floorboards from top quality plywood treated with creosote, the screw and bolt holes drilled in advance. Attaching them took only a few minutes, with a washer or two for adjustment.

Next came the seat supports. The roadster had two bucket seats in front and a rumble seat in back. Only the front buckets were supported directly by the frame. File, fit, bolt, screw. He worked in rhythm with the humming walls.

By noon, after downing a can of soup, he was ready to install the rear quarter panel. This required some thought, and the act of thinking stopped him cold. He stepped back and took a look at his project, amazed at how much he'd accomplished in only a few hours.

"We're *smokin'*, honeys. Why, we're almost —"

And then he was on the floor — flat on his face as if he'd

been clubbed from behind — dirt, grease, and sawdust coating his lips. Hot, cold, weak. He sweat, shivered, gasped for breath. Around him the hum faded in and out. Finally, he rolled over and saw the 200-watt bulb glaring down at him like a desert sun.

Thirsty.

He crawled over to the sink and pulled himself up. Easy. The water tasted like alcohol, burning his throat and stomach. He drank it anyway, then gave himself a shot — thirty units — and collapsed onto his cot.

He slept. When his eyes popped open again he was panting, as if he'd been running in his sleep. When he caught his breath, he noticed something. The hum he'd grown so accustomed to seemed different somehow. Rougher, less melodious. He looked around. Bees flew from hive to pan, pan to hive, same as always. Yet *something* was different.

He looked at the peephole. The beam fell diagonally left to right across his worktable. In a moment the significance of this fact struck him. It was *morning* — a new morning. The morning of the seventh day, if he hadn't lost track. He had slept an entire afternoon, evening, and night.

"Unbelievable," he mumbled.

He opened the ice box and withdrew the vial of insulin. He prepared the shot in no particular hurry, glad to be doing something with his hands. The vial looked low, very low, but he didn't worry about that now. Afterward, he leaned back and let the prickly feeling spread slowly through him. He didn't feel like getting right to work. Or thinking. He'd sort everything out in a little while. Right now his honeys were still emerging from the hive, taking wing, following their regular flight paths, starting a new day. Still . . . the hum sounded different.

Absently, he scanned the room until his gaze fell on the

flap door. Something held his eyes there.

He leaned closer. It was barely visible, but something looked wrong with the flap. The right bottom center looked odd, misshapen, like the wood had been bent or warped.

Quickly, he glanced at the bolt on the main door — it was still padlocked.

He got down on his knees and examined the flap door. The right corner had definitely been tampered with; there were scratches all around. Both hinges also looked off-line. He stuck his fingernail in the seam and tried to lift the flap. It wouldn't budge. Kellerman swallowed. With his index finger he felt the interior mechanism of the rube latch. The latch had been tripped. The flap door was locked shut.

Heart pounding, Kellerman turned and faced a room he no longer recognized. Hood, fenders, columns of boxes, piles of debris. A hundred hiding places.

Then he saw it. A group of bees beginning to hover around and behind a column of boxes near the east wall next to the sink. Bee by bee, the circling cloud grew, looming over something just out of sight.

Kellerman grabbed a hammer off his worktable. The room seemed to move toward him, though he must have taken one step, then another, and another, past the automobile toward the column of boxes. He moved forward without thinking, raising the hammer in his fist as he peeked around the column, then drew back in amazement.

Crouching behind the boxes, beneath the circling cloud of bees, quivering like a frightened rat, was Popeye.

14

POPEYE!

Before Kellerman could scream his name, Popeye backed against the east wall next to the sink and shrank into a shivering knot. His crossed eyes bulged in two different directions at once — one on the hammer raised in Kellerman's fist, the other trying to follow a bee buzzing near his ear.

Somehow Popeye's terror calmed Kellerman. He lowered the hammer, then spoke again, slowly, pausing to make sure each word was clear:

"What . . . are you . . . doing here?"

Popeye did not answer. Now that Kellerman had lowered the hammer, Popeye's left eye looked Kellerman in the face. Or almost — the eye pointed somewhere over Kellerman's right shoulder. Popeye's other eye seemed to move independently, like the eye of a lizard, trying to follow a bee that threatened to land on his ear. Kellerman felt like he had come upon a wild animal caught in a trap.

"What are you doing here?" Kellerman repeated.

Popeye seemed not to hear. He began to tremble even more now, as both his eyes began to follow bees. Several were hovering so close they almost touched him now, and more were approaching, encircling him.

Kellerman realized Popeye was too terrified to speak. Bees began to land on him. He pawed fearfully at the first one — the bee lifted off his arm for only an instant, then landed in the same spot. Another bee landed on his foot. Then another landed, and another. Popeye smashed his back against the wall, trying to push *through* the wall. Kellerman heard plaster cracking.

Now Kellerman was frightened, too. More and more bees were landing on Popeye, coating his wrist, then his forearm. Kellerman had never seen his honeys do anything like this. But then, he suddenly realized, except for himself and the beekeeper, no one else had entered the schoolhouse since his honeys arrived fifteen years ago. Now the hum from the walls grew louder, deeper, almost (was it possible?) *angry*. In another minute a hundred, then a thousand bees would cover Popeye. But before that, Popeye would leap up, go crazy like a rabid rat, and the bees would sting him.

Kellerman looked wildly around the room. In the corner he spotted the folded gray canvas he had used to cover the V-8 engine.

"Don't move!" Kellerman shouted above the hum, but Popeye was past hearing. He was shrinking into a tighter and tighter ball, turning slowly yellow.

In an instant Kellerman retrieved the canvas and flapped it open in front of Popeye with a loud *pow!* The sharp sound and the blast of air knocked half the bees off Popeye, and most of the rest lifted off under their own power. Keller-man snapped the canvas a second time, then a third, sweeping his honeys away from the trembling man. Moving faster than he had in years, Kellerman darted down and brushed the last few bees off Popeye's head and neck, then dropped the canvas over him. Instantly the bees returned, raining down on the gray mound like drops of gold paint.

Kellerman quickly circled the mound, flattening out the edges of the canvas, laying down hammers, wrenches, headlights, small boxes, anything he could find to hold the edges flat and keep his honeys from crawling underneath. Then he stepped back and stared at the sight. The canvas was completely covered with bees, a swarming mound of yellow.

Kellerman wondered if the canvas was thick enough to prevent his honeys' stingers from penetrating.

"Don't move," he said again, but the mound continued to tremble.

What now? He had little time to ponder the question; his honeys were crawling over the canvas like ants searching out their prey. He had to get Popeye out of the schoolhouse right away, or he'd be a dead man.

He looked across the room at the flap door, then back at the canvas. "Stay put!" he shouted at Popeye, then hurried over to the flap door. It took a long time, nearly ten seconds, to unlock the rube latch. In his near panic he almost forgot where the trigger was. He propped the flap open with a long screwdriver, then returned to the mound, quaking beneath the yellow blanket of bees.

"Get hold of yourself and listen! I'm going to pull the front part of the canvas across the floor to the flap door, the same place where you got in." As he shouted the directions to Popeye, Kellerman realized there were probably bees trapped under the canvas with him. Popeye was probably being stung even as he spoke. "I'm going to pull you all the way over there, then lift the canvas over the flap, so you can crawl outside. You're going to have to crawl with me now — all the way across the room. Not too fast, not too slow, or the bees'll get under there. You hear me? Understand?"

No sound issued from beneath the canvas.

"Nod your head if you hear me," Kellerman said, but the mound only trembled. Kellerman looked around and threw up his hands. Nothing to do but go ahead. "OK, I'm going to pull now. You follow me, not too fast, not too slow. OK . . . now!"

He gave the canvas a slow, even tug. The weight of the bees and all the tools and junk piled around the edges made the pulling difficult, and for a moment the mound did not move. Then suddenly, almost too suddenly, the mound lurched toward him.

"Not so fast!" Kellerman screamed. "Follow my lead!"

The mound stopped. Kellerman tugged again, and this time the mound followed, shuddering forward like a dam giving way. "That's better. Follow my lead."

It took a full five minutes to cross the room. When they neared the door Kellerman had to move his body out of the way and pull from the side. "OK now. I'm going to lift the edge of the canvas over the flap so you can crawl out. Get ready!"

He lifted the canvas quickly, praying the screwdriver would hold up the flap and that more of his honeys were not hovering in ambush outside. The moment he slipped the canvas over the flap the mound dove forward.

"Easy now . . . all right!"

Kellerman clapped his hands in triumph and relief, then heard the sound of tiny footsteps scrambling away over the grass.

"Hey, *wait!* Why — what the hell were you doing in here?"

But Popeye was already gone.

Kellerman sighed and wiped the sweat out of his eyes, then looked down at the deflated canvas. Slowly, one by one, without so much as an angry flutter, his honeys began to lift into the air and return to work.

15

WHEN HIS HONEYS had all returned to work, and the hum that filled the room was once again smooth and rhythmical, Kellerman collapsed in the swivel chair.

The casual way his honeys had returned to their regular pattern, once the intruder was gone, impressed Kellerman. It dawned on him that he was safer than he'd realized, here in this old schoolhouse. He decided his honeys had swarmed on Popeye not in anger, as when he had stirred them to flight with a blast of compressed air into the walls, but in the cool, professional manner of personal bodyguards. Yes, he was safe all right. Let anyone try to interrupt him now! Let Vukovich or Hacker or the Crow Woman . . .

A chill stabbed Kellerman in the chest as he realized the Crow Woman's fate if she had taken his bait and crawled through the flap door. He shuddered, then jumped up from the spot where he was hinging the driver's side door to the post support and hurried over to the flap door. He locked the rube latch, then took a putty knife and stuffed plastic wood into the seams around the flap. The trap was sealed permanently.

He turned and faced the room where walls hummed and bees, thousands of them, filled the air, scouting the piles and boxes for something sweet, long lines flying from crack to pan, pan to crack. Until this moment, he'd never truly appreciated just how many bees there were. *Biggest natural hive I ever saw,* the beekeeper had said. The beekeeper had worn a thick rubber poncho tucked into hip boots, plus heavy gloves and a hat with an insect net drooping over his shoulders. He was inside the schoolhouse less than two minutes. The bees, perhaps a hundred of them, landed on the poncho and the net as the beekeeper moved swiftly along each wall in wonder, rapping the plaster gingerly with his knuckles. *You don't even see most of them in here. Most of them hunt for food outside. They enter the hive through the outside cracks in the stone. But with the size of the hive inside these walls, I'd estimate forty or fifty thousand. Maybe more.* Kellerman, who was wearing only khaki pants and a T-shirt, had gasped. *Forty or fifty thousand?* But the figures meant nothing next to the vision of his honeys swarming over Popeye, transforming him into a shrinking, shivering yellow ball.

Kellerman swallowed. He was indeed safe here, in this room with his honeys. But he could let no one else in — ever. Then another chill pricked his skin as he remembered what Curly had said. *I'll be back. And I'll get that door open, if I have to break it down.*

Kellerman looked at the heavy bolt. The door was 2½ inches of solid oak. But the boy might still get in somehow. Popeye had.

Popeye! Kellerman sat rigid in the chair as his thoughts returned, finally, to their original subject. Why the hell had Popeye invaded his workshop? Kellerman turned Popeye's personalities over in his mind: Popeye the sneak, the beggar, the fool, the coward, the snitch.

Suddenly it came to him.

"It's Vukovich, honeys." Kellerman said. "He's hired the sorry little shit to spy on us. Well, he got an eyeful, that's for sure. And the scare of his life to go with it, just to get a look at *this* . . . "

As his eyes fell once again on his project Kellerman felt something begin to happen inside himself. The logical part of his brain told him he should keep his thoughts focused on his problems outside the schoolhouse: Popeye, Vukovich, Ed Hacker, Charley, Curly, the Crow Woman — all the do-gooders, sneaks, and crazies who were trying to invade his sanctuary. But the fact was he was *safe*, safer than he'd ever been in his entire rotten life, in this room with his honeys protecting him, on the morning of the seventh day inside. And he had a job to do.

From the crack in the wall Babe's voice seemed to mock him: *I'll swan, Frank. You've done it now.*

Kellerman shook his head. That's where you're wrong. I ain't done with anything yet.

He picked up a wrench and set to work. It was natural somehow, working without thinking. In a way, the automobile was building itself. Even the rear quarter panel, a tough job, fit snugly, easily, above and below the belt line. Quickly, effortlessly, the body grew, part by part: firewall, fenders, hood, doors. Screws, washers, holding nuts, cotter pins turned and snapped into place.

Minutes, hours passed. Or so he guessed. He could feel the time going by but did not stop to measure it, did not stop to notice the beam of sunlight moving across the floor. He kept going as the walls hummed, bees buzzed, pulleys turned, cables stretched, an automobile grew.

When he finally laid down his wrench and stepped back

against the west wall to have a look and gauge his progress, what he saw before him was no longer a skeleton, no longer a framework, but finally, truly, an automobile. A 1932 Model 18 Deluxe Roadster. A classic open car, the first Ford V-8. It wasn't *finished,* of course. It had no headlights, no seat, no dash. He still had to wire the electrical system and paint the body. But the basic car — body, frame, engine, drive train, suspension, steering — was all assembled. Viewed from the front, the car looked like he could just climb in and drive away, if only the schoolhouse door were wide enough to squeeze the car through.

Kellerman's chest swelled. "We've done it, honeys."

He wondered how long this last spurt had taken him. He glanced through the peephole and did a double take. He lifted his head and checked the angle of the beam. It struck his worktable at a thirty-degree angle from the floor. The sun was low in the eastern sky. It was morning. A *new* morning, twenty-four hours or so from the morning that seemed only moments ago, when he had helped Popeye escape from his honeys.

A new morning. The morning of his eighth day in the schoolhouse.

Kellerman shook his head. Nearly a finished automobile in less than eight days — was it possible? He laughed. "Hell, even God rested on the seventh day, honeys."

He shook his head a second time. Had he done all this, the major body assembly, in a single day? Or had he worked round the clock twice? He eyed the automobile again, skeptically this time, as if he expected it to dissolve before him. It was strange — he felt *good,* alive and alert.

"Shot, better take a shot now. Better safe than sorry."

In his excitement he didn't even glance at the insulin level in the vial. After the shot, after the twinge and the burning

sensation had spread throughout his body, even after the cold
Ravioli-Os he forced down his throat, he felt great.

He took another look at the automobile. Another few days
and his project would be finished. The Model 18 would be
ready to take its place with the other automobiles in his personal history. Only this one would not be lined up outside
with the rest. It would remain right here, in the schoohouse
workshop were he had built it. He smiled. When everything
else was finished, and in perfect working order, the very last
step would be to paint the body. Strawberry red.

You can't relive the past, Frank.

The voice seemed to come from behind Kellerman, from
the hum inside the north wall. He didn't bother to turn
around to answer it.

"I ain't trying to," he said calmly, still gazing at the Model
18. "You never understood why I kept all them old cars
under that tin roof, so you'll never understand this
one, either."

Kellerman stepped over to his worktable and sat down in
the swivel chair. He stared through the peephole at the cars
lined up beneath the tin roof. In his mind's eye he filled in
the missing car, the first Model 18.

"Magic, chaos, hope," he said, checking them off.
"Then what?"

His gaze locked on the fourth car in the line, the third
beneath the tin roof: the old blue GMC pickup, the Jimmie
Truck.

"This stage is tough to name, honeys," he said, staring
at the battered pickup but remembering the trim blue 1954
GMC he'd bought new at the peak of his prospects and his
success when the garage, his family, his whole life seemed
to be on track.

"This one's tough to name," he repeated, "because it's

really two stages in one.''

And they came virtually at the same time, in 1955, when he taught both Curly and Babe to drive. Joy and sorrow. No. Those words weren't quite right. Well, *joy* was right enough. That's what he'd felt with Curly, four years old then, sitting on his lap in the cab of the GMC, holding onto the big blue steering wheel, a wheel as big to Curly as the wheel of a tall ship was to Kellerman. Just the two of them sailing the seas of Kellerman's five acres, round and round the house, the schoolhouse, and the propane tank. *OK, let's make Jimmie go left.*

Yes, it was joy he had felt teaching Curly to drive. But teaching Babe had been something else.

She'd always been afraid of driving, and of cars in general, since the first time Kellerman coaxed her into the passenger seat of the purple Prince of Windsor.

Come on, Babe. You know I'll take care of you.

I trust you, Frank. But is it really safe?

Safe? This is a straight-8!

He drove the streets of West Kansas City — the muscle part of town, the docks, factories, and stockyards — waving to old friends while Babe hung on for dear life.

You always have to suck on that dash like it's a big tit? he fumed, embarrassed when Ninny and Yanny Yorkovich suggested that Lucky's new girlfriend looked like she might die of fright.

Slow down, she pleaded. And he did.

She liked the Hudson better. It was bigger, heavier, seemed slower and safer. Still, she was frightened whenever Kellerman changed lanes, pulled into traffic, or tried to pass another car.

Please *slow down,* she'd beg.

I'm going so fucking slow now we'll never get there, he'd answer.

Kellerman considered himself a master driver as well as mechanic — he'd never gotten a ticket — and Babe's constant whimpering drove him crazy. Her fears were irrational, even destructive, he decided. She had the same scared mouse look he'd seen in her eyes when she was running the stuffer on the Nabisco cookie line. But that wasn't the real Babe, he believed. He remembered the cool, confident way she'd walked barefoot over the lawn around the old willow tree in Penn Valley Park. Why couldn't she be like that all the time?

In the sixth year of their marriage he decided to do something about her fear of automobiles. He decided to teach her to drive.

First they had a talk. *Life's not supposed to be a damn walk in the park,* he began uncertainly, then noticed she was staring at her feet. Look *at me, damn it!*

She did not, but he took her hand and lowered his voice before going on. *Somewhere inside you,* he groped, *there's another, stronger person trying to get out. I want to see that person. I want to hear her talk, watch her move. And I want her to look me right in the eye!* He paused hopefully. *You know what I mean?*

Babe lifted her eyes for an instant. *I think so.*

He decided he would teach her to drive the GMC.

We've got two cars, she'd protested. *How come I have to drive a truck?*

Because it's higher off the ground; you can see the road better. In truth, he was afraid she might wreck the Hudson. *Besides, any woman who can drive a truck won't be afraid to drive anything else.*

To his surprise, she accepted this logic.

Well, let's get going, she said and climbed into the cab of the GMC. He taught her the basics — steering, synchronizing gas and clutch pedals — in the yard. She was slow but determined. After a week of yard practice he let her drive on dirt roads, sitting right beside her in the cab, ready to grab the wheel or stomp the brake. Finally one Saturday night she was ready to solo.

He waited until nearly sunset, then drove her out to a dirt road north of the Canadian River. *No cops, no farmers, nobody at all on this road of an evening,* he said brightly. Babe kept her eyes on the twisting road ahead, following the ruts carved into the red earth.

He stopped at the bottom of a valley next to the river. *Just take Jimmie up to the top of the hill and turn around,* he said and gave the wheel an encouraging thump as he stepped out of the cab. Babe slid over and looked him in the eye before nodding.

Well, let's get going, she said.

He stepped back to give her room. She took a deep breath, then eased off the clutch. Kellerman peered through the rising dust and watched her accelerate the pickup, slowly at first, then faster, shifting smoothly through each gear. Red dust boiled up in a trail behind the tailgate, and the pickup climbed the hill like a rocket lifting off into space. She's coming out of herself now, Kellerman thought, watching the trail of dust rise straight and true. When the truck reached the top of the hill, it kept on going past the spot where he had told her to turn around. Stop! he wanted to shout, but she was too far away. As the pickup topped the hill, the last rays of the sun caught the tailgate for an instant, making it sparkle through the dust cloud, only to drop out of sight, like a falling star. Kellerman felt a chill sweep through his body then, as if he were watching something disappear from his life. The pickup returned a few minutes later, but the feeling did not go away.

"It wasn't sorrow," Kellerman said to the bees. "It was more like *fear.*"

Fear of what? he asked himself now. Fear of change, maybe. Or fear of the new strength she was developing — though he would come to rely on her strength, her prodding and carping, as the years passed. He understood that now.

"Most of that happened later," Kellerman mused aloud. "In the next stage." He stared through the peephole at the fourth automobile beneath the tin roof, the fifth in the complete line of his history, the car he liked to look at least — though it was clearly the most beautiful — the sleek Studebaker Silver Hawk, the car he'd bought new in 1956 when he thought he was still a comer, thought he'd already arrived. He bought the Studebaker strictly for status. Five years later, in the awful summer of 1961, he drove the Studebaker to Afton the day he abandoned his wife and son.

"Shame," Kellerman said.

And having said it, he moved on, to the last automobile in the carport, the sixth stage of his personal history: the dented, ugly, dead mushroom-colored '60 Corvair sedan. The car Ralph Nadar called unsafe at any speed. The car Kellerman bought just to drive to his humiliating job at the capitol — janitor on the maintenance crew. The car he had driven almost every day for nearly twenty years in the longest, most depressing stage of his life. The downhill stage.

He recalled only one incident from those years when he had actually tried to turn things around, to get back on track, if only for a moment. It had cost him his driver's license.

Three years ago, a week before the State of Oklahoma officially retired him, he was driving home from the capitol when he saw Ed Looper's pickup approaching from the south, from Yukon. Looper was probably on some errand for Vukovich. Looper had stayed on at the garage after the bank took it away from Kellerman. For reasons he could never determine, Vukovich kept Looper in line the way Kellerman never could. Together, Vukovich and Looper had made the garage profitable. In fact, Vukovich owned garages in El Reno and Bethany now as well. Vukovich was still a comer and Ed Looper was his right-hand man.

The sight of Looper's pickup, alone and vulnerable, dead ahead, triggered an old eagerness in Kellerman. A sudden strength flowed through his arms to the steering wheel. When Looper's new Ford half-ton was within a quarter mile, Kellerman swung the Corvair into the middle of the road.

He often wondered what must have gone through Looper's mind the instant he saw the Corvair angle toward him. It must have been more than shock, more than fear. For although years had passed since they'd spoken, Looper knew Kellerman and all his automobiles, and he'd always given both a wide berth. This time he could not: flood ditches, filled with four feet of overflow water from the Canadian River, ran along each side of the road, cutting off any escape. Looper hit his brakes but it was too late to stop, and what good would that do anyway? For the Corvair picked up speed as the strength in Kellerman's arms flowed down to his right foot and he jammed the accelerator to the floor. Looper began to zig-zag the pickup, but the Corvair had radar, zeroing in on its target. At fifty feet Kellerman caught a white glint of terror in Looper's eyes. Then Looper did the only thing he could do. He swerved the pickup into the right-side ditch, splashing up a double geyser of brown river water.

Ha! Kellerman cried and drove through the spray beaming, feeling better than he had in years — until he heard a wailing sound and saw the flashing blue lights of Eddie Hacker's patrol car in his rearview mirror.

Looper was unhurt. The judge fined Kellerman five hundred dollars and took his license. A green piece of paper allowed him to drive to work for one more week until the state retired him for good. The day they laid him off was the last time he'd driven the Corvair.

"It was Curly give me the word to describe that stage," Kellerman said aloud as he sat motionless in the swivel chair. "Day he left home for good, left Oklahoma for good. 'Because people waste their lives here,' he said. It was me he meant. 'If the shoe fits,' he said. And then he said, '*Despair.* That's what I feel in this house.' He said that to me, his father that raised him. Despair!"

Kellerman squinted through the peephole at the battered gray Corvair. "The shoe fit."

He sank back in the chair and thought about the line of automobiles, the six stages of his history. From magic to despair, he thought. That summed it up. A history of failure.

But now he'd built another Model 18, the last in line, the seventh stage. What stage was this? he wondered. He hadn't begun his project with failure in mind, and he was *not* going to fail at this, by god. But what stage was this, after all these others? *You can't relive the past,* the voice from the wall had said. But that wasn't his purpose at all.

"I never could make you understand," he whispered. "Neither you nor the boy."

So what now, Frank?

That was the real question, he had to admit, though he didn't even bother to acknowledge the voice that had seemed to come, this time, from the east wall. Was there a word to describe what he was doing, now? He'd always had trouble with words, had never been able to say the words he really needed to say — to Babe, to Curly, to anyone. He had no words when words most needed to be said.

And now he needed a word. He opened his eyes and looked at the automobile before him. Yes, it was another Model 18, like the one his father had destroyed. But he hadn't built this one to relive the past. This automobile was something more than the first one. Not better, exactly, but *more* — an automobile beyond any other in his life. The last in line, the seventh stage.

What now? Kellerman doubled his fists; he strained. If there was a word that meant more than going back, more than starting over, more than going past what was, if there was a word that meant all those things, and more, then Kellerman didn't know it.

"Magic, chaos, hope, joy and fear, shame, despair — then what? What now?" Kellerman asked.

And he leaped from his chair in wonder, as the answer, or so it seemed, arrived with a loud knock at the door.

16

KELLERMAN STAGGERED, grabbed the edge of the worktable and took a slow, deep breath to calm himself.

"Who the hell is it *now*?"

"It's me, Dad. I'm back."

"Back!" Back from where? Kellerman wanted to scream. Back from Yukon? Back from Hawaii? Back from the past?

"I visited Mom this morning."

The words froze Kellerman for a long moment. "You what?"

"I took some day lillies out. And a peperomia to plant beside the marker. Peperomias are house plants, but they were her favorite, you know."

I know! Kellerman wanted to shout.

"The plot's in bad shape, Dad. Grass and weeds a foot high. You haven't kept it up. You haven't been out there at all."

It was true. Kellerman's head drooped as he considered this fact. Then he clenched his fists and looked up at the door. "When you're dead, you're dead."

"What? What did you say?"

"Never mind. Where the hell have you been?"

Curly's voice seemed to harden. "Talking to people. About you and what you're doing locked up in there with those bees. I talked to Charley Bluefire. I talked to Orville. I talked to Ed Hacker and Looper and Vukovich and old man Loudermilk. I even talked to Merle Coats, out at the capitol. They all say the same thing, Dad. They all say you've gone off your nut, like the Crow Woman."

Kellerman flinched.

"Funny thing is," Curly went on, "I don't believe them. Most of them had no idea what you're doing in there. Charley knows, I think, but he's not talking. Vukovich said you stole some kind of motor from him. Says you're doing something to it in the schoolhouse. Is that it, Dad? Is that the game? Are you playing mechanic again?"

Playing mechanic! Kellerman rolled his eyes toward the ceiling and swung his fists at his sides.

"No," Curly went on when Kellerman didn't answer. "I've decided that whatever it is, you know exactly what you're doing in there. And I've got to find out what it is."

Kellerman stared at the door. "What do you mean, 'got to'?"

For the next few moments Kellerman heard only the hum. He sensed his son was bracing himself, getting ready to say something.

"All right, Dad. Here's what I'm going to do. I know you're not going to open that door, so I'm going to tell you something. And then I'm going to do what I have to."

"Have to? What have to?" Kellerman stammered.

"First I want to talk a minute," Curly replied. "I want to tell you something about 'The Dream Game' — and all those TV commercials I'm making now."

"I know all I want to know," Kellerman said. He started to turn his back on the door and slipped, heels swishing out from under him like a clown taking a pratfall. He fell backward, toward the automobile, and caught himself with the heels of his palms. It was the wet floor. He'd noticed the water seeping under the door. Damn ice bags, he thought dimly. Are they still out there?

"Are you all right? What's happening in there?"

Kellerman's bruised foot hurt like hell now. He staggered to his feet. "I'm fine, just fine. Why don't you just go away and leave me be."

Kellerman thought he heard Curly sigh.

"No, Dad. We've never really talked, and I guess there's no point in starting now; but I'm going to say this one thing so maybe you'll understand why I'm going to do what I'm going to do."

"Do *what*?" Kellerman demanded.

"I'll tell you in a minute. Look, I know you think I don't give a damn about all those people that got cheated — "

"I don't care about any of that. That's all — "

"But I *do* care, damn it. Just listen, will you? For years now, even before all the trouble with 'The Dream Game,' I knew something was wrong — with me. With what I was doing. Not legally or morally . . . everything I did on that show I did in good faith, whether you believe it or not. But something began to bother me, right at the peak, right when the show was most successful. At first I couldn't pinpoint it. I mean, hundreds of people were winning their dream trips, and millions more were watching them win. And I was getting rich, a little. But there was something else. I *liked* that show, really liked it, because I thought I was doing something good. I mean, important. I thought I was keeping dreams alive for millions of people. For the players, sure, but mostly for all the people who watched. Millions of them.''

"Yeah, you were hot shit, all right. Your mother loved that fucking game." Kellerman sat down in the swivel chair and hung his head.

"Let me *finish*, will you? Just let me say something for once.''

I never stopped you from talking, Kellerman wanted to say. Tell me one time, since you were ten years old, when you ever had more than two words to say to *me*? And now you want to give me a fucking speech? But Kellerman said nothing as he waited for his son to go on. He had to admit the voice he was hearing through the door didn't sound like the phony, oh-so-smooth voice he'd heard on the TV. Was this Curly's real voice or just another fake one? How, Kellerman wondered, am I supposed to tell?

"All right," Curly finally went on. "For a long time I thought everything was great. Then I started noticing something in the faces of the players. I wasn't sure about it at first. I thought maybe it was my imagination. But it wasn't. You could see it in every face, if you were there, live, on the set with them. I couldn't describe it. I didn't know what it was. I just knew they all had it. They were all the same. And then it hit me. That was it: *They were all the same.* Exactly. No matter who they were or where they were from — Nebraska, Yonkers, Big Sur, black, white, oriental — all the same. Same exact look in their eyes. Same hope, same joy, same disappointment. Win or lose. Exactly the same.''

So everybody's a shit hog, Kellerman thought. So what? Welcome to the world, boy.

"Always the same feelings shining in their eyes," Curly continued. "And all on the surface, like there was nothing at all *behind* their eyes, inside their heads. Just dark. Nothing. Like on the inside none of them was really alive.''

At these words Kellerman's own eyes swelled. He sat erect. ''That's not your fault —''

''I decided it was the game that made them look that way,'' Curly went on without pause. ''Once I realized that, I wanted out. I want you to understand that, Dad. Way before the scandal, I wanted out.''

''It doesn't matter,'' Kellerman replied in a soothing voice. ''Like I told your mother, I forgave you for all that a long time ago.''

Curly's voice exploded through the door: ''I don't want your goddamn forgiveness! That's not why I'm here!''

Kellerman's face flushed a deep red. So I was told, he thought. Then said: ''Why *are* you here?''

''Because you *wanted* me here, goddamn you. But I'll tell you something else: I've got my own reasons now.''

Kellerman felt something cold stab the back of his neck. He shivered for a moment, then shook it off.

''And I'll tell you one more thing,'' Curly said. ''Last time I was home, after Mom died, I could of used some help from you.''

''What kind of help?''

''I'd lost everything,'' Curly said. ''The show, my reputation, my future. Everything. I thought I had, anyway. When I started that deal to make airline commercials I was gambling people could separate me from what went wrong with 'The Dream Game.' I was gambling enough of them could still trust *me*. Well, it looks like they can't. The spots have been running a couple of weeks now, and nobody's buying. The airline's going to cancel the deal, and who can blame them? Because I'll tell you something else making those commericals taught me: It wasn't really the game that made everybody look like they were dead inside. It was me.''

Kellerman leaped to his feet and shook his head vigorously. ''You didn't make the world the way it is . . .''

''I made my own part of it,'' Curly interrupted. ''But that's not the point. A year ago I could have used some help from you. I was starting over. I needed to *talk* to you is all. And I tried. But you were so damn . . . ''

Kellerman felt something welling up inside him. ''I'm sorry . . . ''

''Here's what I wanted to say then,'' Curly finally continued. ''I thought we had something in common, Dad. I thought you felt the same way about your life as I did then. That you'd wasted it, ever since you lost the garage business. But you kept going. Even after you got diabetes. Till the day you retired. I wanted to know what it was that kept you going — because I needed to keep going too. You understand?''

Kellerman tried to speak but made only a rasping sound.

''That's all I fucking wanted to know!'' Curly shouted. ''Not too much to ask, I thought. But you wouldn't talk to me. Wouldn't say a fucking thing. They buried Mom and you sent me packing. Then a year later I get this call from Charley Bluefire who says you've moved into the goddamn schoolhouse with the goddamn bees. So here I am, Dad. But I don't expect you to tell me what it's all about. No sir. No way.''

Kellerman had sunk back into the swivel chair. He turned and looked at his automobile, then back at the door.

''Look,'' he stammered. ''I want to talk to *you*, too. I just can't. Not right now. Not today, I mean. I've got to finish something, or I never will. Stay around a while. Please. Stay in the house, in your old room. I'll finish this thing in a few days. Then I'll come out and we'll talk.''

"No we won't."

"What?" Kellerman leaned forward. "What do you mean?"

"You're not going to tell me anything," Curly said flatly. "You never have. I"m going to have to see for myself."

Something bright and cold flashed through Kellerman. He rose from the chair. "I'm not coming out. Not yet."

"I don't want you to come out. I'm coming in."

"No!" Kellerman looked around the room at his honeys, thousands of them flying from hive to pan, pan to hive. "You *can't* come in. The bees — "

Curly laughed sarcastically. "Come on, Dad. You can't keep it secret. You *want* me to break in there. That's the game, isn't it?"

Kellerman waved his palms at the door. "No. There's no game . . ." He heard a clunking noise, as if Curly had dropped something heavy on the steps outside the door.

Blam!

The sound lifted Kellerman a full inch into the air. "What! What are you doing?"

Blam!

The oak door shuddered. Bees rose from the pans, from the piles of sawdust, from the boxes, from the sink, from the automobile.

Blam!

"Stop! You don't know what you're doing! The bees!"

It was a sledgehammer, Kellerman realized. The one he'd left in the garage across the yard. The heavy oak shook with each blow. Sawdust puffed from piles and cracks in the floor. And bees, more and more bees, filled the air. Kellerman watched them pour out of the cracks in the walls. The hum swelled, deepened.

Blam!

Kellerman leaped for the air hose. When the door gave way, his honeys would swarm on Curly. With no canvas to protect him, the boy would have no chance. Kellerman had to stop him, *now,* any way he could.

The room was nearly black with bees, a roaring cloud blocking out all light. Kellerman felt the electric buzz of his honeys' flight, a hundred thousand wings beating together, as he blasted air through the crack.

Then a scream pierced the roar. Kellerman fell away from the wall as the scream faded quickly away from the school-house, across the yard, and vanished behind the slam of a door.

Kellerman collapsed on the floor.

Minutes later, as he lay on the bare wood, the dark cloud above him began to dissolve; the buzzing roar in his ears faded. As his honeys returned to work, flying from hive to pan to hive, his son's words rang like a clear bell inside his head:

You can't keep it secret. You want me to break in.

It was true, he realized. He wanted Curly to break in here. But not *now.* Not yet. Not when his honeys were still here. Not until years from now when even he was long gone.

Kellerman looked up at his project, his automobile. Almost finished. The last in line, the seventh stage, the stage for which he had no name.

A monument to your first and only love.

Kellerman nodded. "You're right this time, you goddamn bitch. It's a fucking monument to me."

Bees circled his head, but Kellerman paid them no mind. He swallowed, then took a deep breath. A moment later he reached for something beside him, then crawled to his feet, toward the automobile.

With the strength of his heart and soul, Kellerman raised the ax.

17

KELLERMAN SLUMPED on the edge of the army cot. The ax lay at his feet.

For a long time he did not look up at the battered wreck before him. He knew why his eyes remained fixed on the floor, though he tried not to think about it. Looking up would mean facing a question, the question that echoed like the dull thud of a hammer inside his brain: What now?

Finally, he raised his head, focused his eyes on the wreck. The sight reminded him of the old black and white films of bombed and torpedoed battleships he used to watch on "Victory at Sea." Great ships like the *Bismark*, blasted and shelled to ruin, still afloat for the moment, but clearly dead.

What now?

Kellerman heaved a great breath and turned his eyes away from the wreck to columns of boxes, irrelevant now, and the tools and parts scattered over the floor. He looked at his worktable and the boarded-up windows cutting off the light. He hadn't thought beyond this stage, beyond his project, now terminated. There was nothing to keep him in the schoolhouse any longer. He could leave right now, this minute. If he walked out now, maybe he could persuade Curly that there was nothing in here worth seeing. Not anymore. The boy hadn't left, Kellerman was sure of that. No, he was somewhere in the house across the yard. Stung, or maybe just frightened, by the raging bees. And he still wanted in this schoolhouse, still intended to get in, somehow. Kellerman was sure of that, too. The boy needed his father. And there was nothing to stop Kellerman from going to him, right now. He could unlatch that door this instant and just walk on out.

Kellerman imagined himself climbing to his feet, picking his way around the wreck, over the debris-strewn floor to the door. Then opening it, the sunlight drenching him like a bucket of luminous paint. His honeys would go on with their work, never missing a beat, not even after he had gone, when the pans of sugar water were empty and the grains of cedar dust had all been carried away. Eventually his honeys would find their sweet food elsewhere, in the flowers and blossoming trees outside the schoolhouse. Their search would take them further and further from the hive until they finally returned to dance the wag-tail dance deep inside the dark honeycombed walls.

The thought of his honeys searching for sweet food made the space beneath Kellerman's tongue begin to tingle. He could feel the old familiar craving coming back now. His mouth began to water, his skin to itch. He looked over at the boxes of C & H sugar stacked on top of the air compressor.

He reminded himself he could leave now. He could just open that big door and walk right out and leave all those boxes of sugar behind. Or he could tear the boxes open first and pour the sugar out, pour it all over everything — the floor, the wreck, the tools. He could give his honeys one last treat, a sugar-coated workshop. He could make it snow sugar.

Or he could just leave *now*, before the craving became too strong, before it became irresistible. He could get up, open that door, and get out of here. Now.

Let's go, he told himself, and swallowed to drench with saliva the tingle creeping down his throat. He swallowed hard, dry. His tongue made a cracking sound, and the tingle crept further down his throat. Let's go, he told himself, but his feet did not move.

At least he could give himself a shot. The needle lay ready on his worktable. But as he looked at it, the needle grew longer, thicker, sharper. Strength, he prayed. He thought of Babe, giving him the shots for two years, every day, because the needle scared him so. He thought of himself the day after Babe died, taking the needle in his own hands, inserting it into the vial, feeling it puncture the top like it was his own skin.

He filled the syringe to the correct level, though he could hardly bear to look, found the right vein in his arm, one thin line of blue, and inserted the needle quickly, jabbing it in, forcing the pain and the nausea, but getting it over with. In a minute he felt the itch begin to burn away. The nausea passed too, replaced by a gray, empty feeling. He sank into the swivel chair, head back, mouth open, arms dangling helplessly at his sides.

What now?

He thought about it. What came after the seventh stage? Another stage? He turned in the chair to look at the wreck, the metal dented and warped, then shook his head.

"No more automobiles, honeys. This is the end of the line."

Kellerman slumped over his worktable. Get up, he told himself. Leave this place.

He did not move.

A moment later he heard a sound penetrate the humming walls. He jerked up. Curly? Kellerman struggled to his feet, dizzy and disoriented, looking around for the air hose, listening for another sound to pierce the hum. And then he heard it:

Haaa, haaa.

Kellerman sank onto the edge of the army cot and laughed a heaving, humorless laugh. "Mabel!" he cried. "Finally! I've been waiting for you, you sorry old crow. What can I do for you?"

As if in answer, a word rang through the stone:

Hubert.

The word silenced Kellerman for a long moment. What, after all, could he answer? What could he say to the loony bird who'd haunted this schoolhouse for more than thirty years? What the hell could he say to an eighty-one-year-old woman he had tried to trap like a rat and had very nearly lured to her death? What could he say, he wondered now, to a woman who, after more than sixty years, still came to this place to find her Hubert?

"He's not here," Kellerman said.

He waited for a response but heard nothing else through the hum.

"Did you hear me, Mabel? He's not here."

Still no answer through the door, but Kellerman knew the old woman had not left.

"Listen to me, Mabel," Kellerman said, his voice rising now. "There's nothing in this old schoolhouse for you." Or me, either, he thought. "Your Hubert's gone, Mabel. And he ain't coming back. You hear me?"

The answer floated through the oak like a prayer:

Hubert.

Kellerman sighed and stared down at his feet. When he looked up again his fists were clenched. He glared at the door, then screamed, "Hubert is dead!"

When the words had stopped echoing in his own head, Kellerman listened for a reply. He stepped up next to the door but once again heard only the hum.

"You're *free*, Mabel," he said then. "Fly away, girl! Fly away while you still can."

When he heard no response, Kellerman pressed his ear against the oak. To his surprise, he heard the *pat, pat, pat* of footsteps moving quickly away over the grass. The Crow Woman was gone.

A moment later he discovered why, as another sound reached his ears through the oak. More footsteps. Slower, heavier steps. The same steps he had heard circling the schoolhouse before. Measured steps, like the steps of his father, drunk and mean, climbing dark stairs in heavy leather boots, to the bedrooms where Mother and Dottie and he lay waiting in fear. Powerful steps, approaching the schoolhouse, coming right up to the door.

And Kellerman knew them. He took a step backward and faced the door.

"Hello, King," he said.

18

THE KING OF SWING had the biggest voice in the world.

"*Time,* Honker!" the voice boomed through the oak.

"What?" Kellerman rocked back, then recoiled in the chair. The force of the King of Swing's voice had nearly knocked him over. "What did you say?"

"Here to tell you 'bout *time,* Honker. *Free* time, *your* time, time you done paid for."

The oak door seemed to shudder from the strain of carrying the King of Swing's heavy bass voice. A voice louder, deeper than the hum of fifty thousand bees through stone and plaster.

"What do you mean, time?" Kellerman's voice was tiny, a whisper. He shouted to make himself heard. "Time for what?"

"Time to do your thing, man. Whatever it be."

Kellerman felt more than heard the King of Swing's voice. Felt the oak groan, the strong door quake. He tried to ignore the power and keep his own voice calm.

"Thing? What thing?"

"The thing you be makin' in there. I know you're buildin' something *big*. I hear you day and night. I hear you and them bees, workin' and buzzin' and buildin' — until this mornin'. This mornin' come a different sound. This mornin' I hear you chop it all down, Honker. Then I hear everything stop. That's when I know I need to come to your door and discuss with you 'bout *time*."

Kellerman shook his head in bewilderment. "I don't understand. You scared my ass half to death more than once prowling around out there. What do you think you're doing, listening in on me?"

"I know you be on the needle," the King of Swing went on. "Charley Bluefire told me. I *know* 'bout the needle, Honker. I know what it *do*. The needle *make* you *do*, the needle *make* you *see*. Needle made me see the devil himself once. That's right, I saw the devil that night you hauled me down that rotunda. You remember that night, Honker? You remember?"

Kellerman took a quick breath. "I remember."

"I saw the devil, Honker. Up side that room by the big star. He's blood red, that devil. He's big, bad, red, and nasty. He breathed the fire of fear into me that night, Honker. He come to tell me I got no more time."

Kellerman remembered the King of Swing's huge body convulsing in the shafts of sunlight streaming through the leaded glass around the Great Seal.

"But he come too *soon*, Honker. That devil, he's red, he's big and bad, but he don't tell the *time*, Honker. Everybody's time *come*, for sure, but that red devil, he don't wear the watch, he don't set the date."

Behind the oak door, Kellerman frowned. "What's all that got to do with me?"

The answer made him take another breath.

"I kicked it, Honker. Horse. I kicked it for good."

Kellerman bit his lip before answering. "You mean heroin?"

"I *kicked* it. I kicked that horse so he don't ride me no more. I kicked that red devil right between his red legs, right in his red nuts."

Kellerman swallowed. "I'm glad you're off the needle, King, but — "

"I *know* 'bout the needle, man. Needle made me see the devil himself, but I kicked his ass, Honker. No more needle, no more red devil."

"My needle is different, King," Kellerman tried to explain. "It's a regular disease I've got. Every day I need to . . ."

"I *know* 'bout *need*, Honker. What you be needin' now is *time*. Devil come round for you, you need time to *kick* him, time to kick him right back where he come from. You need time like you give me that day in the rotunda. And you got it, man. All the fuckin' time you need."

"Time for what?"

"Time to *build*, Honker. Whatever you been buildin' in there day and night. Days now, I been hearin' the buildin' sounds. But this morning a different sound come to me. A choppin', smashin' sound. *Givin' up* kinda sound. Like you seen the devil. Like he told you got no more time."

Kellerman said nothing. He felt sweat begin to bead above his eyebrows.

"But you *got* time, man! I'll be seein' to that personally. Charley Bluefire, he say Honker don't want no interruptions in his perch. No visitors. So from now on, I'ma be your doorman. No more visitors today. No more visitors tomorrow. *Time*, Honker. You got all you need."

Kellerman's voice rose now. "I don't *need* a goddamn nigger for a guard dog, you hear? You don't understand — I'm *through* in here. It's *over*. I'll be coming out of here directly.''

The King of Swing's thunderous voice softened slightly. ''Whatever you want, Honker. You got all the time in the world. I'm gonna be around till that door opens. But let me ask you just one thing. You think it's so easy?''

Kellerman frowned. ''Think *what's* easy?''

''Comin' out, man. Devil climb up side your perch, ain't so easy a trip down.''

''I can come out of here any time I make my mind up to.''

''I do believe it,'' the King of Swing said. ''I believe it, 'cause you always been good in the clutch, Honker. You ain't no choker. Ain't no choker saved me from that red devil up top that rotunda. Ain't no choker saved Popeye from them bees.''

Kellerman raised his eyebrows. ''How do you know about Popeye?''

The King of Swing laughed a laugh that made the walls shake. ''Popeye, he's my seeing-eye dog. My x-ray vision.''

Kellerman nodded. Of course. Who else could have scared Popeye enough to make him crawl into a room full of bees? ''What'd he tell you?''

The King of Swing laughed again. ''Popeye tell me you been buildin' a giant *bee* in there. A super hornet! He say you got a factory with two million workers. He say Honker fly through the air like he was a bee too!''

Kellerman laughed. Popeye the snitch! Popeye the sneak! Ha!

The King of Swing's voice turned serious again. ''I got to back off now, Honker. Leave you some room to work.''

Kellerman started to say he didn't need any room, but the big bass voice buried his own.

''That devil, Honker, he's big and red. You build you the biggest, baddest bee you can. Sting that devil dead. You got the time. I'll see to that."

Kellerman listened to the King of Swing's heavy, even steps retreat into the distance. He was headed west, Kellerman could tell, toward the patch of high weeds just across the road.

"You're wasting your time!" Kellerman yelled.

For a long time, exactly how long he had no idea, Kellerman just sat. He chewed his lip and the thought returned to him that he needed to talk to Curly. To do that, Kellerman realized, he would have to come out, for the King of Swing would keep Curly and everyone else away from the door.

Kellerman looked over at the latch bolt.

Go. Get up, go.

He remained in the chair. He wondered what held him there. Inertia? Fear? The boy needs me, he told himself. I've got to talk to him, say something.

But what?

"God*damn* it!" he cried aloud. "I'm sixty-five years old. I ought to have somthing to say to my own son."

Still he did not move. Instead, he listened to the steady, monotonous hum, as if expecting to hear any moment a low, mocking voice telling him something he already knew all too well: *You've let him down again.*

But only the relentless hum reached his ears. After a time he tried to rise again. Exhaustion crushed him back into the chair.

Relax a minute, he told himself. Get your strength back. Then get up out of this chair and *leave this place.*

As he sat he felt a strange numbness begin to grow inside his chest, then his left hand, then his right, then both feet, as if his body were slowly falling asleep, part by part. He looked at the syringe on his worktable and wondered if it was time for another shot.

No, just had one.

The numbness continued to spread, up his arms, down his legs. Got to do something, he thought. Got to get the blood going.

He reached down and picked up a ballpeen hammer off the floor. What now? The numbness seemed to reach his head along with the question. He felt the spot behind his eyes grow fuzzy and light. He stood up by reflex. Got to get going, he told himself. But by the time he had crossed the room to the automobile, his head did not know what his hands were doing. He did not feel his hands lift the battered hood, unpin its hinges, and raise the dented shroud off the wreck. The metal creaked and groaned as he flattened the hood out on the floor. The first blow of the ballpeen hammer rang through the old schoolhouse like a bell calling children back to class, but Kellerman didn't hear it. He didn't feel the sting of the hammer in his fist as he pounded out the dents.

If he felt anything at all, it was the pulsing hum of his honeys hard at work.

As time passed, Kellerman became more aware of what was happening. He heard hammering, saw dents flattening, felt bends unbending. He welded cracked metal together, applied body putty, filed ragged places smooth. He replaced broken plugs, redrilled holes, refit seams. He saw a wreck unwrecking, an automobile reassembling.

Why? he asked himself. Why am I doing this again?

He had no answer. He knew only that the wooden handle of the ballpeen hammer fit snugly in the palm of his hand. That his fingers curled perfectly around the smooth shining steel of the ratchet wrench. That the muscles in his two arms flexed and relaxed in synchronized motion as he grasped the crowbar and applied leverage to crumpled metal.

"Why?" he asked aloud. He listened carefully then, but no answer returned.

He kept working. As he welded, hammered, and filed, he couldn't tell how much time was passing, nor even whether it was day or night. He paid no attention to the peephole — until a quiet moment, almost a pause in the hum, when he heard a car pull up outside.

He looked through the hole and saw in the morning light (which morning? he wondered, which day?) that it was a police car. Kellerman leaned back in the swivel chair and waited, but no footsteps approached the schoolhouse. Instead, he heard the voices of several men arguing. Then one voice louder, bigger than all the others, a voice so big and powerful it seemed to swallow up the other voices. Finally there was silence. He looked through the peephole and saw the police car was gone.

Kellerman understood what had happened outside. He had been given more time, just as the King of Swing had promised. But the thought of more time to work made him think of something else, a feeling, sharp and familiar, beneath his tongue. The craving for something sweet.

He opened the icebox and withdrew the vial of insulin. He then inserted the needle into the rubber top of the vial and drew back the handle on the syringe to suck out just the right amount, thirty units, of insulin.

He stared at the scale on the syringe, then blinked. He couldn't find the mark. Damn light in here. He turned and held the syringe up in the light, close to his eyes. Something cold seemed to prick his stomach. The syringe was empty. It had filled only with air. He looked down at the vial. It too was empty. He was out of insulin.

No.

If he had stayed calm and taken time to think, he might have realized that he was in no immediate danger. All he had to do was to open the door in front of him and walk out. Across the yard, in the abandoned house, was a telephone. Maybe Curly was there, too. He could drive Kellerman into Yukon and get insulin.

But the dry, tangy itch beneath Kellerman's tongue was growing, spreading into the rest of his mouth, then down his throat and into his chest, out through his arms and hands, to the tips of his fingers. He closed his eyes and held his breath to try to make the urge go away.

Please. No.

Then Kellerman's eyes popped open and he saw the sacks of sugar piled on top of the air compressor.

No. I won't.

Kellerman's tongue began to throb and sting. His skin burned. No. No. He walked toward the air compressor.

As he reached the sugar an idea formed in his mind: a chance. One chance. He bent all his strength, all his will, toward the thought in his head.

Do it. Now.

With both arms he grabbed the sacks of sugar, all of them — fifteen or twenty — and lifted them off the compressor. He hardly felt the weight as he staggered across the room and dropped the sacks beside the toilet. The nerves in his fingers sizzled as he ripped open the first sack and poured its contents into the water. Then he pulled the handle on the toilet and watched the water swirl until the bowl swallowed up the grainy cloud in a series of gargling gulps.

One by one, Kellerman ripped open the sacks and poured the sugar down the toilet until the last grain was flushed away.

Then he weakened and collapsed back into the swivel chair. Panting, scratching his arms, legs, and neck. Then his arms were too weak, too heavy to hold up. They drooped at his sides as the burning itch roared over his skin, slick with sweat. He closed his eyes. "Strength," he wheezed.

He reopened his eyes and stared at the crack in the wall, where bee after bee buzzed in and out. Kellerman stared through the crack, deep into the wall at something he could not see.

"Babe," he whispered.

It was the hum that finally carried him. It seeped into his skin, soothing the itch as he sagged in the swivel chair. The beat of tiny wings lifted him off the seat and carried him back to the automobile. He grabbed a wrench, bolted bucket seats to their mounts, fit dashboard to frame and firewall, pointed headlights straight ahead. He found strength somehow to wire up the ignition without a hitch. He worked. And worked.

As time passed and the automobile reassembled, it seemed to Kellerman that his strength was lasting longer than it should. He was borrowing the strength and the time somehow. Maybe he could borrow enough to finish.

He did not think about the insulin nor the sugar nor what might be happening outside his workshop. He did not think about the past. His body now seemed to have a will of its own, as if the connection between his own mind and body had been severed. His hands moved independently, it seemed, fitting and tightening metal to metal. He did not understand this, but he accepted it. For whatever reason, he was working again, building his project.

Only one thought kept intruding, reconnecting brain to body, disrupting the smooth movements of his mechanic's hands: *Where was Curly?*

And as more time passed, Kellerman felt something else growing inside himself. Something strange. Neither a thought nor a feeling. Something else. After he attached the cables to the battery, completing the electrical system, he felt it lift him from the automobile and carry him back to the swivel chair. Without knowing why, he leaned forward and looked through the peephole.

It was morning. Which morning, he had no idea. But the morning light made the tall dry bleached grass shine as if the light glowed from the earth itself.

And then he saw it.

Beneath the tin roof of the carport an automobile was missing from the line. The Hudson.

"Where the hell'd it go, honeys?"

Kellerman shook his head, then pressed his eye closer to the peephole to search the yard. An instant later his head snapped back an inch.

The Hudson loomed directly before him, from out of nowhere it seemed, the front of the car facing the schoolhouse. Kellerman felt an eerie sensation as he stared at the Hudson's wide chrome grill, which seemed to spread in a big grin — or was it a leer? — aimed directly at him. Whatever it was, it appeared to be growing, spreading wider as he watched.

Abruptly he realized why. The Hudson was *moving*, picking up speed, barreling straight for the schoolhouse. He gasped. An instant before impact, Kellerman spotted two eyes behind the approaching windshield, two eyes hot with concentration, eyes that saw only one thing, dead ahead. Mickey Mantle's eyes, timing a fastball.

The window exploded in Kellerman's face, propelling him backward into a column of boxes, which toppled onto his head.

When he looked up again, the room he knew so well had vanished. A cloud of bees roared like a thunderhead all around him. Through the dark buzz he could see daylight spilling through the shattered window, a gaping hole above where his worktable was supposed to be. His worktable, he soon discovered, lay on its side across his legs, which were beginning to ache. It was difficult to tell through the swirling cloud of bees, but although the interior plaster walls had been shattered, the stone itself appeared to have held. The cedar planks covering the window had popped off, letting in the light.

The hum inside the room was not a hum anymore but the whining roar of a hurricane. Kellerman leaped in panic as he realized where the storm was heading. He didn't get far. The worktable pinned his legs. He had to pull them slowly, painfully, free. He managed to stand, then stagger toward the window filled with light and bees. Through the window he saw the wrecked Hudson, its hood curled back over the windshield like a dead tongue. Bees swarmed everywhere, but his honeys hadn't yet focused their attack, as they landed on the motor, fenders, and cab. The crumpled hood covered the windshield completely, and Kellerman could not see inside the car, did not *want* to see, but *had* to see. He had to get inside that car *now*, before his honeys found their prey.

He tried to lift his leg to crawl through the window, but pain held him like a trap.

Then something else moved. Something *big*, on the edge of Kellerman's vision, far away from the wreck. A black giant rose from the weeds across the road. The King of Swing seemed to span the road in a single stride. In another he reached the wreck. With powerful hands, he ripped open the driver's side door and pulled out a smaller man, a man who, in Kellerman's eyes, appeared to be only a boy — a thin, nervous boy who, somewhere in the confusion, had lost his Yankee cap.

Instantly bees descended on the two of them as the King of Swing cradled the smaller man, groggy and squirming, in his enormous arms and raced, with giant strides, toward the house.

"Curly!" Kellerman cried.

He tried once more to climb through the window, but couldn't. Then he reeled, dizziness and the pain in his legs overcoming him. More and more bees swarmed around him in a darkening cloud, blotting out the light. The door, he thought, and tried to make his way back through the debris. But the light had disappeared, and he tripped over things he could not see. *The door*, he thought again, but the cloud of bees enveloped him and he turned round and round in confusion. He raised his hands and struck wildly to find the overhead bulb, though it should have been burning already. When his hands brushed the cord, he grabbed the switch, felt a quick, numbing pain — then nothing.

19

THE LIGHT, WHEN it finally returned, illuminated nothing.

A haze, a blur, a sheet of gray. Light tearing through the sheet, silver pouring over gray. Light and sound, a steady whirring sound, humming gray, gray on gray. Then something moving, back and forth overhead, gray spots in a gray sky. And one spot bigger, darker, unmoving. Dead gray moon in a gray sky.

Kellerman blinked and recognized the 200-watt bulb hanging from the ceiling directly above his head. The bulb was scorched black. He took a breath and tried to move. Something else moved, rippled around him. He felt cool, wet — then realized he was lying in a shallow pool of water. He raised his head for a moment and looked around the debris-strewn floor. He squinted — his glasses lost somewhere in the debris — and saw the water was hardly deeper than a sheet, but covered most of the floor. At the base of the oak door he spotted the telltale stain where the water had seeped in.

He sighed and lay back again, looking up at the blackened

light bulb and the bees buzzing through the air flooded
with daylight from the smashed window. He knew what
had happened. Water had leaked under the door from the
bags of melted ice piled outside. When he had reached up
to turn on the overhead light, the current had flowed right
through him to the wet floor. A perfect circuit. Gravity had
saved him.

Kellerman closed his eyes and laughed.

When he looked up again, the light seemed even brighter;
once more he had to squint. He noticed the cloud of bees
had thinned out. The buzzing roar had faded back to a hum.
But not the usual hum. Something was different. Then Kellerman remembered *why* he had grabbed for the bulb, why his
honeys had swarmed, why the sunlight now gushed through
the gaping window into his dazzled eyes.

"Curly!"

Kellerman lurched forward and started to climb to his feet.
The pain — a stabbing, paralyzing pain in his legs — took
him by surprise, spilling him hard onto his knees. He
crashed onto the toppled worktable, the source of his injury,
and hung on.

He looked up, toward the south wall, and gasped.

Before him spread a city of gold. A golden city with golden
towers rising high into the sky. And golden rivers, flowing
down from the sky itself, from the tops of the towers, spilling down their sides, paving the streets with gold, gold on
gold, and golden people with golden wings, climbing the
towers, dancing a golden dance, round and round and round,
flying up into the golden sky.

Kellerman looked on this scene and trembled.

Somewhere deep inside his mind, in the rational part, he
realized that what he saw before him was an illusion.
Somewhere inside his head he knew what the golden city

really was. He knew the actual events that revealed the city to him only now. It was simple. When the Hudson struck the schoolhouse the exterior stone had held, but the impact blasted away the interior plaster, revealing the city behind the wall, the maze of tightly packed honeycomb and the thousands of bees who tended it. The impact had loosened and cracked the comb. Fresh golden honey oozed down the split sides of the comb, down the cellular windows of the towers, pooled around their bases and dripped, layer after layer, onto the floor, gold on gold on gold.

The difference in the hum, he now realized, reflected the discordant sounds of a city disrupted. Normal work had stopped. Panic was developing. Buildings were crumbling, lines were down, food was disappearing, the store bins were cracked open, grain was spilling out. Bees flew everywhere, nowhere. Flight paths had disintegrated. The city was dying.

Kellerman gave a tiny cry and turned away, toward the rest of the debris-strewn room, toward the wreck of his workshop, toward his automobile.

He could not see it very well; his eyes were suddenly clouded. But there it stood on its own four wheels, ready to go. It must have been beautiful — this he knew — needing only a coat of paint to be ready for the road. A perfect coat of strawberry red, and then his project would finally be finished, the line ended, the last stage completed. And then he would have a word for it, the stage which had no name, a word that meant starting over and going beyond and more.

If only he had enough time to finish.

But before he could grab a brush, something grabbed him. A feeling, an urge that gripped him around the throat. An urge like no other he had felt in his life. The same urge, the same dry tingling beneath his tongue, down his throat, crawling around inside his body, prickling his skin: the same urge, but different, stronger, so strong it seemed to lift him off the floor, turning him slowly, slowly, toward something he did not want to see, could not bear to see, not *now*, not when he had no insulin left.

He turned, against all his strength, all his will, toward the honey.

And all his resistance vanished. On his knees he crawled toward the gleaming gold. He felt the irresistible pull of gold, saw its luminous color, smelled its rich sweet scent. He yearned to taste its indescribable sweetness on his lips, his tongue. It was *his*, here, now.

On his knees he reached down to the base of the shattered plaster wall to a pool of gold, dove both hands deep beneath its sticky gleaming surface, and scooped up in his palms a cup of gold.

As he lifted the glittering sweetness toward his lips, he sensed a change in the room. It happened so quickly he had no time to think, no time to react, no time to do anything. The rough, chaotic buzz of the dying city suddenly smoothed and deepened. His honeys, more of them than he had ever seen, ever imagined, began to swarm around him. He felt something touch the tips of his fingers, just above the honey cup of his palms — still inches from his waiting lips — something instantly obscured by the swarming bodies of a hundred, a thousand bees landing on the cup of his palms like drops of golden rain, coating and recoating his hands, forming a ball of living gold, a world of bees, pulsing, growing, only inches from his face.

Inside the swarming globe, he split the cup of his hands, spreading his hands and arms apart until there were two spheres of bees before him. Then bees began to swarm from his left hand to his right, shrinking the left globe and swelling the right, bigger and bigger, until the sphere of bees engulfed his right elbow, then his bicep. With his left hand, still coated with many bees, he began to paw carefully at the swelling globe on his right. He brushed, scooped, dug into the globe of bees forming like a new planet on his extended arm. They did not sting, did not resist his clumsy spade, just kept coming back, refilling the hole as fast as he could dig it, until at last he jabbed his spade hand all the way in, all the way to the honey in his still-cupped palm. With his left hand he split the globe, and there at its naked center, on the tips of his fingers, for just an instant he saw her: the queen.

And in that instant she fluttered, a single royal flick of her stately wings, turned her great golden body around, lifted her queenly head and looked him square in the eye, then spoke:

Well, I'll swan, Frank. What now?

The globe closed instantly, swallowing her up like a mouth. Kellerman's eyes remained on the invisible center, covered over and over by layers of swarming bees. His eyes remained fixed there even as more bees, thousands more, swarmed onto his arms, his chest, his back, his head, his face.

"I want to show you a place down by the creek. A place I tried to show you once before." He whispered the words through the hum, the hum he no longer heard but felt, the hum that was no longer outside him but *in* him.

When he stood he felt no pain. The wrecked workshop was an obstacle course swept clean. Though his eyes were clouded and covered with bees, he found the door easily. Through a cluster of bees his left hand found the bolt, then the knob. His grip was sure. The door opened.

The doorway exploded with light, light so bright he had to squint inside the swarm of bees, had to step without looking. But before he stepped outside, he turned — a soft, graceful turn, completely around — once, twice, three times, rotating the buzzing globe that engulfed him.

And then, as he stepped out into the light, a light brighter than all the other lights he had seen, something began to form on his lips: a word, the word he'd been searching for, the word that meant everything, the word that smelled like fresh strawberries in a musty barn, and gold leather and sweet perfume in the back seat of a speeding Pierce Arrow, the word that sounded like the crack of a Louisville Slugger against horsehide, the word that looked like a slim young woman dancing barefoot around a willow tree, the word that meant starting over and going beyond and more — it was coming to him, finally, here, *now* — he knew it, he felt it, he could *taste* it. It was on the tip of his tongue.

EPILOGUE

FROM A DISTANCE, the figures approaching the schoolhouse looked like monks.

Six hooded figures in gray, moving in a slow gray line, as in a silent ritual, each lost in deep thought or prayer. Their faces were invisible behind the hoods and thick veils. Their cloaks, gloves, and boots concealed every inch of flesh. The first three carried axes, the last three rolls of canvas and fine netting.

As they neared the wrecked automobile on the south side of the building, the line stopped. No sound issued from the schoolhouse. No hum, no buzz. The window in the stone wall above the wreck gaped open, no glass or wood blocking the view. But they did not look inside. Instead they looked around at each other indecisively, as if somehow the ritual had been broken and the consequences were unclear.

Then the first figure, much larger than the others, raised an arm and motioned the rest to follow. They rounded the corner and found the door in the west wall wide open. For a few moments they stared up at the open doorway in silence. Then one by one they dropped their burdens and climbed the steps. Wet plastic bags squished beneath their boots as they crossed the short porch to enter.

The room inside appeared to have suffered an explosion. Nearly all the plaster had come off the walls, exposing a maze of sticky, browning honeycomb. There were no bees. Torn boxes, pieces of broken plaster, tilted tables and chairs, tools, junk, and other debris littered the wet floor.

All this the hooded figures appeared to take in with a glance. Their attention quickly turned to the object in the middle of the room.

It was an old unpainted automobile. An open car without its rag top. A wreck, like the one outside, but different. This one seemed almost deliberately wrecked, the dents and scars repaired — but repaired in such a way that only made them more visible. The car looked like a man with no skin, a wounded man with cuts and bruises and punctures all exposed. A bloody mess that did not bleed. A dead man peeled open for examination. The hooded figures stared at the strange automobile — and something else.

In the passenger seat sat Mabel Zucha.

"Mama!"

In the middle of the line Orville Zucha removed the hood and veil of bee netting from his square head. He began to take another step forward, but the look in Mabel's eyes seemed to freeze him.

Sitting in the passenger seat, she did not crow, did not flap her arms, did not look anything like a bird. The black, unnerving stare had vanished. Instead, she sat with her arms folded like a lady.

"He's *destroyed* it."

Another figure removed hood and veil. "He's destroyed it," Vukovich repeated, staring at the battered hood covering the V-8 engine. He started forward to lift the car hood when a third figure stopped him.

"Hold it right there till I figure out what belongs to who."
Ed Hacker removed his hood. "Everybody just stay right
where you are."

"He got away, the lucky bastard," Vukovich said.

"He didn't take his syringe." It was Charley Bluefire's
voice. The syringe lay on the wet floor next to a wrench.

Then the largest figure, towering head and shoulders above
the others, removed his hood. The King of Swing stared
down at the syringe for a long moment, then bent his great
head forward in a nod. "He kicked it."

Charley shook his head. "Honker's a diabetic, King. He
can't just — "

But the King of Swing folded his massive arms across his
colossal chest and dismissed the thought.

"What I want to know," Ed Hacker interjected, looking around the room, "is where all those damn bees went."

"We're wasting time here," Vukovich said.

"Mama," Orville whispered and started again toward
the automobile.

"Wait."

At the sound of Curly's voice, all motion stopped. For
a long moment the room was silent as Curly's gaze moved
up and down, from the automobile to the old woman to
the automobile again. His dyed blond hair, matted and twisted
from the weight of the hood, glistened in a stream of sunlight
flowing through the open doorway.

"Well?" Ed Hacker said.

Curly did not answer, but fixed his gaze on the automobile.
He chewed his lip for several moments, then stepped forward.

"Don't scare her," Charley Bluefire whispered.

But the old woman did not seem frightened, did not move
at all as Curly climbed slowly into the driver's seat beside

her. Her eyes remained fixed on the road ahead, a road that was not a road but a doorway too narrow to drive through.

"Hold on," Curly said.

And, hand trembling, reached for the key.